I0824549

AMERICAN HAN

AMERICAN HAN

A NOVEL BY

LISA LEE

ALGONQUIN BOOKS OF CHAPEL HILL
AN IMPRINT OF LITTLE, BROWN AND COMPANY

Algonquin Books of Chapel Hill / Little, Brown and Company
Hachette Book Group
1290 Avenue of the Americas, New York, NY 10104
algonquinbooks.com

First Edition: March 2026

Algonquin Books of Chapel Hill is an imprint of Little, Brown and Company, a division of Hachette Book Group, Inc. The Algonquin Books name and logo are trademarks of Hachette Book Group, Inc.

Portions of this novel appeared in slightly different versions in the following publications: "Paradise Cove," Chapter 17, was first published in *Ploughshares*, Fall 2014, Vol. 40, Nos. 2 & 3, Fiction Issue edited by Percival Everett, and reprinted in *The Pushcart Prize XL: Best of the Small Presses 2016*, November 2015. An excerpt from "The Grieving Party," Chapter 5, was first published as "Margaret Cho's Mother" in *New World Writing*, Winter 2015. "House Hunting" and "The Hideout," Chapters 1 and 3, were first published as "The Hunt" in *North American Review*, Issue 295.3, Summer 2010.

ISBN 9781643757254

LCCN 2025948801

Printing 1, 2026

LSC-C

Printed in the United States of America

For Mike and Yuna

Home is where the han is.

—ELAINE H. KIM

AMERICAN HAN

THE TYCOON

1

HOUSE HUNTING

December 2001

I'D BEEN LIVING in San Francisco for a few years when my mom began appearing, mostly unannounced, acting strange and saying unexpected things, talking about her life and wondering about mine. At the beginning, her presence was suspicious, everything cloaked in secrecy.

The first time my mom showed up at my door, she gave me a half hour's notice. She called, declaring that she was already in the city, though she didn't tell me why she'd driven in from Napa and I didn't ask. Our relationship had soured to the point where I'd become almost mute around her, a habit formed out of instinct and anger. It was the weekend and I was home doing nothing, but lately I'd been treating weekdays like weekends, skipping classes for the first time even though it was my final year of law school. With graduation so near, I was finally facing the reality of a life I'd never chosen. The discipline I'd always had was beginning to erode.

My mom appeared at the bottom of the stairs, mink coat swishing at her knee, ankle boots stomping up the steps. At that time, in the early 2000s, South of Market was a grimy place—every morning there was a big, fresh human shit outside the front door—and I hadn't seen a single fur coat in my neighborhood in the four years I'd lived there.

A building over, a college acquaintance was living in a warehouse with floors covered in sawdust, the remains from a business that had crafted chairs out of reclaimed wood. Around the corner was a shelter for the unhoused. Ours was one of the few remaining neighborhoods where residents possessed neither the power nor the desire to protect the value of the homes they'd never own. Warehouses were just beginning to transform into luxury live-work lofts, all glass and steel and high ceilings, fluid space that you could purchase for the cost of a small Australian island.

When we met at the top of the staircase, my mom held up a piece of paper, crumpled and worn, like an ancient document that had changed hands and been folded and opened countless times. It was a flyer with a picture of a house. For months, she said, she'd been driving in from Napa to attend open houses.

"I saw a house today," she said. "I hope I win it."

Her coat billowed like an open parachute. When she took it off and handed it to me, I saw that she'd become so skinny, so narrow, it was like someone had folded her up and ironed her. My dad had warned me that she wasn't healthy, that she hadn't been eating. She checked to see if I noticed her new figure. I was staring, which seemed to satisfy her. She looked me up and down, comparing quietly.

I hung up the coat in the closet, wedging it between stacks of moving boxes that I'd never unpacked, though it had been years since I'd last moved. My mom disappeared into my bedroom where she immediately settled in, curling up in my bed, eyes closed, blanket pulled up to her chin. I knew she couldn't possibly be asleep, but I watched closely, wondering still. Like my mother, I had difficulty trusting my own judgment, but for me this difficulty concerned insignificant things, not big life decisions. Paralyzed by indecision on day-to-day details, overly confident about life-changing choices that you can't take back—perhaps not the best combination.

ABBA floated up from a set of speakers outside. Exuberant voices sang along in terrible unison, exploding at the chorus into pure shouting, lacking melody or any sense of tune, but all heart, free and electrified. The streets were packed with people from the Love Parade dressed in leather chaps with leather briefs, cowboy hats, and disco attire, small gangs dancing nude on floats and all over the streets as if the city was one big nightclub. I looked out onto Folsom from my third-story window and watched a pink float glide by, swanlike, the stage swaying with bodies that gyrated and twirled like spinning tops. I had chosen the neighborhood because it was central, a place where things happened. It was nothing like where I'd grown up, in Napa, where the public parks were empty and you could walk from one neighborhood to the next without seeing a single soul except hired help cleaning yards. I had never thought of my mother as even having a life, but here she was in San Francisco, crashing at my place, and it appeared that something was happening to her, though none of it was anything that I had expected.

I was watching, still, when my mom opened her eyes. She peered at me as if she was looking down a long hall into another room, but I was sitting in a chair right in front of her.

"Do you want some coffee?" I asked.

In the kitchen, I poured my mom a cup from a pot I'd pressed shortly before she'd arrived. When she asked for sugar, I had a moment of mild hostess panic as I remembered that she took sugar and cream with her coffee. I rifled through the cupboard for a bag of sugar.

When I turned around she was holding up the flyer for the open house, waving it like a flag. I took it from her to get a closer look. The house was a narrow salmon-colored three-story walk-up with a driveway the length of one car and so steep I couldn't imagine anyone driving in and out of the garage. On either side, the houses were similarly narrow and stacked, similarly pastel-colored, one lavender and the other pistachio. *Bernal Heights Gem*, the caption read.

"What do you think?" she asked. "Do you like it? Do you think I could live there? Does it look small?"

Her short black hair was a curtain pulled open to the stage of her face: big features announcing big feelings, the undisputed star, the grand finale. She no longer possessed such control of her face; her expressions were all the same—mild surprise, frozen in a state of near shock—recalling the speculation from my dad and his sister about secret injections.

As long as I could remember, my mother had spent money on her face—deep sea creams, vitamin C serums, retinol, snail facials, laser treatments, chemical peels, visits to Korean dermatologists—all for a youth that was unattainable. While watching TV, she'd hold up a hand mirror and examine her lines, pressing with two fingers the areas that had lost firmness. She'd taken to keeping a photograph of herself on her wedding day perched on the table beside her. Once as we watched a game show together, I caught her staring at me.

"Will you trade with me? Your skin is so young," she'd said, hands outstretched, fingers wagging.

I heard a story once about an aging Romanian aristocrat who killed young women for their blood, a clean beauty miracle moisturizer. She smoothed fresh blood on her face, convinced it would return her to the skin of her youth. When she ran out of blood, the face she saw in the mirror reflected her true self—skin loose and lined and beginning to sag. She demanded more blood from young girls.

I'd told my mom that story. She gasped, though not from horror.

"Do you think it works?" she said.

Since turning sixty, my mother's pursuit of youth had taken a new dimension. She was still trying, but there was no more playfulness about it—she seemed sad, or afraid, as if she'd accepted that there was only forward and no going back. My mom had grown up in Korea and could never free herself from impossible expectations of beauty and success. America had its own standards that only confused her. She'd made a life for herself without approval from her family, with America judging her and narrowing her options, so she and my dad just kept treading water until she finally looked up and saw that her life was behind her.

I examined the picture of the pink Bernal Heights Gem.

"You're moving here? Why?" I asked.

"The open house was packed," she said. "I have to win it. Don't you?"

"Don't I what?"

"Don't you think I should have that house?"

"How would you buy that? This flyer says it's over a million dollars. What does Dad think?"

"Maybe I'll live there alone," she said.

I waited for her to elaborate, but she just took a sip of her coffee, set it down on the table, picked it up again. I looked at her quizzically. Considering how distant we were as a family, it shouldn't have mattered to me whether my parents split up, but an animal part of me said that I couldn't survive with a broken family.

"Do you think I could do it?" she said. "I've never been alone before. How do you do it? Will you help me?"

"Why would you?" I said. "What about Dad? How do you have the money? Are you selling the house? Does Dad even know?"

"Don't tell him," she said. "I don't know if I want to live with him anymore. He could get a girlfriend. Someone younger."

"What are you talking about?"

"Do you like living in San Francisco? How do you get around?"

I considered for a moment the information my mom had just revealed to me and all that she was leaving out. There were so many missing pieces. I felt like I'd just returned from a long absence to join my family in the middle of a movie only to learn when the lights came on that I'd been sitting with someone else's family the whole time.

"I take the Muni," I said. "Or walk or ride my bike."

"It must be fun to be a young person living here. You probably have a lot of boyfriends," she said.

The last person I'd had a relationship with was Steve Chen, the brother of a friend of a friend. We dated very briefly, not long enough to call a thing. Steve was an engineer at Google, back when everyone had heard of it, but the name didn't have the kind of effortless power it does today. In truth, I hadn't had a boyfriend, or girlfriend, in four years and I'd never embraced the dating scene, which—pre-Tinder, OkCupid, or what have you—involved getting drunk at bars and parties and smiling and laughing a lot. I've never trusted people who always look like they're having a fabulous time. *No one believes you*, I'd say to myself. I couldn't pretend to be carefree even while drinking. This was one of many things I couldn't talk to my mother about.

"Maybe I'll get a boyfriend. Don't you?" my mom said.

"Don't I what?"

"What do you think?"

MY MOM SAT in the rocking chair, hands cradling her coffee cup. The sun shone through the vinyl blinds, marking parallel lines across her face. She had on a lot of makeup, which I noticed because she'd always been makeup-free. Her mouth was outlined in dark liner, but her lips had been left jarringly colorless. I couldn't tell whether she'd left them that way on purpose or simply forgotten to fill them in. When I asked her about it, she said she'd seen it in a magazine and became indignant when I suggested it wasn't flattering. "It's my choice," she cried out so quickly I suspected I wasn't the first to call attention to it.

When she was quiet, her face was still, so different from her true self that I questioned everything.

"I shouldn't have given Minjoo my jewelry. It should have been yours. You're my daughter, not Minjoo."

I wanted to remind my mother of how differently she'd spoken when my brother Kevin and Minjoo were first married, how she'd called just to announce that I was no longer her daughter, listing all the ways in which Minjoo was perfectly fulfilling the role that I'd failed at my entire life. "Minjoo helped me set up an email account. Why don't you help me like she does? When are you going to at least start making money?" she'd said. It was my first year of law school.

I remembered this as my mom rocked in the chair and talked about the jewelry, and I remembered, bitterly, that she'd offered her diamond ring to Kevin and Minjoo when they announced their engagement, though Minjoo had turned it down because she expected a full carat, at minimum. I'd been upset because for years the ring had been promised to me. As a child, I looked for opportunities to try it on when my mom removed it to scrub the kitchen sink. I'd stare at the diamond on my ring finger, and while the band was far too big, it promised a future of glamour and romance. I'd sometimes get away with wearing it for hours, fingers curled under, careful not to let it slide off, until she realized her ring was missing. By the time Minjoo rejected the diamond ring, I'd decided that I didn't want it either, partly because marriage had come to look like a trap, partly because the ring no longer represented what it had to me as a child: the expectation of getting something you've been assured is your birthright. No such thing should exist for anyone in this world.

"I don't care about the jewelry," I said. "I don't even wear jewelry."

"I don't like Minjoo anymore. She doesn't care about me. Don't you?"

"Don't I what?"

"Don't you think Minjoo is fake? I think she's been tricking me."

My mom set down her mug on the coffee table. She leaned in, face jutting out like a runner at the finish line.

"How long will you be in San Francisco? Do you think you'll stay after you graduate and get a job? I hope you're still here when I move here. When you have time we can do things together, like mother-daughter."

"I might move next summer," I said, even though I'd decided earlier to be low-key. I was intent on keeping my secret a secret until I had something real in motion, no longer stuck in this in-between space, full of half-baked ideas.

"You might move?" she said, alarmed. "To where?"

"I don't know. Maybe I'll leave California," I said.

"Why would you leave?" she shouted, as if she'd driven all through the night to see me only to meet me on my way out, announcing that I wouldn't be back. "Don't you have to take the California bar exam?"

"I can take another state's exam," I said.

"But I'll be living here soon. Who else will tell me how things work? I need help. I can't do it by myself," she said. "This city is so brave."

My mom gazed at her hands. As she spread her fingers apart, I remembered that she hated her hands. To me, they looked like normal hands, but according to my mom, they were large and big-boned and the skin had become loose, wrinkled, and spotted like her own mother's. She'd hold her hands up next to mine, saying she wished we could trade. "Why did you get all the *good* things?" she'd say.

I'm not aware of a surgical procedure that shrinks a woman's hands, but in Korea, it wouldn't be unheard of for a person to consult a plastic surgeon to lengthen the legs. In fact, it was quite common to go under the knife for a seemingly limitless list of elective surgeries, with the focus mostly on the size and shape and features of the face. Eyelid surgery, by far the most common, was the subject of one of the oldest arguments I had with my mother—she couldn't bully me into doing it no matter how many times a day she told me I looked ugly without it, and how my disobedience was keeping me from winning life. The eyes, the nose, the shaving down of the jaw—it all sounded horrible to me, but the procedure for lengthening the legs had always seemed the most grotesque. I'd read how the bones were broken, the limbs stretched—manually or by machine—and afterward the legs healed, a process that took up to a year. It granted a patient an average of one and no more than two inches in height; in some instances, less than one inch. Large calves could be fixed by cutting the nerves in the muscle, causing the muscle to atrophy. Short legs, muscular calves: just a few of our Korean afflictions.

My mom folded her hands, hiding them in her lap. She looked into my eyes, her brows knitted together.

"What do you mean you don't know where you're moving to or whether you're even going to move?" she said. "How can you live your life not knowing where you're going? I always have to know where I'm going to end up."

"Nothing happens the way you plan anyway," I said.

Once, during a cab ride out to North Beach, the driver said to me, "Where did you get your baby confidence?" when I told him my plan to move someplace where no one knew me.

"I wish I could be you. It must be fun," she said, her voice soft. "You can do whatever you want."

She tugged at the skin on the back of her hand, then rubbed it with her fingers.

"It's because of me," she said. "I raised you. I'm your mother."

I supposed that it was true, that I owed my life, my choices, to my mother. But all I saw was someone who'd only held me back, put me down, controlled me, and now that I was going places, she wanted credit for my future of possibility.

It's despite you, I thought, *not because of you*.

I wouldn't say it out loud. Deep down, I knew we were both right.

2

NO MIDDLE NAME

MY NAME IS Jane Kim. Kim is a common name in Korea, and therefore also in the places in America where Koreans live. But for a long time when I was growing up in Napa, as far as I knew there were no Kims—or Parks or Lees or Moons or Chos—to be found anywhere outside the walls of our house. I knew that Koreans lived elsewhere, just not where we lived. I saw these Koreans, including cousins, aunts and uncles, grandparents, hardly ever. It wasn't until fifth grade that I met other Koreans in Napa: a Korean girl adopted by a white family and a Korean boy with a Korean father and a white mother from France. The three of us were simultaneously drawn to and apprehensive of each other. We thought of ourselves as rare. To see myself in someone else was an affirmation, yet somehow horrifying.

I do not have a "Korean name." Sorry to disappoint. My parents thought that a girl born in America should have an "American name." Choosing a name is the first chance to exert control about who a child will be, to apply our own hopes and dreams even if all we're hoping for is a blank canvas—a future with no history, no past. My older brother Kevin, on the other hand, as their only son, was to carry on our legacy. Kevin's birth name is Jun-ho, but when he was ten he stood in front of an old white man in a black robe at the Napa courthouse and requested to change his name. The judge saw no reason to deny an American-born boy permission to change from Jun-ho to Kevin even if he did look more like a Jun-ho than a Kevin. He was all in, no regrets.

His sadness had turned to anger for all the teasing he'd been subjected to, when at the beginning of each school year the teacher called out to Jun-ho from the roll sheet, sounding it out and mispronouncing it every time, causing the other kids to snicker.

"Junn . . . hoe? Hoo? Ha?"

"June. June hoe," Kevin would respond quietly, eyes down.

"*Ho! Ho bag!*" The most boring person always thinks they're the funniest.

It wasn't enough to say: *You can call me Kevin*. He wanted it on the record.

Koreans don't have middle names. So I am one of perhaps thousands of Jane Kims in America. When I recently renewed my driver's license, it was time to upgrade to REAL ID and the nice Latina at the counter with incredible nails told me that she had to input exactly what was on my birth certificate. This woman with tiny figurines of donuts and boba and sushi and pizza lacquered to her fluorescent-painted nails double-checked with her supervisor because the displeasure on my face matched her own displeasure at the idea of NMN on her own ID. I knew this because she told me, her voice all understanding. I felt seen. "You could come back with your passport?" she offered, explaining that my passport likely left the middle-name entry blank, but my passport was expired and since my driver's license was about to expire and I'm too responsible to drive around with an expired license, we had to go with the birth certificate, which is why I'm now, officially, Jane NMN Kim.

My parents weren't thinking about names when they moved here. My mom and dad arrived in California, separately, in the late sixties. They had known each other as friends in Seoul and kept in touch after moving to America. My mom was living in Los Angeles with her mother and many brothers and sisters, her father long dead, probably rolling in his grave about his family leaving him behind in Korea, while my dad was in San Francisco with his parents, his sister and brothers and niece. Koreans tend to live together in tight quarters near other Koreans. For us, family is the point of life. Sure, we like money, capitalism, conformity, hiking, dramas, and pop music, but all of that even is about family—we're doing it for, with, in honor of, family. Because of the distance between Los Angeles and San Francisco, my mom and dad talked on the phone frequently, then spent time together when my dad had a brief stint in Los Angeles's Koreatown, working odd jobs, making connections, learning how to start a business. When they decided to marry, they eloped—both families were vehemently against the marriage.

"I didn't want to marry an ugly doctor, like my sisters," my mom said. "My mom set me up with one, but I didn't like him. I told her that I didn't want to marry him and she didn't care—she told me I had to or she'd disown me. So I ran away with your dad. He didn't have any money, but he was the most handsome man I'd ever met. I wanted to have pretty children. He drove a motorcycle and played the guitar and sang Elvis songs to me. I cried the whole way to San Francisco. I'd disobeyed my family and I knew they wouldn't talk to me again—and they never did, not until Kevin was born."

While my mom's family thought of themselves as superior in class and status to my dad's, my dad's family thought my mom wasn't pretty enough to be one of them. They thought they were the best-looking Koreans to walk the earth. Two things both sides could agree on: hatred for the other and that joining together was not a good match. After a few years in San Francisco, my parents moved to Napa, where they had no family and no friends. Kevin and I were born there, and we became the Kims in Napa. As opposed to the Kims in LA, Oakland, or San Jose, for whom more context had to be given for anyone to be sure which Kims someone was talking about.

Being the best was very important in our family. Kevin's and my successes reflected on us all. When Kevin and I picked up tennis and piano—tennis as soon as we could hold rackets, piano before we could read—and were exceedingly good at both, our parents were determined to make their investment worth it: we would be winners. And we were, though I think I should note that even with our awards and national rankings, we weren't necessarily impressive by the standards of certain Asian Americans, as our parents and aunts and uncles reminded us constantly. For some of us, the bar starts high. I had what was called "natural talent." Piano teachers and tennis coaches were baffled—once-in-a-lifetime talent, they said, truly exceptional, words like "prodigy" and "phenom" were thrown around. They urged my parents to move to places like New York City and Florida, where the right people could mentor me. In New York, I'd continue piano, studying under the best, and I'd be off to Juilliard and Carnegie Hall before we could blink. In Florida, I'd quit school and train under Rick Macci at his namesake academy alongside other children aiming to turn pro by age thirteen. But I must have been nine, and I couldn't choose, nor did I want to move. I wasn't interested in being gifted; giving in meant giving up everything else and how do you ask that of a child? I just wanted to play tennis the way I saw other people do it—for fun—but I was beginning to see that to play for fun, there was a certain level that you couldn't cross, and I'd crossed it by the time I was eight when I double bageled my mom, a lifetime player, and won my first USTA 14-and-under tournament. It was the same with piano. At first, playing the piano had satisfied something in me that I couldn't name, but practicing hours upon hours, day after day, to perfect a program for an upcoming competition took that away.

Lucky for me, my parents didn't know how to uproot themselves and start over again, so we stayed where we were, and that so-called talent, talent that only brought me grief, got me far, but not far enough, because you need the fire to get you the whole way and I didn't have it. Expectations were too high. That's what caused me grief. Expectations and the mix of admiration and envy from the white families in our town who resented me and my family and what our success meant about them. I kept training and practicing and competing, but never fully committed to either, making myself frustrated and bored. I didn't want to quit because tennis and piano felt easy and natural and gave me my identity, but I also didn't want to give up everything I would have had to give up to reach what everyone said was my potential. I felt like a fraud. I wished that I could play for enjoyment, not to win. But for me, there was nothing between winning and quitting, an agony that I wouldn't wish on anyone.

When I turned eighteen, I quit both tennis and piano, went to a respected university, then a mediocre law school on scholarship. Kevin did not have natural talent, but he had the fire. He played tennis for a Division I team and turned pro, but he didn't last a year. In sports, fire will never get you the whole way if you don't have the gift. You must have both. Athletics are stingy that way, not like other vocations where they say it's about talent, but really it's the fire that begets success. Kevin didn't last long on the professional circuit because there's no money in it unless you're winning, and you need financial backing to train and tour. I'd heard our dad lecture Kevin many times over the years that a man supports himself and his family. Kevin announced that upon graduation he'd join the police force. He'd picked up a part-time job with the campus police, pinning parking tickets underneath the windshield wipers of illegally parked cars, and the cops he worked under praised him and encouraged him to follow in their footsteps. With a college degree, a police officer's starting salary was higher than most office jobs. While our mom had wanted him to be a lawyer or doctor if he couldn't be the next Michael Chang, our dad was proud. He'd wanted to be a policeman himself, but citizenship was a prerequisite and America didn't grant it to him until he'd reached middle age. Our parents both worried that policing was a dangerous job, that Kevin would get hurt or even killed. Neither of them thought of the possibility that Kevin could be the one to cause harm in the line of duty. I didn't know what to think of any of it, too preoccupied with making something of my life that was separate from all of them.

My dad was like me, or I was like my dad. But unlike me, he was self-taught at everything, all instinct, all desire. Musically gifted, he learned to play the piano by watching his sister at piano lessons, taught himself the guitar, and sang in a beautiful deep baritone, like the Korean Elvis he dreamed of being. When I heard him sing, it was as if he had been saving up all his softness just for those moments. He was even better than most people I knew at tennis, though he'd never had a lesson in his life. He'd never gotten to pursue anything he really cared about. You go your whole life like that and you feel like you wasted your time on earth. That's the story I've been learning about my family. My mom and my dad wanted to get back what they'd lost. All either of them wished for was the chance to choose. My dad had always wanted to see all of America and make money doing something he enjoyed, not work that was just work. He got pushed into owning and running a string of small businesses, starting with a carwash and a 7-Eleven, then a diner in Sacramento, which helped him work his way up to our town's beloved Swensen's diner/ice cream shop, and ending his career with an auto shop, which was supposed to ease him into retirement. Swensen's was strongest in our memories because we owned it the longest, it was the most difficult to run, and because we all worked there, making it our one true family business. Now that my dad was retired, he'd picked up a job as a long-haul truck driver and was finally getting to tour America. My mom wanted to be young again, free to dream of a future as a city-girl business tycoon. I was trying to avoid the kinds of regrets my whole family had, regrets from choosing money and stability over happiness and then convincing yourself that you'd never had a choice. Kevin had been stuck for a long time. I think it started from the day he was born, before he was even named.

3

THE HIDEOUT

December 2001

AFTER ALL THE talk about houses, about moving and not moving, and the energy it took to try to keep our secrets from slipping out, my mom and I decided to head out and grab an early dinner. Little Italy, my mom requested, so I suggested the place on Columbus for those Roman pizzas that come out thin and light, a small round pie on a white dinner plate, served by fast-talking Italian men with singsong voices, making such a fuss that I'd find myself blushing every time. I offered to drive, since the Muni didn't reach that far and the bus took forever. I'd often walk up to North Beach through Chinatown and pick up an egg custard tart on the way, but a good daughter wouldn't make her mom walk two miles uphill.

I was lucky to have a car, but it wasn't reliable and was a pain in the ass because my building didn't have parking. I moved the car almost every other day to avoid parking tickets for street sweeping. I drove a Beetle, an old model from the late seventies that my dad had restored at his auto shop as a college graduation gift. He'd asked me if I wanted a new Beetle, the modern version with the little flower vase on the dash. I'd told him: "New cars are obscene." That was a few years earlier, and by the time I'd put a thousand miles on it I learned that the problem with old cars is that they require constant maintenance. Only a young person who's been given many things she didn't have to work for would turn down the gift of a new car. That turned out to be one of my many stupid decisions.

A few minutes into our drive to the restaurant, I was regretting having volunteered to drive. I'd been ignoring the clanking sound coming from underneath the car, hoping it would go away. That year I'd taken the car to the shop numerous times for not inexpensive work—new battery and tires, new brake pads and rotors, new fuel pump, alternator, and starter. I'd never learned to have parts replaced before they stopped working.

On our way home from dinner, the clanking under the car got so loud and constant, my mom stopped talking about the pink house. "What's that?" she said, ear turned forward. Soon, the car was shaking. I held my breath as I searched the dashboard for lights or warning signs. The arrow on the temperature gauge trembled in the red danger zone. I must have done something right to counteract the day's bad karma with good karma because a car pulled out of a parking spot only a few feet ahead at the corner of the intersection. I turned on the hazard lights and we coasted to the curb, right into the spot the other car had just left. The car shuddered, then died. I was overcome with relief. Not only had I magically found legal parking, the place where we'd broken down was also fairly flat. I could see that a couple blocks further, the street swooped dramatically.

I got out and looked underneath the car. I didn't know what I was looking for. I was afraid to open the hood. After a minute I gave up and called a tow truck. I couldn't lose this car. If I kept skipping classes, I could lose my student health insurance, not to mention my scholarship that paid me a living stipend, but I was determined to hold on to my car. It was illegal to drive without car insurance, but health insurance was optional and having it was a privilege. Since I knew I wouldn't be penalized, except possibly with my own life, I'd let the health coverage go, but as long as I had a car, I'd buy good auto insurance because I was young and priorities and risks were out of whack.

Back in the car, my mom was on the phone, asking to speak to a Mr. Kwan. My gomo—my aunt on my dad's side—had told me that my mom had been spending time with a Chinese real-estate investor named Stan Kwan. I wasn't sure what she meant by "spending time." I could hear Mr. Kwan's voice coming from the receiver, reciting the address of an auto shop. My mom repeated it slowly, calling out the numbers one at a time and spelling out the street name, then waited for his confirmation, even though the name of the street was Moss, the one-block alleyway where my apartment was located and where my mom had met me earlier. Mr. Kwan's voice was sharp with annoyance as he called out the address again, loud and deliberate, as if he was talking to a child, though there was nothing to correct—she'd gotten it right. I wanted to punch him in the face.

My mom pressed a piece of paper into my hand and didn't let go. I'd already grasped it, but she held the note in place, pinning it to my palm with her thumb and closing my fingers into a fist around it.

"Stan gave me the name of an auto shop, the best in San Francisco. We have to take the car here," she said, still pressing into my hand.

"I just called a tow truck," I said.

I took the note and held it up. My mom's oversized cursive covered the entire sheet. I handed it back.

"This is too far," I said. "It's back at my apartment. The tow truck will just take us to the nearest place."

I found myself feeling pleased about dismissing her attempt to be helpful. My mom was always overstepping, sabotaging ambitions, ruining relationships. She couldn't just let things be. A few years earlier, I'd been wait-listed at a top law school. When she found out, she called everyone in our Korean network for help with getting me in. A friend of a friend knew someone whose son had just joined the faculty—he was an assistant law professor, tenure was a ways off. My mom called him and who knows what she said, but I imagine the phone call from a Korean woman he'd never met panicking about getting her daughter in off the waitlist wasn't too surprising—he was Korean American, after all, raised by Korean immigrants, and he'd made it into that elite space. But I know my mom, her relentless tyrannical fear—he would have wanted to get her off the phone. He passed on the number of a tenured faculty member who was on the admissions committee.

"You *must* call," my mom shouted into the phone before I'd even said hello. "Her name is Marianne Spitko. Call her 'professor.' Tell her they must let you in."

I'd applied to law school when I didn't want to because I thought I owed it to my mom and my dad. They'd given me their lives. Didn't I owe them this? When I dialed the number for Professor Spitko, I felt weak with dread. I hadn't even thought out what I'd say, but I made sure to call after hours—that way I wouldn't have to talk to anyone. Worst thing I'd have to do was leave a message. To my surprise, Professor Spitko picked up the phone, though it was almost 8 p.m. She was as surprised as I was. She was expecting a call from her daughter because it was about time to pick her up from a friend's house.

"I didn't think you'd answer," I'd said.

"Who *is* this?" she asked.

I told her my name.

"Why are you calling me?"

I told her I was on the waitlist.

"What is it that you want from me?"

I didn't know, but I must have said something about wanting to get in off the waitlist.

"How did you get this number?" she demanded.

I bungled through the conversation while Professor Spitko spoke with confusion and suspicion and irritation. At one point, she even sounded scared—I could have been a scammer or even a stalker. She asked me to repeat my name and spell it out. I could tell she was writing it down so she wouldn't forget. I did not get in off the waitlist. I'm sure my name was crossed off the list that very night. But when my mom asked me that night if I'd called the professor, I was able to report yes, I'd done what she'd asked.

"Good," she said.

When I was younger, I'd learned to freeze my mother out so she couldn't try to do "helpful" things behind my back that almost always ended up making things worse. Of course, she didn't mean to cause harm, but it was mind-boggling that she couldn't tell the effect she was having and still didn't notice after the fact that what she'd done to try to make things go her way had caused a devastating reaction. The problem had become that I couldn't tell the difference between my mother's harmless presence and her harmful presence. Keeping her out had become a habit, but here was my mom seemingly trying to fix things.

My mom took back the note with the address of the auto shop and slipped it into her purse.

"Okay," she said, folding her hands in her lap. "How long do we wait?"

"About an hour. Maybe more," I said.

"An hour? I can't wait that long! How will I get home? I need to get to my car! Don't you? I have to get up early tomorrow! Can I walk to my car from here?"

My mom opened the passenger door and swung her legs out. Her feet stomped on the curb, making a hollow sound, and she pushed herself up and out of the car. I'd thought, just for a day, that the old mom was gone. I thought she'd been replaced with a new mom, who was sticking by me, even if for her own survival.

"MOM! What are you doing?" I shouted.

My mom froze. She whipped her body back inside and slammed the door shut. I felt like I was in a cave, hollering through a tunnel to my mom at the other end, peering at me from another cave.

"We're not close to my apartment," I said, calm now. "You can't walk there. You don't know where you're going. You'll just get lost."

We'd pulled over just beyond the eastern edge of Golden Gate Park, along the tip of the Panhandle. Cars swooped around the bend, flashing streaks of rear brake lights. The fog rolled over us like milk.

I wanted to shout at my mom. I felt like a deep well that had filled to the brim with grievances, either unsaid or said and unanswered, my body just a container to carry memory and bad feelings and make room for more. Any minute the thing could explode and shatter outward, reverberating across the world. I kept pushing it down. This wasn't the option that I preferred, but I'd become good at it and speaking my mind had never worked out.

I should have let her wander off and get lost, let her see what it was like out there alone in the world. I waited for her to scream, something predictable, accusatory. *You've put me in hell!* or *I should jump off the bridge!* Something so relentlessly oppressive and designed to stir up so much guilt, I'd give in to whatever she wanted. It's how I saw my mother because that's the mother she'd shown me so far. There were reasons for the walls I'd built, reasons why when she'd try to get through, the version of me that greeted her was my meanest self.

For once, my mom surprised me. She didn't say a word. I watched, trying to make sense of her silence, and in that moment I felt a power over her that I didn't know I had. She looked like a twig someone had stepped on. I thought she would do anything I said. In my eyes, my mother had transformed. It was me who was supposed to be obedient, and shamed for not being a good daughter, not living up to expectations. My mom should have been scolding me, connecting everything that was going wrong that day to everything that had gone wrong her whole life, then connecting it back to me, the person who was to blame for all her grief. But here was my mom following my directives, staying put like I said, waiting for instruction and saying nothing, as quiet as I'd once been when I was a child under her thumb. The change in power was a trick, making me see her as a nice mother.

I wanted the old mom back. I wanted the old mom so I could tell her that she fucked me up. Then I would be satisfied in hating her. This was someone who used to tell me that she got nothing out of being my mother, who pushed me in front of a horse when she was afraid it was attacking her, who said it was my fault for being spoiled the time my dad beat me with the handle of a golf club (*Not her face!* she screamed, because she didn't want anyone to know), who blamed me when my brother broke down my bedroom door and again when he crashed the car into a tree while I sat in the passenger seat, who removed the photos of me from the family picture frames and replaced them with photos of her younger self while telling me I was fat and ugly, who told me she had a dream that she accidentally killed me when she meant to poison my sheepdog, who convinced me that she had cancer (though she was not sick) and that I'd given it to her by being mean, who made me run miles with weights strapped on to train for tennis tournaments, who gave me pep talks backstage at piano competitions by telling me that I better not make any mistakes, otherwise an entire year of practicing, preparing for this very moment, would go to waste. This was someone who'd demand that you trust her, betray you, and then say, "Why do you think I'm against you?"

Please don't change. Don't be nice to me now. I wanted the mom who'd made me who I was, the mom who I could predict and understand, whose consistent cruelty and chaos-making and inability to relate made life easier: I knew where I stood and could keep my dignity. No one else could see me. There was no one so penetrating yet remarkably oblivious. If she was gone, how would I know who I was anymore?

THE TOW TRUCK got stuck a few blocks down—the Love Parade had cut off access—so we had no choice but to ditch the car. We walked down to the Muni, intending to head over to my place where my mom had parked nearby, what I thought was her last stop before the drive home to Napa.

"Can I show you my apartment? That's where I stay the night when I'm in the city to look at open houses. It's in North Beach," she said.

"North Beach? We were just there," I said. "For dinner. Remember?"

"We were?" she said. "I didn't know."

Was she trying to keep it a secret before or was she just confused? She'd always been bad with geography, with remembering the names of people, places, and things, which was probably why those were areas in which I'd become proficient. I didn't know whether it was the language barrier and never feeling at ease in America, or if she was similarly inefficient in her native language and home country. The fact that we were fluent in different languages and cultures and knew just enough of the other was like having the wrong set of keys to your own house.

We hopped on the Muni and rode underground. The subway was packed with sweaty people from the parade, each car filled tight like an overstuffed bookcase. The air conditioner wasn't working. It felt and smelled like we were inside someone's sour mouth. A small group got off the train, throwing glitter and rainbow confetti as if we were all getting married. Now that there was enough space to be near without talking directly into each other's faces, my mom spilled the details on her supposed apartment: on the weekends while house hunting in San Francisco, she'd been crashing in a vacant studio in a building that Mr. Kwan owned.

"I don't do anything else when I'm here," she said, "because I don't know what I'm supposed to do and I don't have any friends yet. I don't go out anywhere. Maybe when I move here you can help me."

She described the neighborhood, listing the tourist attractions, including Lombard Street, "the crookedest street in the world," which was constantly being photographed, sometimes, she said, with hordes of people climbing off tour buses and waiting in neat lines for the chance to take a picture. I nodded as she exclaimed how expensive the rent was, how beautiful and wonderfully high and scenically located the building was.

"I can't wait for you to see it," she said, her face instantly animated, despite the tightness. The closer we got, her excitement became more palpable, expressions more exaggerated.

"There's a beautiful view," she said, "and a wonderful high high ceiling. It's so big. I can't wait to show it to you."

"Are you okay?" I asked. "It's like you've lost your mind."

My mom wouldn't look me in the eye.

"Are you leaving Dad?"

She wasn't ready to tell me or thought I wasn't ready to hear it. Maybe she hoped I'd just figure it out and no one would have to say anything. She went back to describing the apartment, her exuberance about her perfect place in a perfect neighborhood filling up all the space between us.

Everything about my mom was an expression of her inner life: her face and gestures, her clothing, her manner of speech, the way she lived in the world. She had a lot to say, arms lifting for emphasis. Her eyes opened wide and her voice raised a pitch. Even her mouth was doing things that would have felt difficult for me, her lips forming the shapes of the vowels that she spoke, turning into a perfect O, Ah, and Oo. The habits that made us unalike sometimes produced similar outcomes: I had resting bitch face, for which there were consequences, but my mother was proof that there were also consequences for going the other way. We both paid, each of us put in our place for not getting it right.

The subway climbed up and out of a tunnel as we headed further north, rising from shadow to light, darkness to pastel Victorians and cool green parks. We passed the quiet bookstores, ceramics, and noodle shops of Japantown, hopped off at Union Square's bustling village of upscale shopping and glittery sidewalks, walked up through Chinatown into Little Italy where my mom could finally show me the hideout she'd talked up on the ride over.

The neighborhood was crisscrossed with streets that were so close to vertical, cars parked in rows facing the curb. My mom and I leaned forward, arms pumping, as we worked our way up an incline. I could hear her panting. The heels of her shoes barely touched the ground.

"People who live in San Francisco must have the best butts in the world. Don't you?" she said.

There was a cold wind blowing, moist with fog. My mom asked if another day I'd take her to Twin Peaks, Coit Tower, the cable cars, the Ferry Building, the MOMA, the Palace of Fine Arts, the Painted Ladies, dim sum in Chinatown. She kept going, as if she'd committed a list to memory, surprising me that she remembered the names of so many landmarks.

"What do people do here?" she asked. "What do *you* do here?"

It felt like we'd never reach the end of the block, though the whole time I could see it—the intersection ahead so near to the sky that it might as well have been a mountaintop. Like snails, we made our way past Victorian houses that had the appearance of leaning to one side.

"You've been to France. My friend says San Francisco is like Paris. Is it true?" she asked. "Everyone here wears blue jeans. How come all the young people are wearing blue jeans? I don't know anyone who wears blue jeans. I like yours. Where did you get them?" If it had been someone else's mother, I would have gotten a kick out of all the questions and would have happily answered them. But this mother was mine; her questions annoyed me. I had just gotten free of her and here she was like a creature from *Invasion of the Body Snatchers*, trying to usurp the life I'd made for myself.

I expected my mom's hideout would be a beautiful aerie overlooking the Bay. She stopped at an ordinary building that was not on a hilltop, as she'd claimed, and we walked past the main entrance to the side gate. I peeked through the windows of the front doors as we passed, noting the ornate common room with Spanish tiles, large framed mirrors, and a chandelier. My mom led me down a narrow stairway adjacent to the dumpster, picked up an empty milk carton and threw it in the blue recycling bin. She pressed the lever on top of a gate, releasing us to the backside of the building.

"Careful," she whispered. "The light went out."

I began to worry that we were trespassing.

"Why are you whispering?" I said, my voice low.

"Stan gave me the keys. He said I can stay here," she said, still whispering, "but the tenants who live here, they don't know. I don't want to get him in trouble."

"But he owns the building."

"Yes, but there are rules," she said.

Behind the building, there was a little strip of dirt along a paved walkway. My mom stopped at a plain door that had no peephole or doorbell. The door was completely flat—no panels, molding, or trim—and had the appearance of the entrance to a storage unit or janitor's room. What it didn't look like was the door of someone's living quarters. My mom rummaged through her purse in the dark until she fished out a set of keys. She tried them one after another until the last one fit. She jiggled the lock. We were in.

We emerged into a renovated basement room with a white tile floor and walls with fresh white paint. It looked like a vacant office used to store broken household appliances and discarded furniture—a disconnected washing machine, a vacuum cleaner that was missing a hose, a yellow couch with a dark wine stain. The room had no kitchen, but on the far end there was a finished storage closet and a full bath with a marble countertop and new fixtures. One of those college dorm mini fridges hummed beneath a lopsided desk missing one of its casters.

The room was windowless except for the one located next to the front door, which was small and square—even a child couldn't fit through it—with frosted glass and a metal grate instead of a screen. Inside with the door closed, I noticed that the door didn't fit properly. It had either been mistakenly purchased in the wrong size, or a well-fitting door wasn't a priority for units not designed as living space. There was a huge gap between the bottom of the door and the tile floor, allowing a sharp draft to sweep in, keeping the room almost frigid. My mom pointed at a space heater and a row of small circular nightlights stuck to the wall.

"Stan got these for me. He's a nice man," she said, pressing the lights on and off one at a time.

The ceiling was unusually high at the room's entrance, a set of barn doors placed oddly near the top, but throughout most of the room the ceiling was quite low, definitely not vaulted as my mom had claimed. She pulled out the seat of the stained couch, converting it into a bed, and got a sleeping bag and a yellow boombox from the closet. I had slept in our backyard in that very sleeping bag. I'd lie down in the middle of the lawn, zip it up to my chin, and try to count the stars as our dog padded all over me.

"Lie down," my mom said. "Rest your back."

She unzipped the sleeping bag, spreading it flat on the pullout bed. She plugged in the radio, which was tuned in to KOIT 96.5 ("light rock, less talk"). Elton John filled the room as she lay down next to me.

"Remember this radio?" she asked. "It's yours, from high school."

"I thought I recognized it," I said. "I can't believe it still works. Why is it here?"

"I'm here all by myself. I'm lonely!" she said, laughing as if I'd asked where babies come from. "I don't have anyone to talk to and there's no TV, so I listen to the radio."

We were looking up at the ceiling, which somehow seemed even lower than before. An old striped pocket T that I used to wear was flung over the couch's armrest with a pair of flannel pajama pants. My mom pulled the sleeping bag around herself, hugging it tightly.

"Why are you staying here?" I asked.

My mom curled onto her side. She was so close, I could almost feel her breath.

"You don't like it?" she asked.

"Mom," I said. "This is a basement or a storage room or something. Maybe an office? It's cold in here and it's full of old furniture and appliances that nobody wants. That closet has a bunch of cleaning supplies and old carpeting. It's kind of depressing."

"I like it!" she said. "See those doors near the ceiling? The doors that look like they're for a barn," she said, pointing to the front of the room, the one section where the ceiling was high. "This used to be a wine cellar. They'd drop down crates through those doors from the garage. That's why it's cold in here. Nobody uses the doors anymore, but they're part of the history."

"Is that why I can hear cars up there?" I asked.

My mom loosened the sleeping bag from her body and draped it across me.

"I can stuff a towel under the door. I've done it before," she said. "There's the space heater, too. I turn it on when I go to sleep."

I should have told her that I liked the basement office janitor storage room. If anyone else had shown it to me, I would have thought that for free rent, it was a gem. But this was my mother, and I couldn't see past our own long history and her failures as a parent. I could see that the world had abused her—Korea had told her that she wasn't pretty or thin or smart or successful, America had said she was inscrutably Korean, her family had disowned her, her husband had turned violent and tyrannical, her friends wouldn't help her when she wanted to escape him, she'd never been able to pursue a career that she wanted and couldn't picture stability in old age, and her children were grown and didn't want her around. Knowing this, I still couldn't look past my own pain to acknowledge hers. I could trace mine back to my earliest memories, and she had caused it. My own lifelong pain was far more tangible than hers, and that's how I failed as a daughter.

"I could probably live here," I said. "But not you."

"Why not me?"

"Because. It's sad," I said. "You're sixty. You live in a house in the suburbs. I don't know any other mothers who are sixty who are trying to leave their lives in the suburbs and move to the city to live in a storage room even if it's temporary. What are you doing? Why are you going to open houses? You can't afford any of those houses. Why are you staying here in this sad room? You're calling it 'my apartment,' like you actually live here."

I wasn't telling my mom what she needed to hear.

"If you think I shouldn't stay here, then where am I supposed to stay?" she asked.

"You could stay at my apartment once in a while," I said.

"You never offered! I don't want to, anyway. I want to stay here. I like my apartment and I like this neighborhood. I've gotten used to coming here. Do you want to stay with me tonight?"

"I should go home," I said.

"Why? You can stay here," she said. "Then I don't have to be alone."

I didn't have a good reason, since the following day was a Sunday and I had no plans. The days of the week were losing significance for me anyway. I couldn't seem to make myself attend classes anymore, when I'd once been so disciplined. I didn't know if it was that graduation was looming or if I feared the three-month BARBRI course that everyone described as death and as necessary to pass the grueling three-day bar exam. It was finally dawning on me that completing these milestones meant that I'd really be a lawyer, at least once I made it through the job market, survived the application and interview process, and convinced a firm to hire me. Never in my life had I dreamed of being a lawyer. How had I gotten here? I knew how. Pressure from my parents, which was a kind way of putting it. In truth, it was unhinged bullying, the kind that made me numb, unable to think straight. Now I was trying to find a way out. But I was too afraid to quit because I'd stop getting checks from school and wouldn't be able to make rent. I'd need to pick up a temp job or figure out something else to make ends meet once the money ran out.

I didn't want to stay the night with my mom, especially in that basement room sharing a convertible sofa bed. I felt the way I used to when I was a child and my mom would sneak into my bed at night, because, she said, it reminded her of a time when she was younger and I'd just come into the world, or of when she was very young and I didn't yet exist. She'd whisper in the dark, her voice light and bouncy like a schoolgirl, telling me that she wished she could go back—to when I was a baby and she was a young mother—and back even further—to when she was a child herself, giggling and sharing stories under the covers with her sister in Korea. Before falling asleep, every time, she'd tell me that my life seemed fun—easy, open. *Will you switch places with me?* she'd ask, begging almost, as if my consent could make everything change.

"I'm supposed to meet up with my roommate tonight," I said. This was a lie, but lies came easy for me.

"Your roommate? You mean . . ." my mom said, trailing off. "Is he your boyfriend?"

"Samir's not my boyfriend. He's my best friend," I said. "Anyway, Samir doesn't like girls."

"Okay," she said.

Two of my male cousins had already announced that they didn't like girls—one was even caught in bed with a boy in high school—but everyone from my mother's generation had chosen to ignore them. *Kee still doesn't want to get married,* they said.

"I'm sure you have a lot of friends," she said. "You should go out with your friends."

We lay there in silence, absorbing the discomfort of our conflicting needs and desires. My mom wanted me to stay, but I had to get away from her, and she didn't want to make me do anything anymore. My mom explained quietly that the basement room couldn't be rented legally as living space—it didn't meet the city's building codes—but could be leased for business purposes or office space. As far as she knew, Mr. Kwan had used the room only for storage.

"He's losing money," she said. "It's ready to go. Why doesn't he rent it? I guess he doesn't need the money."

I remembered the voicemail she'd left the previous month, saying that she was in the city and maybe she'd stop by. I could see that the message was extremely long, based on the minutes displayed on my phone, but this was one of my mom's habits that had always annoyed me. Who habitually leaves ten-minute messages? I hadn't played the whole thing, and at the point when she mentioned the possibility of staying over, I'd stopped listening. In fact, the moment I heard her voice, I'd already had my finger ready, hovering above the delete button. It wasn't that I didn't want to have her over, or that I wanted her out on the streets. I was so angry about so many things and had been for so long that any thought of her was completely incoherent in my mind. I wanted her to suffer and feel rejection as I had.

"The people upstairs pay five thousand dollars a month for a two-bedroom flat," my mom said. "Can you believe it? It's because of the location! How much do you pay?"

"Not that much," I said.

"What, you won't tell me?"

My mom folded her hands behind her head, sighing as she looked at the ceiling.

"I love it here," she said. "When I'm driving to the city, as I cross the bridge, all my worry disappears. You know, me and your appa, we lived in San Francisco before you were born, when we first came to America."

"Yeah, I know," I said.

A car started its engine above us, revving, then idling. It sounded distant and near at once, like a voice underwater.

"Appa was in San Francisco, and I was in LA with my family. I ran away with him. He came and got me in the middle of the night. He waited outside in his car—a Bug, same as the one he got for you—while I snuck out. We drove to San Francisco and got married a week later."

My mom slid closer, brought herself so near that I could see every pore on her face. She was staring at my skin like it was a new dress that she was checking for defects before purchasing.

"It's still like baby skin. So soft," she said. She caressed my cheek tenderly and patted it with the tips of her fingers. She poked and pulled the skin gently, checking for elasticity. She'd often told me that my face was so small it was like a walnut, which she demonstrated by holding up her hand wadded into a fist, shaking it for emphasis.

"What do you use?" she asked. "Maybe I'll use it too."

"Nothing special," I said.

"I remember when you were little, you said you wanted to be just like me," she said.

"I don't remember that," I said. This was not a lie. I didn't remember, though later I recalled that for much of my life I'd craved her approval. It had been so long, I could barely remember the feeling.

We were so close, I could feel my mother's breath on my face. Her wistful and tender mood made me feel gentle toward her. With no warning, everything shifted, but that's often how things worked in my family, otherwise how would a surprise be a surprise? It was time to remind me of where I stood, where my place was and had been all this time. There was power that other people had, could have, but it wasn't mine, would never be mine. This was a reality that had to be announced on occasion. How else does someone at the bottom know how little they're valued in this world? All my life, everything connected to the idea of what I could and couldn't have, in small and big ways, quietly setting the tone, determining the range of my choices without my even knowing it.

"I'm leaving everything to Kevin. He's my son," she said. "He's supposed to get everything." She waited a moment for my response. Hearing none, she continued.

"My mother did the same thing—to me and my sisters," she said.

It shouldn't have been news to me, neither her intention about her own will nor the execution of her late mother's. My mom had divulged both many times before, mostly when I'd been very young and under different circumstances, when money problems had sparked panic and blame and regret about her life choices.

A few years earlier, her mother had died, leaving everything to her two brothers, both surgeons living in Orange County, but nothing to my mom and her four sisters. The bulk of my grandmother's estate consisted of a very old house in Seoul and two equally old but smaller houses on the same piece of property. A popular K-drama had been filmed in the main house during the rise of the Korean wave, greatly increasing the value of the compound. My mom and her sisters, like me, had been told since birth that, as daughters, they'd inherit nothing.

I shouldn't have been surprised, but I'd never let myself believe she would really follow such an obviously archaic and unfair tradition. It was clear now, however, that it had never been an idle threat. There was no reason to be telling me now, except as a warning. It felt like I was hearing it for the first time, except that I wasn't. I remembered each time she'd told me, but I'd chosen to forget. It was like getting punched in the gut in the same spot again and again.

I stared at my mom. I'd learned from my father and brother that lack of emotion can be the cruelest presence. My eyes burned into her face, and in that moment I thought she was ugly beyond description. In no universe could I have any resemblance to my mother.

"Why would you do that to me?" I said. "Do you know how stupid that is?"

My mom acted like I hadn't said anything.

We gazed at the ceiling. I could hear voices muffled above us, car doors slamming shut, and the hum of an engine, warm and smooth, like the car my dad drove.

We were both avoiding the big issue: Kevin, who was supposed to get everything, wasn't ready to deal with anything. If my mother and I seemed dysfunctional, I don't know what you'd call my brother. We were all wrapped up in our own lives, not paying attention to Kevin. None of us mentioned that he'd stopped returning phone calls and had gotten very slow responding to emails, when he responded at all. When I sent him an IM asking why he hadn't shown up to the get-together at our gomo's house, his response was one word: "Forgot."

"Do you want to go to the roof?" my mom asked. "The view is beautiful!"

I looked at her with repulsion, but she continued to ignore me.

"Don't you?" she said.

"Don't I what?"

"It's beautiful at night. Lights everywhere! You can see the whole city and Golden Gate Bridge and the ocean. I love to go up there. As soon as I step onto the roof, all my stress is gone. I don't have to think about anything. Can I show you?"

I figured that the real thing would not match what was in her imagination, or what she wanted me to believe and that she knew was not true. I remembered how she'd once tried to give me a canvas tote bag, a freebie she'd picked up at a home renovation convention. She kept showing it to me, holding up the blank side in different poses while obviously trying to conceal the other side, which it turned out was screen printed with an unironic picture of George W. Bush.

I didn't want to share something beautiful with her, especially after she'd made everything ugly by reminding me of my disinheritance. Financial insecurity had always compelled my mom to exclude me—the daughter, at the bottom of the ladder—so that she could support my brother—the son, at the top, who was supposed to save her. I understand now that this is the way the world works on a much larger scale. Neither of us knew then that Kevin wouldn't be saving anyone.

Something was holding me back from saying no to my mom, even though, if you'd held a gun to my head, I would have told you to just shoot. I wanted her to feel disappointed, but more than anything, I wanted her to know what she was doing to me without my having to tell her.

"What can you see up there?" I asked, undecided, still. I wasn't giving in, but I wasn't completely gone. Still on the fence. That's where I was. It was the best I could do.

"Everything!"

I looked at her—reclined on the pullout couch, eyes focused on the ceiling, arms open wide as if ready to catch anything. She said it again. "Everything!"

Her enthusiasm made me wonder if there was something I'd missed the last time I'd taken in the same view from a friend's apartment one block up. I'd only been to my friend's place in the daytime after all. Maybe it was different at night.

A moment earlier I was so certain you'd never find me hanging out on the roof with my mom unless I'd been drugged and kidnapped, but of course it's exactly where I ended up, and of my own volition. We climbed several flights of stairs, and then a doorway spilled us into the crisp night. Out of breath, I looked around. There was a little patio set and a narrow herb garden. Our hair danced in the wind and whipped our faces. I pulled my jacket tightly around me. My mom spun in circles, arms stretched out. We were alone.

It did look different at night. There were lights everywhere, as far as I could see. The whole city was lit up, bodegas and skyscrapers glowing, the streets winking with traffic lights. The roads looked like a game of Pac-Man, headlights crawling in straight lines like dots on a screen. I could see all the way across the city to distant neighborhoods, where the roofs had lights turned on as if they knew people like us came out at night to look across the way. The Golden Gate Bridge was illuminated, a flood of gold-tinged light brightening the sky, little red lamps lining the cables strung above. Underneath, boats and ships cut through the ocean, blinking lights navigating the night. In the distance I thought I could see the hazy outline of mountains, electrical towers in the foreground lit in the shape of triangles. Nearby, Coit Tower had left a light on for us. The city was beautiful and ridiculous, a spectacle, all that light polluting the sky, allowing us to see nothing but artificial energy that obscured the billions of stars above us. But I loved it. The city would never be mine—I hadn't grown up here and I wasn't staying and I had a feeling I wouldn't be back. One day I'd want to find a place to settle down and I knew it wouldn't be here, based on what I'd gleaned about the real estate market from my mom. But my internal map of the city was like a map of myself, the streets and parks and neighborhoods carrying memories of friends and laughter, late nights and bad dates. This city was where I had escaped my mom's obsessions and learned to see myself with my own eyes.

My mom stood closer to the edge. I watched her as she took in the vista, her face glowing with the city light. She looked so happy and content. When I looked back at the landscape, I tried to see what my mom saw. The expanse lit up so bright and glittery looked like my mother's future: a second chance, freedom, a return to her youth. I didn't know if she'd get what she wanted from the city, but I hoped that it would change her as it had changed me.

4

BAD ENERGY

March 2002

SPENDING TIME WITH my mom had left me adrift and disoriented, as if I'd survived a game show where the losers had all died. I started taking walks alone, thinking of all the changes in my parents' lives and in my own. Sometimes I'd find myself lost in thought several neighborhoods over and, too tired to walk back, I'd hop on the Muni and space out as we passed tidy rows of tall, narrow houses, the bus bending like an accordion, the pivoting joint stretching and wiggling at each turn. On the way home one night, I got a text from Samir: *Just got in from work. Where are you? Par-tay in the Mission.* He was the only person who texted me back then. I barely knew how to do it. Without hesitation, I agreed to meet him at the corner of 16th and Mission. I needed a pick-me-up, and as I headed toward the steps to the subway, closer to Samir and our circle of friends, I could feel myself detach from my family, as if they were a coat I could slip on and off, replace with a sparkly new one when it was time to be the Jane I wanted to be.

As I came up the escalator in the Mission, Samir was already there waiting at the top. He'd never say that he was looking out for me, but I could always feel his protective nature. We walked together, matching each other's strides for several blocks. We were so in sync that people often thought we were a couple. I'd always understood our closeness to be a result of sex never entering the equation—because he was gay, it didn't hurt my feelings that he wasn't romantically interested in me, though I was attracted to his dark wavy hair and the fact that he always looked grouchy and unapproachable, like an Arab Mr. Darcy, even when he was in a cheerful mood.

We passed taquerías and falafel joints and Latino bodegas. The neighborhood's grungy bars had become hip, bouncing with new bands and young professionals and money. Every block seemed to offer a shiny new shop: artisanal doughnuts, artisanal axes, farm-to-table crêpes, alpaca wool, new old stock workwear.

"Who's gonna be there?" I asked.

"The usuals," he said.

For the rest of the walk, all the way to the front door of a friend of a friend's house on Guerrero, we gossiped about the latest hookups and breakups, new and old faces. A respite from the chaos of my family, a safe place where moods and behavior were predictable. Samir was a software engineer, a career often described as suitable for the steady and levelheaded, which he was, or for the boring, which he wasn't. He commuted to Redwood City (Deadwood City, he called it), where he worked for one of those companies that has so many employees, the office is an entire campus with a cafeteria, a gym, daycare facilities, multiple parking lots, and shuttles. He had the kind of job that my mom coveted because it was so often held by the young couples who were always outbidding her on the houses she wanted. Samir was my only friend who knew the whole story about my family and the truth about law school. Without him, I would have had no one to talk to about my mom crashing my life in the city and my dad's new life as a truck driver, about my strained relationship with Kevin. It was funny how he knew so much about them, but they knew so little about him. No matter what I told her, my mom still thought he was secretly my boyfriend.

MY MOTHER WAS certain that owning a home in San Francisco was the key to her fortune. One day when its value doubled, she could sell, marking the beginning of an upward trajectory. Perhaps the proceeds would get her a complex with a few units and she could collect rent from the leases. From there, a bigger building with more units, and maybe a spacious house—who knew how far she'd go. She was the next tycoon. It was why she admired Stan Kwan. He'd been doing it for so long now, he'd become a real estate mogul by his thirties. My mom wished that she'd started when she was still young like he had, back when everybody was fleeing the city, not trying to get in.

Life with my father hadn't turned out the way she'd pictured it. She'd never gotten comfortable financially, never felt that there was enough, always ten steps behind. The years that we owned Swensen's were hard on her. Our new house had a big mortgage, we'd bought one too many luxury cars, there was Kevin's private school tuition, our tennis and piano lessons, our tutors and SAT prep, the country club membership, and college was only a couple years away. The restaurant wasn't making enough to cover all our expenses, so she and my father had laid off a few employees and she did all their jobs herself, unwilling to give up anything we'd gained, on her feet from morning until night waiting tables, bussing tables, scooping ice cream into cones and milkshakes and sundaes, grilling burgers and frying chicken, washing dishes, mopping floors. She'd never expected that to be her life. She'd thought she'd get to brunch and shop and play tennis all day. My dad had been a good father and husband—in the sense that he was responsible and hardworking and would never leave us—but he'd never shown us love in obvious ways, and even when he was there it was like he wasn't, his silence so pervasive that his bouts of rage felt all the more surprising. He'd never wanted to try anything new. He enjoyed camping and being on the road, driving to national parks, but he wouldn't consider Paris or Rome, places that my mom wished she could visit. He'd once told me that he didn't feel comfortable as an Asian man traveling to Europe, but I'd wondered: Then why Kentucky? Why Utah, Oklahoma, Idaho? Why live in Napa? Wouldn't you come across more Asians in Paris or Rome than in most places in America? On top of everything, my brother had gotten married and now answered to his wife, not his mother. She could no longer depend on him to secure her future. At sixty she was taking stock of her life. She hadn't gotten what she'd wanted, but it wasn't too late, she could still turn things around. She had big energy and the rest of her life to go.

So my mom kept going to open houses. Nearly anything for sale was snatched up immediately, sometimes sight unseen, before a single viewing, and everything was out of her range, even apartments, condos, and tenancies in common. But nothing was going to stop her from moving to San Francisco. When Stan Kwan offered her free rent in exchange for serving as the on-site manager in one of his buildings, my mom moved in the next day with a suitcase and a futon she and my dad used to take camping. I stopped by the basement storage unit in North Beach where she'd been crashing and picked up the few things she'd been keeping there. The furniture and the rest of her stuff from Napa came later, when my dad and I spent a weekend carrying everything up two flights of stairs into the first place she'd ever lived alone. Maybe it was strange for my dad to help her move, as Samir had said, but that was just the way they did things. They'd known each other their whole lives. Even though my mom was leaving my dad, it didn't mean he wouldn't be there for her when she needed him. He'd never been ambitious enough for her, but on a good day, he admired her ambition. He just didn't like when she blamed him for not giving her enough. The apartment was on California Street at the edge of Chinatown—a great location and a nice building, much better than my situation, and she didn't even have to pay for it. "My apartment is better than yours," she said to me gleefully. My mom was back on top.

As a new city dweller and especially because she was living alone, my mom needed help with a lot of things, and she expected that I'd visit periodically to give her guidance and company. I came each time bearing gifts. Korean persimmons for collagen, inflammation, and regularity. Jeju citrus tea for digestion. Red bean buns from the bakery down the block to satisfy the carbs-lover in both of us. Picking up treats for my mom was annoying, but I didn't mind the inconvenience if it meant my visits started out on the right foot.

I'd managed to attend my law school classes about half the time that semester and I'd failed most of my midterms. When I was supposed to be studying, I was researching PhD programs in American Studies, or what was called Ethnic Studies at some schools. Back in college, I'd taken a class on Korean Americans. I'd wanted to learn more about the history of Koreans in America, to understand what we'd inherited from generations of war and immigration, but to stay on track and graduate on time I'd had to complete my coursework in English, my chosen major. In the Korean Americans class, I'd met a TA who had answered all my questions about grad school during office hours. I'd wondered if academia was a life that I could pursue, but my parents had been haranguing me about my future since my first week of college. To get them off my back I'd given them an answer that I knew would make them happy. The problem was once I'd said "law school," they wouldn't let me change my mind. Now law school was almost over, and I was having to face the choice I'd made that I'd never felt was mine. I was becoming obsessed with the idea of going to grad school—not only did it seem like a way out, a change that could save me, it was the only thing I could remember that I'd wanted on my own, that no one had a stake in. But I couldn't tell my parents, not unless I had an actual plan in motion. And I'd already brought up the grad school idea my junior year of college right before enrolling in an expensive LSAT prep course that my parents had found. Once my parents put down the first installment, I knew I'd have to commit—I couldn't let their money go to waste. But when I mentioned the possibility of grad school, my parents broke down simultaneously into panicked shouting about money—who would pay for it and what kind of living would I make when I finished the degree. So now, as I secretly submitted applications to grad school and waited to hear back, I told my dad that I was moving. I needed a change, I said, I wanted to get out of California. I'd graduate, get my law degree, and move to another state, take that other state's bar exam. It was a complicated lie. I suppose I was providing a distraction while I ironed things out and got my life set up the way I wanted. And it wasn't really a lie. I wanted to graduate; I was afraid not to. My plan was to keep going to class, more or less, pass my exams and graduate, maybe even take the bar exam, but all the while I'd get myself into a PhD program, figure out how to pay for it, and set myself up wherever that might be. I'd never thought that a life in academia could work for someone like me, but now I wondered.

While I'd told my dad I was moving during one of his calls from the road, I had yet to tell my mom. It was the type of news that required an in-person conversation. Her voice sounding directly in my ear through the phone when she was unhappy could be harder to take than face to face. I could block out anything that was too insulting or melodramatic if I could focus on other things about her—the way her hair curled inward into twin Cs on either side of her face, the scent of her homemade lemon verbena cleaning solution, her silk rug squishing under my toes. Whatever she said, in whatever tone or volume, I would keep my objections to myself. The powerless are often the people who shout the most, and after a lifetime of never being heard, my mom could shout the loudest, which was often self-defeating, but she deserved to have the satisfaction of a good spell of ranting.

I purchased the red bean buns and persimmons on the walk up Grant Street. The tea I'd picked up in San Jose, the closest place that had the supermarkets necessary for a good Asian American—H Mart, 99 Ranch, Lion, Đai-Thành. My mom's apartment was located at the border of Nob Hill and Chinatown, an area that probably had a name in the form of a portmanteau (NobChin?) or something quirky like the

Pink Triangle or the Rainbow Patch. New neighborhood designations continued to pop up everywhere, even though the city itself never got any bigger.

My mom's new building was on an incline so steep and panoramic that Hollywood had been filming car chase scenes down her street since the sixties. One block up, the sidewalk turned into a staircase that climbed so high, nearly vertical, the street disappeared into the sky. Athletic types in high-tech spandex and fluorescent running shoes, heart rate monitors strapped to their chests, ran up and down the steps, resembling killing machines. While my mom's apartment wasn't at the very top where the street peaked off, the view from her building reached across the city and out over the bay, sunlight streaming up from the water and bouncing off the glass walls of the skyscrapers and the hoods of cars and the glittering sidewalks, dazzling me.

I could smell the incense wafting from her apartment, a woody scent, tinged with musk and powder. Inside, it was overwhelming. There were two white pillar candles in the living room, the little flames flickering.

"They are magic," my mom said.

They referred to the incense and the candles, all purchased from her psychic.

"They push out negativity. I lit an extra candle because I knew you were coming."

My mom followed her psychic's instructions faithfully, lighting the incense and the candle for exactly an hour twice a day, every morning and evening at eight, stubbing out the incense stick and snuffing the candlewick with pinched fingertips—*Never blow out the candle*—at nine o'clock on the dot.

"Because the gypsy told me to," my mom said when I asked why. "It protects against negative power and bad energy. She said I need to block out bad luck and spells and jealous people."

"Stop calling her a gypsy," I said.

"She won't stop calling me," she said. "I shouldn't have given that gypsy my phone number." My mom and the psychic were on the outs.

We sat in the living room, all that burning and energy working to push out the negativity that was me. I told her the bad news.

My mom listened quietly. She took a bite of the persimmon I'd brought, which she'd pared and sliced into wedges. She waited until I finished talking before asking questions. She had only one.

"Will you come with me to see the gypsy?"

"I thought you were avoiding her," I said.

"This is important. Will you come with me?"

"I don't think so," I said, shaking my head.

My mom's face tightened, then dropped, muscles loose, slack.

"I never could say no to my mother," she said, chewing slowly. "I wasn't allowed. If she asked for something, I had to do it. I didn't have a choice."

I'd always thought that defiance was a trait some people were born with, but I was beginning to think that it was something we learned or unlearned in response to the invisible rules of the world. I didn't want to do what my mom was asking of me. I'd never gone to see a psychic, despite my mom's efforts. My mom, on the other hand, regularly consulted psychics for financial advice and guidance on decisions big and small: Should she sell her house and when? Which season is best to invite her sister for a visit? Should she go on the trip to Palm Springs with her tennis team? Occasionally, she visited the psychic out of boredom. My mom enjoyed the suspense, the hope, even the fear, of all the possible futures the psychic promised. Many of my Asian friends' mothers also consulted psychics, as regularly as some women got their nails done. Once while visiting a Vietnamese friend in Long Beach, I was turned away at the front door, after having originally been invited, because my friend's mom had since consulted a psychic who advised her to keep strangers out of the house until Mercury was out of retrograde. Even President Park Geun-hye, the first female president of South Korea, relied on a spiritual advisor, though she was eventually impeached and sentenced to prison for the criminal activity arising from the relationship.

My mom sensed that I was about to say something. Which is probably why she spoke first.

"The gypsy said this would happen," she said, her voice low.

"What?"

"That one of you would disappear. I was afraid it would be Kevin."

"Good thing it's not Kevin," I said.

"I haven't heard from him in a while."

"So maybe it *is* him."

"I had a bad dream," she said. "I dreamt that a porcupine was stuck in the toilet and it wouldn't come out! I used a toilet plunger, but the porcupine wouldn't go down or come out. When I woke up, I was crying," she said. Her eyes teared up. "I went to the gypsy. You know what she said?" my mom asked. "She said that something bad is about to happen. She knew. That's what the candles are for. She gave them to me to burn out the bad energy."

"I don't think it worked," I said.

"Why do you have to be so negative?" she said. "You've always been like that. I don't know why. Kevin's not like you. You're the reason why I had to light two candles today. Why can't you talk in a more joyful way?"

When I was growing up, my mother favored Kevin to such a degree that even other parents noticed. When I was a teenager in high school, my friend Gemma Olson's mother often pulled me aside. Gemma and I were friends because we were the same age and lived in the same neighborhood, though she often complained that her mom pushed her to be friends with me because she wished that Gemma had my discipline and athletic talent.

"Mothers always deny having a favorite," Ms. Olson said. "We even deny it to ourselves, but we all have one."

I don't remember what prompted the attention in that particular moment. Perhaps I was standing apart from Gemma and our friends, a kind of self-isolation arising from conscious and unconscious aggressions, not surprising or particularly interesting considering the racial and socioeconomic makeup of our insular and unremarkable social world. Gemma's mom had talked to my mom enough times to notice a pattern—she was always bragging about my brother, always putting me down.

During those years and for many years forward, my mom was obsessed with her only son. She had a big stake in who he'd become since in her cultural understanding, he was responsible to care for her in her old age. A kind of parallel and contrasting philosophy applied to me, along with an unreasonable disdain—her daughter's success or failure would neither benefit nor hurt her, since a Korean woman's daughter belonged to the family she married into, and since women are belongings and the people they belong to are men, any caregiving that might be extended to her birth family, if at all, was granted only to her father.

I didn't know how much was cultural, how much was generational, whether some rules applied only within my own family. But I'd seen the most selfless Korean women shamed as spoiled, selfish, high maintenance. It was reflexive. Claiming that Korean daughters were spoiled felt like an assertion of status and class, and while one could say it was a compliment—"We're *lifting* our daughters!"—it felt rooted in the hatred of women. Korean mothers like mine had to put down their own daughters, make us know our place, be sure that we didn't have too much confidence, never, ever compliment us, otherwise a Korean mother was a bad mother.

People who weren't Korean didn't understand. I barely did. I was always forgetting and remembering again—that was our job, as Korean Americans, to remember, to keep remembering. The alternative was to spiral, become lost, take the wrong side.

Ms. Olson was divorced, a single mom. She was in her mid-forties, like my mom. She had white blonde hair that she'd passed down to Gemma, their most noticeable trait because the shade was so rare. They also shared the same ice blue eyes, but beyond hair and eye color they didn't look alike. Ms. Olson was tall, lean, and athletic, her face as angular and muscular as her physique. Gemma was on the short side, like me, and while not large, she was soft, not thin and sinewy like her mother, and her oval face was more open, with wide-set eyes and a mouth like a bow. She tried out for every sports team at our high school because she craved her mother's approval. You don't need talent to join a high school athletics team, but it was clear to anyone at the meets for tennis and volleyball and basketball and soccer, even to those who didn't know the rules of the games, that Gemma was no athlete. Ms. Olson ran for miles and miles, training for this or that marathon, tennis and swimming on her off days, cycling and yoga on occasion. She was the fittest mom I'd ever seen. To have the time for the kind of working out that molds a body to look like that, a person would either have to not have a job, which she didn't, or be a professional athlete. The only work she knew was the work of staying in shape. Gemma and her brother were latchkey kids, because their mother was always away from home participating in a sport or a tournament or a race. At home, the fridge and pantry were nearly empty. There were bags of microwave popcorn, raisins, and Lipton iced tea mix. Occasionally some avocadoes or a little basket of berries. Never anything resembling the makings of a meal.

Ms. Olson's brother was a pioneer of mountain biking, having established the first mountain bike company in the world after spending the second half of the nineteen seventies riding balloon-tired hoopties down Marin's Mt. Tamalpais with other pot-smoking, jean-shorted hippies. Her ex-husband was a retired stockbroker turned winemaker, though not a particularly successful one, the kind where the business was just staying afloat and in thirty years would ride a self-promoted story about being one of the original wineries in the valley before the town became Beverly Hillsified, before it began to diversify and introduce progressive ideas and businesses, even allowing for a Black family-owned winery, though nobody would talk about the time when a group of Black women got kicked off the Wine Train for talking too loud, or when real estate agents took down FOR RENT signs if a Black person came up the walkway, or when selling your house to a Black family was explicitly discouraged. Last I heard, the winemaker ex-husband was still calling Mexicans Spics and Asians Chinks. He thought it was the same as calling a person wearing glasses Four Eyes, which he also did. Saying "Ching Chong Ching Chong" at the mention of anything Asian was fair game and he encouraged Gemma to do it too. I knew because she told me so when she tried to defend herself regarding the many times she said "Ching Chong Ching Chong" in my presence, sometimes directed at others and sometimes at me. If anyone had a problem with any of the above, they were "too PC." He thought he deserved things because he was a white man and bragged often about subscribing to *The New Yorker.* To this day, if someone mentions *The New Yorker*, there's a moment where I can't tell the difference between the person in front of me and my memory of this despicable man.

Inheritance got Ms. Olson a modest house in the same desirable neighborhood where my family lived. She received spousal support, though it didn't seem to be enough for herself and her two towheaded children—they wouldn't turn on the heat, the lights only when necessary, everything was secondhand, there was never enough food in the house. At the same time, she still didn't have to work, got to enjoy the rare privilege of free time.

I always thought that it was my competitive tennis training that drew her attention—she'd taken to cutting out and posting on the fridge mentions of me in *Tennis* magazine, and often I'd spied her at the club standing alone on a neighboring court, watching me drill with my coach, mouth open—but I was beginning to realize that there was more to it, a bond forged by something we didn't understand, a shared melancholy that neither of us ever recognized.

If I met Ms. Olson today, I wouldn't give her a second thought, would think of her as someone not worth my time, but the truth is: she was one of the few adults who treated me like a person, who respected me. Maybe it was for this reason that Gemma, who was my friend, wanted to see me fail. Maybe it was the influence of her father, or of America. In any case, I prefer to remember Gemma's mother, and not Gemma.

"All mothers have a secret favorite, but your mother is different," Ms. Olson said. "She *wants* her favorite to be Kevin, explicitly."

She sat on a patio chair in the backyard wearing just a sports bra with jogging shorts and sneakers, having just returned from running the backroads along the vineyards. Her freckled skin was browned a golden shade of toasted white bread, the way very light-haired people tan, if they tan at all. Her eyes were closed, face pushed toward the sun, like a houseplant.

"I think we have a lot in common," she said.

She looked at me kindly. Gemma stood nearby, drinking iced tea and petting a neighbor's cat that had leaped onto the potting bench. She watched us suspiciously.

"We both have mothers who don't understand us," Ms. Olson said.

Those of us who carry too much guilt can sense it in others, a bond that can't be explained. Memory is printed in our cells, fires in the synapses of our brains, manifests in the way we think and the way we talk.

This other mother could see my mom's faults, but couldn't understand why my mom felt no shame. She sensed my own guilt, which is why she confided in me, though I tend to believe that she didn't know where mine came from.

My guilt stemmed from different sources. How I fit into America with more ease than my mother, my father, or Kevin, operating like a spy, moving in and out, taking and withholding and pretending. My particular type of oppression—young, Asian, a woman—that made certain people want to save me. A long history of being put down and put in my place, shamed and insulted from every side for any action or lack thereof, for speaking or failing to speak, for being too successful or mediocre or a failure, for any preference and any choice—in short, a person who's been subjected to too much victimization will feel guilty all the time, both for her compliance and her resistance.

Another source of guilt: my mother's need for Kevin, and how it gave me space that Kevin didn't get. I never wanted that kind of attention. I could see what it was doing to him.

Last: I was about to leave my mom behind.

"WHY WON'T YOU come with me to see the gypsy?" my mom said. "You say you're moving, but you don't even know where you're moving. The gypsy can tell us what direction you should avoid and which way you can go that's safe and will bring you luck."

"I can't let a psychic decide where I end up."

"How can you not know? How are you going to get a job? How will you be ready to take the bar exam? I thought the exam is different in every state. How will I know what's going on?"

"I'll tell you."

"Will you tell the whole true?"

"So help me God," I said.

My mom watched me with an unwavering gaze, so intense it felt as if she was peering into my soul. Could she see my lies? She kept staring in silence, not even blinking—I wondered if she was trying to cast a spell. I became so uncomfortable that I had to say something to change the mood.

"You could visit me," I said with too much enthusiasm.

"But where?"

"I have to figure it out. I'll know soon."

My mother looked angry and hurt, as if I'd stolen a family heirloom and sold it. Soon I'd receive the results from my grad school applications and I could tell her more then—I could tell her the truth. For now, all I could do was get her ready for the big change that was coming, though it would turn out that I was as unprepared for what was coming as she was.

"I want to live somewhere new," I said. "I've been here my whole life. Nobody wants to stay near their hometown. People move far away all the time."

"Not everyone," she said. My mother's pained expression made the room shrink. I thought I could see the smoke from the incense and candles thicken and swirl around us, summoning all the negative power and bad energy, and pushing it away from me and my mother. She walked to the table where the candles and incense burned, her hand up with pinched fingertips. There was a final puff of smoke, dense and marbly, that hung above my mom's head like a question mark.

THE LAST COUPLE months that Samir and I lived together we took a lot of walks, like a middle-aged couple. We dressed in layers, jacket over sweatshirt over T-shirt, because walking in San Francisco can feel menopausal—hot and cold, back and forth and back again. You can go from a warm, sunny spot of the city to frigid wind on a hill up high. Walking up an incline, the layers come off. The longer you stand still, the clothes go back on.

At first, we walked to specific destinations, our stomachs guiding us. The donut shop in the Tenderloin, the bakery in Chinatown, Indian ice cream in the Mission. Then we walked aimlessly, from one neighborhood to the next, and sometimes we'd end up at the shore, the ocean waves lapping at our feet. On weekends, we walked during the day; on weekdays, in the evening, because Samir had his job in the South Bay. We often found ourselves sitting down for ramen at our favorite noodle place that had no sign or menu and was up a cobblestone staircase in a hidden alleyway. We called it No Name Noodles because we didn't know what it was called. The joint was small and crowded, and the room filled with steam from the hotpots and noodle soups and shabu-shabu enjoyed at every table.

On the way home one night, we took a detour through Alamo Square, where there was a park with a very high peak that overlooked the city. The wind had picked up, making my eyes fill with tears. We zipped up our jackets and hopped in place, trying to shake off the cold. I pointed at the Painted Ladies and their perfect triangular roofs, the pastel Victorians glowing like lanterns. I could never remember which one was the Tanner house from *Full House*, since the red door had been painted over. All around us, the city lights glittered, the buildings and streets twinkling, alive. It all looked so far away, as if we were ghosts looking down on the world we'd left behind.

"I want a different life," I said.

"Well, you're working on it, right?" Samir said.

"I guess so. But nothing's happened yet." I gazed at the lights blinking in the distance. "We'll keep being friends, right?" I asked.

"Why wouldn't we?"

"It just happens."

"It's not gonna happen," Samir said. "We won't change. We'll visit each other. We could even meet up somewhere different every year." Samir named the destinations on his bucket list, all the places he wanted to see while he was still young.

I hoped that Samir was right, but the travel he described had a price tag and I didn't see money in my future. I squeezed his arm and hooked mine through his as we walked down the grassy hill toward the Painted Ladies. When Samir began humming the theme song to *Full House*, I snorted and rolled my eyes, but we'd only walked a few steps before I chimed in, singing along. At the chorus, we screamed the lyrics at the top of our lungs. We were stupid kids shouting a stupid song from a show we both hated from the eighties. We'd watched a few reruns together on TV, mostly to make fun of the bad acting and the terrible script. I couldn't believe we could remember the lyrics.

We fell to the ground, doubled over in laughter, and tried to catch our breath, the grass cool and crunchy and pungent. When I looked up, Samir was rolling down the hill, screaming in a terrible high-pitched voice that I'd never believe was him except there was no one else there. I pulled my arms in close, made myself straight as a rolling pin, and I tumbled down right after him, the knoll steeper and craggier than I'd expected, laughing the whole way.

5

THE GRIEVING PARTY

March 2002

AFTER MY PARENTS' house in Napa was sold and before the new family moved in, while the house was in escrow, my mom had a party—part going-away, part grieving party about my going away.

Invitations went out on little white note cards letterpressed with pink hibiscus and a purple border, addressed to her friends, six Korean women who had immigrated to America in the sixties and seventies, after the Immigration Act of 1965 removed restrictions on Asian immigration. Some had arrived in the US already married, others had met Korean men who had also immigrated. They'd started families and opened small businesses, though their jobs were unrelated to anything they'd dreamed of doing or studied for while working toward degrees in Korea, which were often highly specialized. Many became greengrocers and owners of bodegas, bookstores, dry-cleaning and shoe repair businesses, which they managed themselves. They were successful businesspeople and masters of frugality and bought homes in the Bay Area that through the years rose exponentially in value. Since the sixties, my mom and the six women had kept in touch through an extended Korean network, long phone conversations, Korean church events, and the highways and transportation systems that joined us all from Berkeley to Oakland, San Jose, Cupertino, Marin, and San Francisco.

On the invitations, my mom wrote in Korean a message that translates to:

Party for Jane
Saturday, 12:30
Please wear black

I had never heard of a grieving party. I wasn't sure if it was a Korean thing.

"It's not like I'm dead," I said. "What's the party for?"

"If enough Korean mothers think about you at the same time in the same place, maybe you'll know," she said.

"Know what?"

"That we're *thinking* about you."

"But I'll be at the party. I'll know you're thinking about me."

"When you're gone, you'll know."

"Then why don't you have the party when I'm gone?"

My mom licked an envelope and scrunched her face in distaste.

On the day of the party, I peeked out the window as six women stepped carefully up the walkway. I wasn't surprised by their simultaneous arrival even though they'd driven separately from different locations. Korean aunties have a way like that. They make impossible things happen, magic seeming to sprinkle around them wherever they go. I could see the tops of their heads, gray dyed black, and the swishing of six sets of black coats. There was a flurry of black slacks and black skirts with black stockings and black shoes.

When I opened the door, the women greeted me, huddled together like penguins in the cold—Mrs. Chang, Mrs. Park, Mrs. Lee, Mrs. Oh, Mrs. Eom, Mrs. Cho. They all spoke at once:

"Ahhh! Jane-ah!"

"Waaaaaah! It's Jane-ah!"

"You got big!"

"You still look young!"

"Do you diet?"

"Aigoo!"

Six sets of hands touched me—my head, my hair, my back, shoulders, arms, and hands. "Do you remember me?" someone said. I smiled through the discomfort, but when they began taking off their black shoes, I missed the attention they'd showered on me. One by one, the loafers and sensible stacked heels lined up neatly in a row in the little nook off the foyer. I handed over six pairs of little velvet slippers from an old Korean cabinet that resembled an oversized pirate's treasure chest.

I noticed a toddler hiding behind Mrs. Park's legs, hands clutching one saggy knee. The girl's hair moved like water, her shiny bangs blunt-cut across the eyebrows. She had wide-set eyes, a round face, and a small mouth. She reminded me of fluffy kittens and stuffed toys, strawberry season and cotton candy, though even she was dressed in all black.

"My granddaughter, Yeon-ah," said Mrs. Park.

I was beginning to feel self-conscious in my jeans and flannel shirt, neither of which was black. I couldn't help but feel regretful in the face of all the guests who'd followed the rules. I worried that they thought I was being disrespectful to my mother.

A flurry of hands pushed one of the women forward.

"Jane, do you know who I am?"

I remembered the woman from my grandfather's funeral, the way she popped out from behind a family crypt, hedges trimmed all around it, bonsai-like, into little domes, the rounded caps of mushrooms. She sported an old lady perm and oversized chunky black glasses, the temples curlicued into thick baroque scrolls.

"I'm Maggie Cho's mother," she said, at the cemetery and again now, twenty years later at my parents' house, which in a matter of days would no longer belong to them. Her current eyewear was slightly less ostentatious, wire-rimmed eyeglasses with gold temples chain-linked in interlocking Cs, and she looked as if she'd barely aged even half the amount of time that had passed.

THE BAY AREA spans far and wide, from the city of San Francisco to the surrounding counties, extending, officially, from the wine country, the headlands, the parks and campgrounds in the north, to Silicon Valley in the south, with its strip malls and tech headquarters and massive parking structures and Asian grocery stores, and from the East Bay with its clusters of immigrant suburban communities and mini cities, the little crunchy haven of scholars and social progress, next door to the Bay's old refuge of hip-hop now gentrified by tech overflow and hipsters and artists, all the way over to the Peninsula with its preppy, athletic spirit, sanitized by technology, industry, and the future.

In the San Francisco Bay Area, the Korean population now included 60,000 residents. It would have been impossible for one Korean to personally know the 59,999 other Koreans living in the Bay Area, but out of seven million people, 60,000 is still not that many. When my parents' generation arrived, they were fewer still, and as new immigrants to a strange country with inscrutable customs, overly salted food, and a tedious language, they longed for community. My parents claimed that Koreans all knew each other or had at least heard of each other through word of mouth, each of us accounted for, connected by the shared history of a century of war and immigration, our families linked across the Bay and down into Southern California, strung together from LA to Atlanta to Queens, beyond the Pacific and back to the homeland, South Korea, the only Korea acknowledged by Korean Americans and the diaspora.

Over the decades, we had multiplied, but at the beginning we were only the first immigrant generation, without the comforts of Koreatowns, extended family, or a sense of community. The early Mr. and Mrs. Changs, the Parks, the Lees, the Ohs, the Eoms, the Chos, and the Kims needed each other to confirm our existence, to speak our shared language and compare winters in California to winters in Seoul, where trees were shaped like umbrellas and it snowed for days on end, where children walked home from school in wool mittens and bonnets, chomping roasted chestnuts purchased from street vendors. We needed to distinguish ourselves from the Chinese and Japanese, the Vietnamese, the Filipinos, who we were always being lumped in with as if our histories didn't exist, never mind the intercontinental wars or how Koreans were loathed throughout Asia, how Asians from the South and Southeast were loathed as well—it was arguable who'd win the prize for the most despised—and, of course the loathing was often directed at each other, amongst those of us who had come from those places where people have been the most historically powerless and victimized. Never mind that Korea took pride in the purity of the Korean race, called itself a monoracial nation. Maybe it had something to do with how the Japanese had tried to wipe out the Korean culture, as well as much of the rest of Asia, or it could have been the comfort women and the resulting shame and grief, or all those babies born out of wedlock sent overseas to be raised by white families, or how the Korean language had been outlawed, or any number of massacres, many unmemorialized and erased from memory.

Koreans in America share an allegiance to each other, to our presence as a whole, whether or not we want to, and even if some of us wish to deny it. We have a sense of loyalty, of obligation, as if we came into the world with it programmed in our DNA: responsibility reaches beyond the filial, beyond members of our own families, encompassing an entire network of people with whom we share shame and grief and pride and a way of seeing something funny in the bleakest situations.

The Changs, the Parks, the Lees, the Ohs, the Eoms, the Chos, and the Kims of the Bay Area always showed up when called upon. At weddings and funerals, even going-away grieving parties, these men and women appeared after years of absence, the way I know that I will when they're dead and buried and I've replaced them as the oldest living generation, when it's become my duty to represent my family and my people.

"DO YOU REMEMBER me?" Mrs. Cho asked.

"Yes," I said.

I smiled and extended my right hand. Mrs. Cho brushed my hand aside and hugged me, resting her head on my shoulder.

"I met you when you were born. You were a new baby, so you probably don't remember."

Mrs. Cho was at least four inches shorter than me. I was five foot four. The experience of literally looking down on someone while speaking to them made me feel both empowered and guilty.

"Do you know who Maggie Cho is?" Mrs. Cho asked, peering up at me.

"Yes," I said.

Maggie was several years older than me. Despite the age gap, my mom and Mrs. Cho had managed to keep a lively competition going between the two of us, probably beginning when I was still in the womb.

Behind Mrs. Cho, the others began to bustle. Mrs. Chang, Mrs. Park, Mrs. Lee, Mrs. Oh, Mrs. Eom, and the little girl Yeon-ah sprung forward, herding the throng of us inside.

"*Everybody* knows who Maggie Cho is!"

"Maggie was almost *famous*!"

"She could have had her own TV show, that's how almost famous she was."

"Where's your mother?"

I took the lead, guiding us all to the dining room, where I'd last seen my mom at work at the dining table arranging the dishes of food that she'd spent all morning and the previous day preparing.

"I heard you get good grades," a voice called out behind me.

"Soon you'll be a fancy lawyer!"

"Jane-ah, you got prettier, did you know?"

"That happens to Korean women. We get prettier with age."

"You're still skinny!"

"Aigoo, Jane is a good girl."

"She's a good daughter."

The dining room table was covered with all my mom's specialties. Pickled cucumber, three different kinds of kimchi, kimbap, stir-fried squid, grilled fish with heads attached, bulgogi, kalbi, fried chicken, jajangmyeon, cold buckwheat noodles, vegetable pancakes, soondubu stew, seaweed soup, a platter piled high with leaves of fresh green lettuce as large as fans, fried zucchini, gochujang and other sauces, purple rice with beans. The toddler was playing Rachmaninoff on the grand piano.

My mom was busy rearranging dishes, switching their places to make the spread more visually pleasing, as if stitching together panels of a quilt. The dishes covered nearly the entire surface of the table, which had been custom-made from reclaimed teak by a Japanese woodworker living in Berkeley. I remembered that my dad had not supported the purchase. He had many things to say about the Japanese—none of it nice—like plenty of Koreans from his generation, having grown up during and in the aftermath of Japanese occupation. My mom felt differently, preferring to think of Asians in America as connected by invisible thread, as if we owed a duty to one another, and disavowing the other was disavowing oneself. After some bickering, my mom had hired Takumi without telling my dad, and the new dining set appeared while he was at work. When he got home, he'd stopped in the hallway, observing the new piece of furniture from a distance, as if he'd discovered a hornet's nest in the yard. He never spoke of it.

Above the dining table hung a crystal chandelier, my mother's best-loved possession. My mom had a fascination with the piano showman Liberace. In the eighties and nineties, when multiple Liberace documentaries were making the rounds on prime-time television, my mom whooped for joy whenever she found one while flipping through the channels. I couldn't deny Liberace. I got sucked in, too. The mansions with ceiling murals depicting the Sistine Chapel, cherubs dancing on piano keys, jeweled hands floating next to an image of Liberace's own face. The gold staircases, the velvet and silk brocade sofas, the piano-shaped pool, the real pianos: white pianos, mirrored pianos, pianos with ornate carvings, gold leaf and rhinestone and crystal pianos, a gold candelabra placed on each one. Every room of every house glittered with multiple chandeliers, including the bathrooms. His Vegas house had a chandelier above a marble bathtub with marble pillars and gold faucets in the shape of swans.

My mom adjusted the dimmer, turning the chandelier lights down low. The crystals sparkled softly, and the fractured light made the whole room glow. The platters of food and the sauces on the table seemed to shift and shimmer, as if their image had been projected through a prism.

"Kevin Kim's mother! This is beautiful," said Mrs. Cho. "I wish Maggie could have been here. You made that fried chicken she loves and that's her favorite kind of kimchi," she said, pointing at the little cubed radishes.

"Maggie Cho's mother, Maggie really likes to eat," my mom said. "I remember when she was small, she was the chubbiest Korean girl. She hasn't changed at all."

Mrs. Cho laughed, unperturbed.

"Jane has always been skinny," Mrs. Cho said. "She never had a problem with her weight. It must have been all that tennis," she said, nodding. "Maggie just started her residency at the children's hospital at Johns Hopkins. What's Jane doing now?"

Mrs. Cho knew full well that I was still a student, making my way through law school, not making a salary, not yet a respectable member of society, not buying my parents lavish gifts to show my gratitude for their sacrifices. She knew, as well, that the party at my mom's house was an occasion to see me off to a new city—New York, I'd decided—where I planned to take the bar exam and find a job, or so I said. Certainly by now they had been filled in on the details of my departure, surely exaggerated to make me—us—appear as successful as possible.

"Maggie is *working* at the hospital? I thought she was *in* the hospital," my mom said. "What do you call it? Re...*hab*?"

My mom swapped the gochujang with the soy sauce. The chopped scallions dipped down and floated back to the surface, little green ducks. She looked up, one finger pointing toward the ceiling, as if she'd just remembered something important.

"Is Maggie still fat?" she said. My mom couldn't resist bringing it up again.

Upon hearing the conversation, I let a single plate from the bottom of the stack of plates I was carrying drop to the floor. The porcelain shattered on the hardwood, startling everyone. My mom and Mrs. Cho immediately got down to pick up the pieces.

"Jane! Be more careful!" my mom said. She held a piece of the broken plate, turning it over carefully in her hands. "This is the good china," she said sadly.

"It's beautiful," Mrs. Cho said. "Too bad it's broken."

Mrs. Cho examined a shard that covered the surface of her palm all the way to the tips of her fingers. The dish was white, hand-painted with a floral pattern in shades of blue and 24-karat gold detailing.

"How much did it cost?" she asked.

"It's a dinner plate," my mom said. She clicked her tongue, sounding the sharp *tsk-tsk* that my people are fond of making. "These are two hundred and thirty dollars each," she announced.

"Sorry," I said, sheepish. I felt bad about having broken something so expensive, though I knew that there was no way my mom had paid full price. She rarely bought anything that wasn't more than half off or secondhand, and finding bargains was one of her talents that I later realized I'd inherited, unknowingly.

"These are from England," my mom said, squatting over the broken plate.

"Ah," said Mrs. Cho. "I have a set from France."

"Let's eat," I said. "I bet everybody's hungry."

I cleaned up the mess. Mrs. Chang, Mrs. Park, Mrs. Lee, Mrs. Oh, and Mrs. Eom disappeared into the kitchen, where they busied themselves preparing the boricha and tidying up, washing dirty dishes, though we hadn't even eaten yet. I got out the vacuum and ran it over the dining room floor, the little fragments of porcelain pinging their way up into the machine's dust canister. My mom called the guests into the dining room, her voice high and singsong, using the proper form of address to show respect, which I understood partially from the language but mostly from the cadences, tone, and extra syllables. We gathered around the table, sitting on the curved-back chairs made by the Japanese woodworker, and without prompting, each one of us tilted our heads down, as if in prayer. It was just a moment, a nonreligious gesture of thanks for the food. No one said a word. The toddler was still playing Rachmaninoff on the grand piano.

Dishes passed hands and voices murmured in approval. My mother spoke.

"Grace Chang's mother! It's wonderful that Grace got married. To a doctor! Jane still doesn't even have a boyfriend. It's because I spoiled her. It's my fault. She can't get along with anyone. Maybe if she lost weight and got her eyes done, someone would want to marry her."

"But Jane is skinny," said Mrs. Chang. "Grace is the chubby one. Jane is prettier than Grace and she's a lawyer. Grace only teaches piano."

"Jane isn't a lawyer yet, remember? She has to finish this semester and pass the bar exam and then she has to get a job. I don't know what she's doing moving to New York this summer. How is she going to afford to move there and get an apartment? She's almost done with law school and she didn't even find someone who'd marry her. If nothing works out, at least she'd be married to a lawyer. It's because she won't get her eyes done. She never listens to me. Grace listened to you and she looked beautiful at the wedding."

"No, Mrs. Kim, Jane is better than my daughter."

"No, Grace is."

I excused myself by getting up from the table quietly. I went out to the backyard, settling under the oak tree where I'd retreated countless times—the spot had a viewpoint from which I could see the interior of the house while no one inside could see me. If I closed my eyes and breathed deeply, I couldn't hear the voices of my mom and the aunties or the tiny piano prodigy, who was now pounding out a Bach fugue.

It was late afternoon. The sun reflected off the pool, kidney-shaped and impossible for swimming laps. It would be another few hours before the roof of the house would shade the pool from the setting sun. I noticed an old wheelbarrow in the yard and wondered when it had last been moved. My dad was the only person in our family who would have used it, and it looked as if he'd forgotten about it in the middle of a task. The wheelbarrow was full of leaves and weeds and dried-up soil. He'd always enjoyed using outdoor tools; he appreciated how the objects connected him to the earth.

My dad only felt comfortable in wide, open land—the fewer people around, the more he felt at ease. Once, while driving on a deserted road flanked by rolling hills, mountains in the distance, no person or structure in sight, he said, "Did you know everything used to look like this? No roads or cars, no buildings. Just land and water and wild animals. There were hardly any people around, just Native Americans before white people came and killed them and stole the land from them."

Truck driving took my dad through the plains of Kansas and Montana, the hills of Wyoming. I pictured him driving past tumbleweeds, his truck sweeping by cattle and cowboys. A shovel leaned against the wheelbarrow, the blade caked with dirt, the long wooden handle dry and split.

My mom saw it as her job to stomp all confidence out of me. If she failed to do so, she wasn't a good mother. This parenting philosophy was obviously counterproductive, since a lack of ego worked against everything she wanted me to achieve. I couldn't be who she wanted me to be while at the same time getting what she wanted me to get. Nowhere did what I want figure into this equation.

I stayed put in the spot under the tree, feeling small, childish. I could see no end to my anger at my mother.

"You can't just do whatever you want," she'd said when I graduated from college and told her I didn't want to apply to law school, which is how I ended up going to law school.

I imagined my mom dead, her ghost haunting me, offering unwanted advice in a panicked shriek. I pictured her in my apartment in San Francisco, hovering in the hallway screaming, "You can't just do whatever you want! You can't just do whatever you want! You can't just do whatever you want!"

My mouth moved silently as I enacted the dialogue in my mind. My armpits itched.

I tried to imagine my mom as a friendly ghost, visiting me to offer support and helpful guidance. I remained completely still but couldn't conjure a scene that didn't immediately become tinged with bad memories.

I crossed the yard to the wheelbarrow and tried to topple it, pushing halfheartedly with the palms of my hands, but it didn't budge. I took a step back and gave it a solid kick with the sole of my shoe, hands up like I was trained in karate, causing it to fall over to the side. I looked pointedly at the spilled soil, the mess I'd made. *Ha!* I said under my breath. I picked up the shovel that had fallen to the ground and threw it across the yard as hard as I could. The muscles in my shoulders stretched, my elbow joints popped. The shovel disappeared into the darkness behind the trees. I heard it swish and thunk into the brush.

"Fuck everyone!" I said, loud enough to be shouting, though not enough to feel satisfying. Soft enough that I wouldn't have to worry that anyone inside could hear me.

I WAS WASHING dishes at the kitchen sink when Maggie Cho's mother snuck up behind me and tapped my shoulder, her short hair swept back in neat waves.

"I saw you," she said. "I saw you throw that shovel and I heard you say the *F* word. You shouldn't swear."

"You were spying on me?"

"I'm always telling Maggie to stop swearing too."

"But no one was supposed to hear me."

"*I* heard you."

"I thought I was alone!" I said, raising my voice, only to soften a moment later.

"Mrs. Cho," I said as I turned off the faucet and removed my mom's fuchsia rubber gloves. "Let's go to the living room. Everybody's probably wondering where we are."

I placed my hands on her shoulders, patting gently. Mrs. Cho didn't budge.

"This is how it started with Maggie," she said. "First it was the cursing, then the comedy, then the drugs."

"She's a doctor now. Everything worked out," I said. "She quit doing stand-up."

"Why did she think she could do that? A fat Korean girl. A comedian? An actress?" Mrs. Cho held her hands up, for emphasis, palms facing toward the ceiling.

"Do you think I *just* started saying bad words, Mrs. Cho?"

"You're too pretty. You're a good girl."

"I'm not a girl."

"Then what are you? You're not a boy. Are you a tomboy? Don't be a tomboy."

I turned her around and gave her a shove. Not too hard, but not soft either. Koreans had been pushed around for centuries, always with some level of violence, physical or emotional. For some of us, this had made us into people who ourselves pushed, rushing around, impatient, in a hurry to get things done when there was no real urgency, people who imposed our will on others no matter what anyone actually wanted, people who might react with violence, hitting, pushing, smashing things, who might speak in a way that was too direct, too frank, that left nothing unsaid.

This is to say that Mrs. Cho wasn't startled when I gave her a shove. A push here, a shove there—it came with the territory. I'd learned to be less forceful around non-Koreans, both in speech and manner, even tried to gauge when a more gentle approach was appropriate with a younger generation of Koreans and Korean Americans, though obviously I had my moments when my true Korean self was irrepressible.

We entered the living room, our slippered feet sinking into the peach carpet. We sat down on the peach floral couch. Mrs. Cho's feet swung like pendulums, a few inches above the ground. The room was empty. Where was everyone?

"Where is everyone?" I said.

"In your room."

"What are they doing in my room?"

"Something about the gypsy."

"You mean the psychic."

"The gypsy gave your mom something to put in your room."

Candles? I wondered. Incense?

"I don't want to go in there," I said. "Let's stay here."

"Okay."

"What are they doing that for?"

"It's for you."

"But I'm not dead."

"Your mother wants you to find your way back home."

There was a pot of boricha on the coffee table, arranged on a tray with saucers and teacups. It was still fresh and warm from post-lunch, so I poured it for us, careful to prepare a cup for Mrs. Cho first and pass it to her with both hands.

"How's Maggie?" I asked.

"Maggie's doing very well," Mrs. Cho said. "She works in Baltimore. She was having a hard time for a while, but she's back on track. I hope when she's done with her residency she'll get a job in San Francisco at the children's hospital."

Mrs. Cho smiled, her gold eyeglasses lifting with her full cheeks.

"I just want her to be the best," she said.

"At what?"

"At being."

I wondered if Mrs. Cho was like my mom, afraid that Maggie would believe in herself too much. *You were too confident*, my mom had said to me once. *If you think I was mean to you, that's why. I just wanted you to be the best.* But I didn't want to bring my mom into it. If she heard that I'd been talking about her, she might think I was making her look bad.

"Do you want to go with me to the store?" I asked.

"Do you need something?"

"We're out of apples," I said.

I needed a reason to get out of the house. I gestured at the silver platter, which contained plentiful oranges, kiwis, pears, and melon, all carefully pared and sliced, though there were no more apples.

"We should get more," I said. "My mom doesn't like it when we're out of fuji apples."

"Okay," Mrs. Cho said. "Let's go."

She pushed herself off the couch, jumping onto the floor with both feet planted in unison, as if landing a flip off a pommel horse.

"You seem athletic. Did you do gymnastics as a child?" I asked.

"I was a professional basketball player in Korea," she said.

"You were?"

"Well not *professional* professional. Almost professional!" said Mrs. Cho. "I was famous in Seoul, you know. Women weren't really allowed to play basketball, but I went to a women's college and we had a girls' basketball team and played against other women's colleges. I was the point guard, so I called the shots. I was the star! I was famous!"

"Interesting," I said. "I had no idea."

⁂

AS WE WALKED outside, I imagined Maggie Cho's mother wearing a jersey and mesh nylon shorts, dribbling a basketball and hopping into the air, shooting the ball with a flick of her wrist. In my mind, she made the shot, easy. The ball traveled clear across the court in a smooth arc and swished through the hoop, no rim.

I discovered that my car was blocked in the driveway by two other cars parked haphazardly behind me.

"Let's take mine!" Mrs. Cho said, happily.

She held up a set of keys, triumphant, and pressed a button. The headlights of a silver Porsche convertible flashed on and off, and the horn squawked briefly, a high-pitched yelp. Maggie had bought the car for her mom in the nineties, shortly after marrying the chief of medicine of the hospital in St. Louis, where she was a resident at the time. They divorced within two years, something about his grown children from a former marriage who resented her and thought she had her eye on their inheritance.

We slid into Mrs. Cho's car, the black leather smooth and warm to the touch, the heat from the afternoon sun lingering. Though the space was tight, she pulled the car out of the driveway in only two moves. She shifted gears so seamlessly, it felt as if we were drifting into a future that had already happened. Mrs. Cho took tight, quick turns. Once we were on the main road, she accelerated around the curves. The driver's seat was elevated, pushed close to the steering wheel and adjusted forward at a seventy-degree angle, which she explained was an ideal driving position that eliminated blind spots. Whoever says Asian women can't drive has never gone for a ride with Maggie Cho's mother.

"I should have been a race car driver!" she said. "Do you watch Formula One?"

Mrs. Cho was speeding efficiently, spectacularly, with high-wire competence, coming to a full stop at stop signs, using her blinker, checking her blind spots.

"I don't like how the race car drivers are all men," I said, "and have you noticed that they all look the same? It's like they're brothers, from the same Mormon family. And there's always a twenty-year-old Barbie handing the winner a trophy."

"Jane, you're so serious. All you have to do is watch those little cars drive around the track. They're so fast! And then they crash. *Waaaaaaaahhhh—psssshhhh*!" she shouted, taking her hands off the wheel to demonstrate an explosion.

We drove with the top down. The wind whipped through our hair and flattened out my voice as I shouted directions into town. At the store, we picked out several apples, two baguettes, and some soft, rotting cheese. The sun was setting as we drove home, casting an amber glow. Mrs. Cho took a detour through the tree-lined back roads and pulled over to watch the sun disappear behind the mountains. Row upon row of grapevines sprawled as far as we could see. Looking out across the vineyard and the rolling hills, watching the line where the mountains met the sky, I wondered if I'd ever achieve the easy confidence that Maggie Cho's mother seemed to have. She accepted herself exactly as she was, but she didn't seem to extend that grace to her daughter. I wondered whether Mrs. Cho's mother, too, had made her feel that she was never good enough, and I wondered when Mrs. Cho had escaped that feeling. I wondered whether Maggie ever would, and whether I would.

I reclined my seat and gazed up through the open roof. Mrs. Cho put her seat back too, parallel to mine. The sky was mottled with patches of clouds that I could only tell were moving when I watched closely. We lay there for a while in silence as the earth began to darken and the temperature began to cool, the dry air becoming drier yet as the heat lifted. I thought about the sight of us, two Korean women—one in her sixties, the other less than thirty—reclined in a convertible sports car at the foot of a vineyard. I could have been her daughter, she my mother.

"I remember Kevin's first birthday party, his doljanchi. Do you know about it?" Mrs. Cho asked. She raised her arms and put her hands behind her head, elbows bent out. "You wouldn't remember because you weren't born yet," she said.

"I saw pictures of my dol," I said, recalling my fat round face, nearly a perfect circle, the way my features disappeared into it. In the photograph, I wore a rainbow-striped hanbok and a black hat embroidered with flowers, a string of pearls looped at the crown. It hugged my head and covered my ears like a little helmet. As a teenager I'd found pictures from Kevin's and my dol celebrations in a bag on a closet shelf. I fanned out the photos on the coffee table and asked my dad about them as he watched the evening news. He picked up one of the photographs, squinting for a moment before his eyes widened in recognition. He laughed, pressing the picture to his chest.

"I didn't want you or Kevin to have a dol," he said. "It was your mom. She thought we had to because we're Korean, so we did, for Kevin and for you. Koreans we knew from all over brought food and presents. But I thought, why would we come all the way to America and have a dol?"

In the photos of my dol, I sat on a miniature throne at a low-set lacquer table carved with folktale figures and inlaid with mother-of-pearl. On top of the table, rice cake and whole fruits were stacked into pyramids: persimmons, peaches, apples, oranges, pears, kiwis, avocados, and bananas, with pineapples and melons on either end; in front center, rainbow-striped ddeok and several other types of rice cake—filled with red bean or sesame seeds and honey, dusted with crushed red, green, and yellow beans, pocked with dried black beans, speckled with black sesame seeds, dyed in pastel green, yellow, and pink. In front of the food was a display of money: crisp twenties fanned out in a semicircle, a one-hundred-dollar bill placed in the middle. On a separate table, a collection of objects for the doljabi ceremony: a long piece of string, a pencil, a book, a golf ball, a stethoscope, a paintbrush, a peach, a twenty-dollar bill, a music box. In the fortune-telling ritual, the one-year-old baby reaches for an object, and the first one they choose predicts what they'll have luck with in the future.

My dad saw the whole concept of the dol party as old-fashioned, superstitious. It came from a time when Korea had been a poor country and babies often didn't make it to their first year. There were others from his generation who felt the same: a tradition from the past born out of poverty and oppression was better left in the past, left behind in Korea, if one wanted to become American. He even thought it strange that families in Korea were still celebrating first birthdays with the dol.

"Korea is rich now," he said. "My best friend growing up is the richest man I know. He's also the handsomest man I know. He could have been a movie star. If I'd stayed and become his business partner, I'd be rich like him, but then I wouldn't be American."

When my dad talked about Korea, it was usually about money—how everyone he knew used to be poor, how many were now rich, how all anyone cared about in Korea was money and plastic surgery, though you could say the same about America.

"My friends in Korea didn't have much when I came to America, and they were all having a hard time when I was making the most. They couldn't believe I owned a big house and three cars. But now a lot of them have more money than me. I could never get rich like that in America because I'm not from here. You could, because you were born here," he said.

He expounded on the class system and inequality in Korea, how for many, it was still hard. He described poor families living in tiny, windowless basement apartments—banjihas—with micro concrete bathrooms raised from the floor and the ceiling so low you couldn't stand upright, no sink and no enclosed shower, just a shower head. Yet, he was exceedingly proud of Korea's growing cultural power, its seemingly rich and glamorous present.

"Everybody likes Korea now," he said. "Even Americans. So why do they still want to have a dol?" His statement only became more true in the coming years with the Korean wave, K-pop, K-dramas, Korean movies, and Korean food sweeping across the world and into America.

After showing the photos to my dad, I brought them to my mom.

"Ha ha ha! Your dol," she said, laughing. "You chose the peach and ate the whole thing right at the table. I had to pry the pit out of your hands because you were trying to eat that too. You were covered in peach juice! It was all over your face and hanbok."

I asked her what choosing the peach meant. I should have known better. But I was a teenager then and hadn't learned how to anticipate what my mom might say—a skill that became necessary for my survival.

"The peach means that you'll grow up to be fat and poor," she said, her voice stern. "So you should go on a diet and start making money now."

I'VE SINCE LEARNED the traditional meaning of the peach: the child will never go hungry, she'll enjoy a life of abundance. I've also come to realize that my mom's interpretation, at least the narrative she chose to tell when she announced my fortune, was a method of deterrence, of prevention, before the future happened in such a way that I'd become a lazy person in need of reforming. If I've learned anything at all, it's this: cruelty is born from a desire for power, but it can also come from a place of fear.

Had I chosen the thread, I would have been destined to live a long life. The pencil and book: I'd become an intellectual. Ball: an athlete. Stethoscope: a doctor. Paintbrush: an artist. Music box: a musician.

"What did Kevin choose?" I asked Mrs. Cho.

"Kevin picked the money," she said. "When he was a baby, he didn't have a big appetite, like you did. He had a digestion problem that babies get sometimes. That's why you were always the strong one. You never got sick. He was too picky."

"He took the money? So he was supposed to be rich. Interesting," I said.

"I think your mom pushed the money in front of him," she said, laughing. "Mothers always do that."

Kevin had always worried that he'd never make as much money as our dad. I learned that his insecurity wasn't uncommon among the sons of Korean immigrant men who'd gotten middle-class rich from becoming American doctors, dentists, pharmacists, software engineers, or more commonly, and in our dad's case, from the grueling, tedious, unstable, and little-respected work of owning and running a convenience store, grocery store, restaurant, auto repair shop, shoe repair shop, laundromat, dry cleaner, car wash, or gas station.

"We hoped that he would be like Michael Chang," Mrs. Cho said.

"He tried," I said.

Michael Chang hadn't been as famous as Agassi, Sampras, or Lendl, but he was—and remains—the youngest male player and the only Asian man to win a Grand Slam singles title, having won the French Open in 1989 at age seventeen. Michael Chang had been Kevin's hero.

"He should have picked the peach, like you, to be strong," she said.

"How did you know that? Did you come to my dol?" I said, surprised.

I'd assumed that she hadn't attended mine. It wouldn't have been expected for many people to attend or even be invited, especially outside the family, since I was a girl and not the eldest.

"I did! Maggie was there too. Remember? She tried to eat the ddeok before the ceremony. She still eats too much. She loves ddeok and biscuits and mochi."

"I don't remember," I said. "I was one."

"When Kevin was little, he saved a jar full of coins and gave it to you," she said. "Do you remember that?"

"He was mad because our parents made him give it to me," I said. "I didn't even want it. I think they were training him to be a provider because he was a boy."

Maggie Cho's mother and I watched the sky. One lone cloud dragged above us, lengthening.

"In Korea, people respect police officers," she said.

"They do?"

"I don't know if they still do, but they used to, a long time ago," she said. "Everything is different now. Korea changed so much. We don't fit in there anymore."

"Who?"

"Me. Your parents. All of us who came here instead of staying there. We thought it would be better here. Maggie says that we came to America and stayed the same, while in Korea everyone changed and modernized."

She paused, seeming to study the clouds changing shape above us.

"I don't think that's true," she said. "It's not fair."

Mrs. Cho was making a mistake that people make all the time: conflating fairness with truth. It was unfair that her generation had gotten stuck in the past when they came looking for the future, but just because it wasn't fair didn't mean that it wasn't true.

I wondered what I could say to make her feel better. Did Mrs. Cho and my parents and their friends think they would have been better off if they'd stayed in Korea? I remembered overhearing conversations about this when they didn't know I was listening. After lamenting the way life could have been if they'd never come to America, the discussion always ended on the fact that they were certain made it all worth it: *Our children have a better life here*. But I was never so sure it was true. Maybe for some of us it was harder in some ways and easier in others. For someone like my brother, it didn't seem better.

I turned to Mrs. Cho. She was still watching the clouds shift in the sky. She looked drowsy. "When Kevin became a cop, he found out that people in America don't respect cops," I said. "He was surprised. He heard about it somewhere and he was so mad. He thought that everyone was going to respect him. In TV and movies, they're always making cops into heroes. When have you watched a show about cops who are bad?" As I said this, I recalled a movie I'd seen about a morally corrupt and violent cop, but it was a lesser-known film, not the kind of thing Kevin would have heard of. He watched blockbusters starring Clint Eastwood and Steven Seagal that had clear messages about good and evil, America versus foreigners, hero cop versus corrupt drug dealers, murderers, gangbangers, and lowlifes. Even the rare TV series that depicted a questionable cop would have us rooting for him. Shows about moral ambiguity where neither cops nor criminals were good or bad weren't yet common. Mrs. Cho didn't disagree with me. I wasn't sure if she was still listening. "Kevin asked me if I'd known what people actually think of cops and when I told him that I did, he just got more angry. How had I known that?"

Mrs. Cho was nodding off, eyes fluttering, lips parted. She felt like a sister, rather than a mother. With my mom, we existed as prisoners of the past, our long and fraught history seeping into our daily lives and into the future, as if time was made up entirely of things that had already happened. I couldn't remember a time when I wasn't having an argument with my mother in my head. I resented what she had passed down to me, what she kept passing down, through the food she fed me, the stories she told and didn't tell me, the way I was warned that choices were not my privilege, the insistence that I must come last. But it wasn't just me. My mom, my dad, my brother—we all felt that everyone else came first, causing us to resent each other, to want to be the one on top.

This mutual resentment was the gift our grandfather had given us through a lifetime of dislocation. He'd been living in America for more than twenty years when he killed himself at seventy-five—ingested some combination of pills and toxic chemicals—after the names of the dead were finally released and he received word that his entire family in North Korea had been killed. By then, his grandchildren were grown, American-born, in college or graduates pursuing careers. He couldn't speak English. I try to imagine his guilt, the knowledge that all that time had passed and he hadn't known that the family left behind in the North had been killed, all because of how he'd wanted more. If that's your history—if you've survived war after war, served a sentence working in a concentration camp, crossed a border illegally carrying a baby in your arms and a child on your back while your wife holds two more and in the dark you cannot see whether guns are pointed at you or your wife or your children, and immigrated again, to a country of excess and laziness and ennui, where people laugh at your foreignness, your ratty, faded clothes from another era, your tai chi in the park, your cultural and language illiteracy—doesn't it make sense that a grandfather might not feel happy and grateful, might not make us feel safe, that he could be cruel and resentful toward his grandchildren, jealous even, with only salty thoughts about how spoiled we were, how little we knew about the cruelty of the world, how we didn't appreciate or even have to know the sacrifices that were made for us?

I felt a tug on my sleeve. Mrs. Cho tapped my arm with the back of her hand, palm up, opening and closing. I put my hand inside hers and she wrapped her fingers around mine. We held hands like that, across the center console, both of us closing our eyes at the sky.

BY THE TIME we returned home, my mom and her friends had finished whatever ceremony they'd been performing in my bedroom. My mom, Mrs. Chang, Mrs. Park, Mrs. Lee, Mrs. Oh, and Mrs. Eom were in the living room, chatting and drinking from a fresh pot of boricha, while toddler Yeon-ah sat on the floor flipping through a mail-order catalog, legs crossed. Mrs. Cho and I waved hello on our way to the kitchen to put away the groceries. My mom followed.

"Where did you go?" she demanded, eyes shifting between us.

"Kevin Kim's mother, we just went to get more apples," Mrs. Cho said as she held up the evidence, the plastic bag of apples dangling in front of her.

"You were gone a long time," my mom said.

"We went for a drive around town," I said. "I showed Mrs. Cho the scenery. I thought you like it when I do that."

"What did you talk about?" my mom asked.

Mrs. Cho and I locked eyes.

"Nothing," I said. "I don't remember. We pulled over and took a nap."

My mom washed and pared the apples in silence, slicing them with too much force. When she was gone, Mrs. Cho looked at me, eyebrows raised. I breathed a sigh of relief.

"I think she was jealous," Mrs. Cho said.

"Of what?"

"That we were together, without her," she said.

"I thought she was being paranoid, like she thought we were talking about her."

"That too," Mrs. Cho said.

THE IMPENDING DARKNESS crept into the house, haunting the dusty corners and invisible cracks, the empty spaces between us. With the well run dry of comparisons to draw, shade to throw around, and shared memories to recall, my mom became tired, her face drawn in. My mom's guests were getting restless, no doubt worrying about the possibility of traffic on the drive home.

Mrs. Chang, Mrs. Park, Mrs. Lee, Mrs. Oh, Mrs. Eom, and Mrs. Cho bustled out of the house much the same way they'd bustled in. We piled into the entryway—all six aunties, my mom, me, and Yeon-ah. As the black shoes were sorted and each pair put on the feet of the rightful owner, six pairs of velvet slippers were passed to me, which I put back into the old Korean chest.

My mom and I hugged each person, including Yeon-ah. My mom handed every hugging guest a plastic bag filled with zip-locked and foil-wrapped leftovers from lunch. This kept her busy. She didn't notice when the aunties whispered in my ear.

"Don't forget to call your mom."

"Be a good girl."

"Make sure you visit often."

"Your mom is proud of you."

"You're better than my daughter."

"We're thinking about you."

"Aigoo."

I stood in the driveway with my mom as she waved goodbye. She looked tired and relieved. We stayed in the same spot, waving intermittently, until the last car was out of sight.

The house became quiet. There was no toddler playing Rachmaninoff on the grand piano. No voices speaking at once, the conversations overlapping and weaving into each other. The house smelled of sandalwood incense, which had been left burning in my old bedroom, per the psychic's instructions. The scent would linger for days. We rinsed the dishes and stacked them in the dishwasher.

"How did it go?" I asked, though by *it*, I wasn't even sure what I was referring to: the party itself, the rapport with her friends, or whatever it was that they'd been doing in my bedroom. I sat down at the kitchen table as my mom wiped the countertops.

She rinsed the crumbs from the sponge, squeezed out the water, and placed it in the little tray next to the sink. She spun around, looking directly at me from across the counter.

"What did you do?" she said.

"What are you talking about?"

"Did you do something?"

"About what?"

"Kevin. Why didn't he come?"

"I don't know. I didn't even know you invited him."

"You must have done something."

"I can't even remember when I last talked to him."

"I thought you saw him last month."

"I didn't. You asked me to drop off a box of his stuff, but no one was home, so I left it on the porch."

"Maybe it's Minjoo's fault."

"I have no idea."

My mom opened a cupboard door and angrily moved around jars of spices before slamming the door shut.

"Why isn't he here?" she said.

"How would I know?" I said. "He's not very happy."

"Of course he's happy. Why wouldn't he be happy? There's nothing wrong with him."

"I didn't say that. I just said he's not happy."

"Of course he's happy," she repeated. "He's probably just busy. He has a lot of friends, like you."

"Whatever friends you're thinking of, they're not his friends anymore."

"That's not true. Remember that time he visited his friends in LA? They went to Disneyland."

"That was almost ten years ago."

"He needs a vacation. He has too much stress. He likes the bitch. Maybe he should go to the bitch. He needs to get some sun. Last time I saw him he looked sick, like he needs blood. Maybe vitamin D will help."

"I'm sure he goes to the beach."

"Why do you have to move so far away?"

"I have to," I said.

"No, you don't."

I wished for my mother that she could have had the perfect son. I wished that my brother could have had a different mother. And I wished I had control of my own life, the power to shed the baggage of family and history, become free to dream up my own future and my own identity. I longed for the same thing as each member of my family—beyond our shared genetic material, wanting more was what we had most in common.

THERE WAS A table placed in the middle of my old bedroom that my mom had brought in for some purpose unknown to me. Several chairs encircled the table and a dark linen cloth was laid out on top. The incense had burned out, leaving a trail of ash on the wooden holder, and the candles had long since been snuffed. What my mom and the aunties had been doing in my bedroom was still unclear to me.

I had a tendency to look down on all forms of New Age spiritualism, although my disdain was rooted in fear and distrust. To believe in magic and destiny and the power of our souls, you must be open, vulnerable, and trust people, which, for someone like me back then, was nothing short of ridiculous. Only now can I acknowledge the parts of my nature—competitive, petty, sarcastic, and contemptuous—that both protected me and kept me at a distance from everyone.

I sat down at the table that had been set up in my bedroom, feeling at once superior and excluded, a confluence of emotions that I didn't yet recognize as endemic to myself. I folded my hands and closed my eyes. For a moment, I tried to meditate, though never in my life had I succeeded. Who were these people who could successfully empty their minds? I imagined it must feel something like death.

My concentration was interrupted by a sound outside my bedroom window. I peered into the darkness, squinting at the shadowy outlines of trees, the branches full and overgrown. I crossed the room quickly to turn off the light switch and returned to the window, my face an inch from the glass, breath held to keep it from fogging up.

The bamboo bush shook vigorously, the stalks tall and leafy, having grown back years earlier after my grandfather died. Whenever he visited, he had spent days cleaning up the yard, despite my parents' protests. Raking and weeding, mowing the lawn, trimming every bush and tree. There wasn't a single branch or leaf or weed that escaped his attention. My grandfather couldn't relax. He had to earn his keep. When he wasn't making himself useful, he was raiding my gomo's medicine cabinet for painkillers, she'd told me after he died.

"He was a drug addict," she said. "Did you know he did drugs during the wartimes? Opium. A lot of people did." We never spoke of it again.

When my grandfather first discovered the bamboo bush, he called me over, pointing excitedly.

"Daenamu!" he said, motioning at the wall of bamboo that flourished in a nook of the backyard. The tall green stalks were planted in clusters, long narrow leaves sprouting at knee height to three feet above my head. "Someone planted bamboo here. Why would Americans plant bamboo?" He began hacking away with a long gardening knife, hunched over, elbows out. He didn't stop until the stalks were cut down to little pointy stubs. It looked worse than it had before. I didn't know why he did that. I'm not sure he knew either.

Now lengthened, lush, and green, the bamboo stalks were nearly effective camouflage for a small person in what looked like red flannel pajamas. Two hands separated a section of bamboo, creating an opening. The figure emerged and walked toward me, stopping at the other side of the window. For a moment, I didn't recognize her. The light of the moon softened her features and she looked tinier than usual, childlike, emphasized by the red pajamas a size too large and which I could now see were printed with Scottie dogs.

It was my mother, appearing young and ethereal, holding a shovel.

"WHAT ARE YOU doing?" I said loudly through the windowpane.

"Can you help me?" my mom shouted. She held up the shovel for emphasis.

In the backyard, I approached with caution.

"I'm looking for something," she said. "I had forgotten about it. Now I can't find it."

My mom entered the bamboo again, disappearing to the other side. I followed, like walking through a waterfall. When I joined her, I saw that there were several holes in the ground, freshly excavated, which shouldn't have surprised me since my mom was standing beside me holding a shovel, but, still, the sight of the holes and the clumps of soil thrown about, combined with the late hour and the ghostly moonlight, was making me uncomfortable, spooked, like I'd walked into the prelude of a horror movie.

My mom began to dig, stooped, knees bent. She dumped the fresh dirt haphazardly around us.

"What are you looking for?" I asked.

"The kimchi," she said. "I forgot about it."

My mom had stopped burying kimchi in the yard many years earlier, but now that the house was sold, she'd suddenly remembered the last jar she'd left in the ground. What would it taste like after ten years?

I went around the house to look for the other shovel, the one I'd thrown into the yard earlier that day, when Maggie Cho's mother was spying on me. By the time I came back, my mom had dug up several more holes.

"Are you sure it's here?" I asked, digging beside her.

"I always buried them here," she said, brow furrowed. "I put rocks on top, but they're gone now."

We kept digging. The holes were beginning to merge. My mother was gone, lost in concentration, burrowing, lifting, and depositing, like a machine. Our shoes were filthy, covered in dirt and little rocks, and I could already feel blisters beginning to form in the palms of my hands. My back and my left knee were sore. The longer we kept at it, the less I believed that the jar of kimchi was even there, and I knew that I should just keep my mouth shut and continue digging, but it was becoming obvious to me that the task was futile.

"It's not here," I announced. I put the shovel down.

"It's here. I know it is," she said.

"Who cares?" I said. "Just leave it! Everybody just buys kimchi now. Only white people make it at home."

"I can't leave it here," she said, burrowing and emptying. "Once we move out, we can't come back. A new family will be living here, remember?"

"But they'll never know there's a jar of kimchi buried in the ground," I said. "What does it matter?"

"It's your fault, you know," my mom said. "You're the reason why it's still down there. I never took it out because you yelled at me for being too Korean."

"No, I didn't," I said, denying the accusation even while remembering how badly I'd shamed my mother growing up.

"You were always hurting my feelings!" she shouted. "You wanted me to be like your friends' mothers, but I'm not like them!"

Unspoken memories crowded at the back of my throat, and I had to push them down. I knew what she said was true, but I could have said the exact same about her and it would be equally true.

My mom kept digging. "It's my kimchi," she said, growling, interspersed with sounds of exasperation and swearing in Korean, which to me always sounded more civilized than swearing in English.

"You know what's wrong with you?" she said. "You're selfish. You don't care about anyone but yourself. You don't care about me, you don't care about your family, you don't care about how much we sacrificed for you."

I'd heard her own mother say the same thing to her. I looked at my mom's rounded back as she hunched over in the dark, elbows out, digging like she was possessed. I imagined she must have felt the same way I did, that it was both true and unfair.

"Kevin appreciates us. He's not like you, he tries to understand us. He's soft and patient and calm. You've always been picky and difficult. It's my fault for spoiling you. You're negative and mean. All you do is remember bad things, you never remember any good memories. What is wrong with you?"

She paused, as if I'd really answer her question. I just stood there, watching, my own shovel still on the ground. The air filled with the damp unearthed soil and my mother's heavy breath.

"Everything has to be your way," she said. "You think you're better than everyone—you think you're too good for us! You never help, all you do is take. When are you going to give back?"

She thrust the shovel deep into the earth again, grunting loudly, the signal that she was finished—with what she had to say, not with digging, which she continued. I just stood there, not helping, just like she'd said.

"I just want to be free of you," I said.

My mom laughed.

"You want to be *free*? Of *me*? After everything I did for you?"

She kept laughing, was now waving the shovel in the air.

"I killed myself working at Swensen's so we wouldn't lose the house, so I could pay for your lessons and Kevin's lessons. My life got turned upside down when we had Swensen's. I was in hell." Every time she said that about her life turning upside down, I couldn't help but think of the Fresh Prince of Bel-Air. I didn't mention that I'd worked at Swensen's too—we all had—and at the same time I was expected to excel at school and win piano competitions and not let my national tennis ranking slide. I didn't mention that I'd never cared about the house and I hadn't wanted the lessons and we'd all been in our own kinds of hell. "I feel like I've been your slave ever since you were born. You're my daughter—you're supposed to serve *me*! My mother didn't have to do anything. My sisters and I did all the cooking, all the housework, like we were serving a queen. That was supposed to be me when I became a mother, but instead I had to treat you like a queen so you could have a good life. What about me?"

My mom's angry laughing and shovel waving was beginning to make me nervous. The holes in the ground merged into one giant grave.

"You wouldn't have been able to do anything you've done if it wasn't for me. I don't get any credit! Everyone always blames the mother when something's wrong, but whenever everything's right, everyone forgets about us!"

My mom brought the shovel down and continued to dig. I wished that I could yell freely, but I'd been trained not to. She wanted *me* to act as mother to *her*, I wanted to say, when it was *she* who was the mother. But it was obvious that we had different ideas about the roles of mother and daughter, who was responsible for who, who was the caretaker and who should be taken care of. My anger dropped into a hole to live with all my other angers, united into one little ball. I wanted to remind her that I was not included in the family will, that she'd decided to continue the tradition of excluding the daughters, which meant that Kevin would get everything and I would get nothing, so why should I give her the attention she thought she deserved if I couldn't ever rise from the bottom of the totem pole?

She had rolled the sleeves of her flannel pajamas past her elbows. She was sweating profusely, digging in silence as I argued with her in my head.

"It's the end of my life now," she said, her breath quick. "Soon I'll be dead."

Two topics that Koreans discuss freely: death and poo. I could be assured that in most interactions with my mom, either the fact of impending death or the state of her bowel movements would be discussed at length.

"People live to one hundred," I said. "Especially Asian women."

"My generation, we're starting to die off."

"Asian women never die," I said. "We have too much to avenge. We just start to look our age."

I picked up the shovel, choosing to avoid the conflict that had flared up moments earlier.

"I don't think we need to go wider," I said, standing in the middle of the great shallow hole. I got down, concentrated on digging in one spot.

"You don't know how lucky you are," she said. "I could've become anyone! My parents never let me do anything. I wanted piano lessons and tennis lessons and dance lessons, but the money was for my brothers so they could become doctors. I wanted to do something too. I wasn't even allowed to go swimming! I started diving in secret—you know those really high diving boards? I did that! I was so brave!"

My mom looked up at the sky, mouth open, as if she was watching Greg Louganis flipping and twirling in tight, perfect spins, disappearing into the deep end with hardly a splash.

"When my dad found out, I got in so much trouble. He was so mean to me. I wasn't supposed to go out in public in a bathing suit—he said it was low class. I was his least favorite daughter. He said I was stupid and fat and ugly. I never stayed out of the sun, like he told me to. But I never told you to stop tanning when you were a teenager. I let you do whatever you wanted because you're the only daughter, but you got spoiled. I had four sisters!

"I didn't want to come to America. My family made me. I loved Korea. All my friends were there—I didn't want to leave them. Korea is beautiful, you know? They have beautiful old architecture, they have trees that you don't see here, and mountains and islands and seasons! In the fall, the leaves turn different colors and cover the ground like a blanket. In the spring, there's flowers everywhere, bright purple and pink. In the winter, it's cold—so cold!—and there's snow, snow, snow. In the summer, it's so hot and humid it's hard to breathe. My mother said I had no choice. My brothers were in med school and we had to stay together, we all had to come to America. Then I disobeyed them and ran away with your dad. They were trying to set me up with a doctor in LA but I didn't like him—he was mean and ugly."

Her face contorted into disgust as she remembered the mean, ugly doctor, as she recounted how he'd called her disobedient and ugly. But I wondered if she regretted her choice. The man she'd married had lost his good looks and turned out to be at least as mean as the mean, ugly doctor. You could hardly say he'd given her an easy life, even though everyone kept insisting she should be happy with what she'd gotten. I wondered if she'd ever stop talking. Her memories were overwhelming both her and me—her eyes kept tearing up as she spoke, making me feel sorrier by the minute.

"Your dad didn't make enough money so I thought I could help by becoming a businesswoman. I enrolled in business classes at Napa Valley College. You know what he did? The first time I didn't have dinner ready on time because I was studying, he threw my books in the fireplace and burned them! Textbooks! You know textbooks are expensive!"

"I know," I said.

"You don't remember, but he was mean to me when you were a baby. I had to go to the hospital. The police came for him. I took you and Kevin to my brother's house in Newport Beach for two weeks."

"Why didn't you leave him?"

"I didn't have a choice," she said. "Nobody would help me. The nurses brought in a social worker and they wanted me to stay in a women's shelter, but I didn't want to. I was afraid of losing you and Kevin and our house. I didn't have any money. I begged my brother to let us live with him, but his wife said they couldn't keep us—they already had three children and your halmoni was living with them too. They said they would only take you, but I couldn't leave you there. I asked my sisters and my Korean friends to help me. Nobody would take us. I even said I'd be a nanny, a maid, and they said no. My best friend in Boston said I was lying. Everybody said I had to go back to him because he was my husband and your father, that children couldn't be raised without their father. I had to stay with him no matter what, even if he tried to kill me."

"You're leaving him now. Why doesn't anyone care?"

"Because I'm old," she said.

My mom was standing by herself in the middle of the big hole. She leaned on the shovel. The slant light flashed on her dark hair, glowing silver. The anger that I'd felt earlier, that was linked to the anger I'd felt all my life, was still there—but I felt the waves recede and change direction, leaving only my mother, an unrealized woman, all that potential still bubbling over. She was right that mothers got blamed for everything, that we expected more from them than from our fathers. How could we not? They're as close to God as you can get.

My mom moved to a corner of the big hole, where she got to work digging again, intent on working her way in.

"My family didn't like your dad because he was from the North," she said. "They said that's why he was bad, that I should have listened. They said that I made my choice, so I had to live with it."

"Why are Koreans so afraid of divorce?" I asked.

"Divorce was illegal in Korea," she said, stooped over. Her feet disappeared into the dirt.

"My side isn't like his side," she said. "My dad was a professor and my brothers are doctors. Your dad's family was poor, but they lied and said they were rich. It's not true. Your haraboji was a bad person."

"Why, because he was poor? Or because he killed himself?"

"He didn't kill himself!" she said, digging, her face turned sideways.

"I know it's true. Gomo told me."

"Your haraboji was bad. He had affairs. He did drugs," she said, shaking her head. "It was the war. There are a lot of things you don't know."

It was my mom who found the kimchi. The blade of my mom's shovel clanged on the metal lid of the big glass jar. She struck gold in the far corner of our ten-foot hole under the jacaranda tree blooming with purple flowers, sweet little trumpets that fell and scattered beneath our feet. We should have known. It was obvious that she would choose a spot like that to bury the jar, deep in the cool earth under the shade of a leafy tree.

We got down in the dirt, knees pressing into the damp earth, and we dug it out with our hands, trying to release the compacted soil that had been holding the jar in place all those years. Once we removed most of the dirt from one side, I was able to push it toward my mom so she could pull it out in one big heave. The jar was so big that when it came up we had to carry it together. We held it solemnly, holding our breath. In the dark hole where the jar had been tucked away, a roly-poly and a centipede squirmed and burrowed. We inspected the jar, holding it still with dirt-caked hands, neither of us ready to make the next move.

I couldn't tell what state the ten-year-old kimchi was in. The lid had rusted and the glass was filmy and coated with dirt, creating an illusion, or not, that the kimchi was no longer white and red but smoky brown. What happens to vegetables that have fermented much longer than necessary?

Together, we put the jar down. My mom squatted, her butt an inch from the ground. She twisted the lid, the muscles in her arms taut, the tendons in her neck rising like vines. A suction sound resounded at length as the lid began to give, then—POP!—a little explosion like a cork from a wine bottle, and a long hiss as if a balloon was releasing its air.

The fragrance that filled the space between us was the familiar scent of my childhood—cabbage and radish and anchovies, fermented in salt and garlic and red chili peppers. Kimchi was our family's staple that became a topping on all American cuisine—pizza, hotdogs, hamburgers, pasta, sandwiches, salad—transforming everything we ate into food that contained more of us.

The old jar of kimchi smelled fine. It didn't seem like there was anything wrong with it. My mom and I peered inside, the tops of our heads nearly touching.

6

STOCKING UP ON AIR

April 2002

THE FOYER OF my mom's building appeared larger than its actual size because of the floor-to-ceiling mirrors. I'd look at myself in one mirror, only to see my backside reflected from the mirror opposite, as well as an image of myself looking at myself into infinity. A common design trick, creating an illusion of a room without borders that could make a person go either way: serenity or panic.

My mom had assigned me the task of consolidating all of our storage bins of clothing, yearbooks, and odds and ends that we'd held on to over the years. The responsibility of managing our family's history in stuff and archiving our memories had fallen on her, the mother, though she'd never been the kind of person who organized and cataloged, which my dad and Kevin and I had always noted, another item to add to her long list of failures. It was just another one of those things that boxed her in and made her crazy. She passed the duty on to me, as well as, eventually, that particular brand of crazy feeling. It was now my job to sort through all the stuff that had been packed haphazardly into plastic storage bins. I had to make decisions about everything—keep, donate, throw out—a task I was to complete before moving away.

My mom met me in the mirrored foyer, where she waited near a row of locked mailboxes. A mini chandelier dangled from the ceiling near an arched entryway. She gestured at a table with a basket set on top, filled with samples of skincare products. A folded piece of paper was propped next to it. FREE, the sign read.

“The woman on the second floor is a dermatologist,” my mom explained. “She lives in that big apartment all alone. I think she’s around your age. She makes enough money to pay for that apartment on her own. You could be like her if you wanted to,” she said.

I took all the samples but one and tucked them in my bag. My mom laughed.

“Even *I* only took two!” she exclaimed.

We took the stairs up to the third floor, where my mom lived alone in a large two-bedroom, just like the dermatologist, though my mom was the building manager and didn’t pay rent, while the dermatologist paid several thousand a month. My mom’s floor was the ceiling to a woman half her age who had power and freedom and a future that my mom couldn’t imagine.

As we walked up the communal staircase, my mom bent over to pick up clumps of lint that had accumulated in the corners. It was part of her job to vacuum the common space every few days. Instead, she’d walk around hunched over with pinched fingertips, gathering dust bunnies and strands of hair, candy wrappers, and leaves and pebbles that had been tracked in from outside. It seemed easier to just run a vacuum, but my mom loathed cleaning.

The boxes were stacked up along the far wall of the bedroom. There were almost twenty—oversized clear plastic boxes full of scratchy wool sweaters and prairie dresses from the seventies that my mom could never let go of; file folders bulging with paperwork; tennis trophies from the eighties and nineties that belonged to me and Kevin; leather-bound, gilt-edged high school yearbooks; an assortment of knickknacks: flattened pennies, souvenir spoons, magnets, keychains, arrowheads, crystals, erasers, stuffed toys. I predicted a long day ahead of me and at least one or two return visits.

“Kevin said he doesn’t want anything,” my mom said. “He’ll take whatever’s left to the Goodwill.”

My mom disappeared and returned with a tray of boricha and a plate of fruit and crackers. She set the tray on a dresser and sat down on the bed, watching as I threw her dated clothing into a pile on the opposite side of the room.

"You don't want to keep any of it?" she asked. "Everything comes back in style."

I looked at the pile for a moment, then crossed the room and took a prairie skirt and a fisherman sweater.

"You're right," I said. "A lot of this is good quality, just out of style."

There were few things in life that I could give my mom credit for being right about.

"Liz is having a baby," my mom said quietly.

"Who's Liz?"

"Liz Choi, remember? Stan's business partner. She's having a baby," my mom said. "Can you believe it? She must be forty, at least, maybe forty-five, but I thought she was in her fifties. I didn't think she could have a baby anymore. Everybody says Asian women look half their age, but nobody would say that if they met Liz Choi. She doesn't care at all what she looks like."

"Did she get married?"

"No. She's having Stan's baby," she said. "They're not getting married. They're not even dating. They're business partners. That's it!"

My mom held her hands out in front of her, palms up, as if to show me that they were empty.

"Are you sure they're not a couple?" I asked.

She let out a long sigh.

"Liz convinced Stan to have a baby with her. Neither of them ever married or had children. They just worked worked worked," my mom said. "Stan's a workaholic. All he does is work. I don't think he's ever even had a girlfriend!"

Calling someone a workaholic might have been a criticism in some circles, but for a Korean of my mother's generation, even overachieving Korean Americans of mine, it was the highest compliment.

"He's always on the phone, headset on, three conversations at the same time. *Ba ba ba ba*," she said, nodding her head with her hands held up, fingers opening and closing together like Pac-Man mouths. "How does he keep track? He switches between calls so fast! All he ever talks about is money this, money that, calling out numbers and making deals."

I'd seen it for myself when we'd stopped at Stan's office to drop off some paperwork. She'd tilted her face toward mine, eyes widening.

"Look at his face," she whispered. "It's all muscle, from talking nonstop."

It was true. Stan looked like someone who exercised too much, but in the face. There he was, sitting at his desk, fast-talking into his headset while eating an apple. His lower cheeks were little bulbs of muscle, like radishes. His jaw and the area around his mouth were strong and sinewy, as tight as a gymnast's ass.

Stan was short and bald, and his teeth were noticeably crooked. He wasn't what I expected, but he was in very good shape, an avid swimmer and hiker and a lifelong health food nut, my mom said. Every morning, he swallowed cloves of raw garlic wrapped in bananas and he commuted by bicycle with front and rear flashing lights, a bright orange backpack with reflectors hugging his shoulders, a neon helmet on his head. He looked like one of the grandpas shopping for produce in Chinatown with his tweed flat cap and his old, ratty clothes, but in fact he'd quietly made an untold fortune in real estate. I was never really sure what his job was. All I knew was that he was loaded, because my mom wouldn't stop talking about it.

Stan was Chinatown, born and raised. His parents had run an electronics repair shop on Grant and Jackson, in a hidden alcove between the Wok Shop and the bakery famous for its steamed pork buns and egg custard tarts, and they'd sent him to Berkeley for an MBA. By the age of forty, my mom said, he owned several buildings in some of the most coveted parts of the city—Presidio Heights, North Beach, Nob Hill. That spring that I was readying to move, the neighborhoods were already becoming indistinguishable, the housing affordable only to a tiny cross-section of Americans with specialized training in service of the tech world. Stan had once been a real estate agent and had helped my parents find their first house in the seventies, in Napa, the town where Kevin and I were born.

"Stan and Liz have been only business partners all this time," my mom said. "But now Liz wants a baby and Stan's sixty-five and doesn't have children, so he went along with it. They didn't even . . . you know." My mom tilted her head, looking at me knowingly. "She got his sperm and a doctor did something."

"IVF?"

"Something like that," she said. "Did I tell you that Stan is sixty-five?"

"Yes," I said.

"When he dies, Liz will get all his money and all the properties they bought together as business partners. He owns others, separately, on his own. Those will be hers too. She didn't even have to marry him!"

My mom sat on the edge of the bed, sighing in exasperation.

"It's because Liz can have a baby. I can't believe it. I never thought that somebody could do that. She's very tricky," my mom said, shaking her head. "She's so smart. She knew that Stan is getting old and doesn't have anyone to leave his money to. He has no family! His parents are dead and he's an only child. Liz and the baby will end up with everything."

"But she'll be alone," I said. "It'll be hard to do everything by herself."

"She can pay someone to help her," my mom said, scowling.

I took the box of clothes and dumped it in the pile across the room. I stood there with the empty box, rethinking the situation, and put all the clothes back into the box.

"This one is done," I said, pointing. "Donation box."

My mom nodded, seeming to look right through me. It was startling how little she cared that all the stuff she'd collected over a lifetime and previously couldn't bear to part with was getting dumped in one cruel swoop.

"You can have children too, like Liz," she said. "So can that dermatologist downstairs. You can make money, just like them."

My mom was looking at me like I was on the other side of a glass wall, and on my side it was a sunny day in a field of flowers, while on hers it was just a dark room with no door. Something about seeing me on the other side, a world where you get to stay if you do everything right, made her panic.

"Don't you want to have children? When I was your age, I was already married and Kevin had just been born. What about buying a house? It's time you start saving money. Why are you moving to New York? You can make as much money here and doesn't it cost even more to live there? Why did you break up with that boyfriend who works at Google? He has a good job and I bet he has good benefits. He even went to MIT. Do you know how hard it is to get into MIT? He's not Korean, but at least he's Chinese. It's better than nothing. You could get married and buy a house close to home. When you have children, he can support you while you take time off from work. You should keep him as a backup."

"I don't need a backup," I said. "And he was never my boyfriend. We went out a few times."

"He could be! You could hold on to him. I'm just trying to help you, Jane. You don't know it now, but you're going to regret it."

"That's not what people regret," I said.

"It's too risky," she said. "You could end up alone. He would be a good husband and he has a dependable job."

"How would you know he'd be a good husband? You never even met him! I've never told you anything about him. You only heard about him through a friend of a friend who told their mom who told you. All you know is he went to MIT and works at Google."

"What about children?"

"What about them?"

"Don't you want to have a family?"

"Not right now."

"I was already married and had Kevin when I was your age," she said.

"You already said that."

"I didn't think I had a choice," she said. "Maybe if I'd never had children, I could've been a businessperson like Stan or Liz. By now I'd own properties in San Francisco and I'd be so rich."

My mom hadn't moved from the edge of the bed. She sat perched with her feet on the wooden frame, frowning. The way she was talking and looking at me as if I wasn't there made me wonder if she was still in that glass room with no door.

"When I lived in San Francisco, before you and Kevin were born, houses were cheap. I could've bought a house in the Marina, right on the shore, for thirty thousand dollars. Can you believe it? 'What if there's a tsunami,' your dad said. Do you know what that house is worth now? Many millions! If I'd bought that house, I wouldn't have to worry for the rest of my life! What if I owned an apartment building? Imagine! Houses in the city didn't cost that much back then because nobody wanted to live here. Everybody wanted to be in the suburbs, especially families. Too much crime in the city, they said. Too many Black people. Too many Mexicans. Too many Chinese. But we're

Asian! I wanted to stay because I had friends and a job. I was a bank teller at the big Wells Fargo in the financial district and your dad was working at a gas station, trying to save enough money to open a convenience store. I loved having a job and making my own money. I was good at it because I liked working at a bank, I liked being around money. I could've stayed in San Francisco and kept working. Maybe I would've been promoted, or I could've ended up like Stan and Liz, buying, selling, making millions.

"Your dad hated San Francisco. Everyone thought we were Chinese, it made him crazy! He didn't like to live somewhere so crowded. He couldn't stand the traffic. In Napa, it was easy to drive around, the roads were wide, there weren't a lot of people around. There was so much space and places to go hiking. We used to visit national parks when you were small, but you probably don't remember. The reason he loves camping and hiking is because he doesn't like to be around people! He's never liked everybody living on top of each other in buildings that are squashed together. He grew up in Seoul in a tiny apartment with no windows and had to share a room with his brother and sister. He always dreamed of having a big house with a big yard. He didn't care that we didn't know anyone in Napa and there weren't many Koreans nearby. Now look at San Francisco. Everyone wants to buy something here. There are no affordable neighborhoods anymore. Everything is too expensive. I wish I could live and work here and be a businesswoman. I should've done it a long time ago."

My mom hadn't yet given up on house hunting, on finding her fortune. She was still making offers on houses she couldn't afford, still getting outbid by young dual-income couples with graduate degrees from elite schools that had gotten them high-paying jobs at tech companies she'd never heard of, that existed in a network of code and links and invisible connectors. Her plan to make a killing flipping a house so she wouldn't have to worry about retirement was looking more unlikely with each passing day. Her worst fear was that she'd live to a hundred, with no money and no one to take care of her. Who was I to think that unreasonable?

"I could have made money by myself. I didn't have to get married," she said. "But I don't know what I would have done without children. How could I have a life? Who would I be? I'd be alone! I was so happy when I became a mother. I thought: Finally! *I'm* the mother of my own family!"

MY MOM'S APARTMENT was railroad-style, the master bedroom at the front end, a picture window looking out the face of the building onto California Street, and the second bedroom at the tail end like the last car of a train, with a door that led down a spiral staircase to the basement laundry room and a narrow alleyway at the rear of the building.

We convened in the second bedroom, which had been converted into a storage room long before my mom had moved in and which she had been using as a place for her many plants to grow and thrive. It was a shame, though not for the plants. The room was a city apartment dweller's dream, with two walls of windows that let natural light stream in unobstructed. The previous renter had been using the room to store a collection of bicycles, thus the bike racks and shelving units and hooks installed on the walls. For my mom, the room served as a very large pantry and greenhouse. She stored huge quantities of household essentials from Costco—toilet paper and paper towels, jugs of olive oil, giant bags of Korean rice, cans of oatmeal, economy-sized boxes of high-fiber cereal—all of which was stacked on the shelves behind her garden. Vines dangled from the ceiling, potted ficuses swayed with large cello-shaped leaves, glossy and fanlike, and small branches sprouted everywhere, as if growing from the building itself.

The greenery winked, happy and cozy in the warm room, the little hot house, an apartment jungle.

"Anything you think we should keep, we'll put it in here," she said. "There's also a storage room in the basement that Stan said I can use."

"Are those tomatoes?" I said, pointing at a pot, plump red cherry tomatoes dangling from the vines. "When did you get all these plants?"

"I never had a garden before," she said. "I was always too busy. I had to work at the restaurant. Your friends' moms were always gardening."

"Can you plant a garden in the backyard down there?" I asked. I peeked out the window down the winding staircase. At the bottom, there was a narrow yard with soil.

"I can't use that space," she said. "I already asked Stan."

My mom joined me at the window, pressing her forehead against the glass. When she stepped back, there was a smudge on the pane, which she immediately noticed and rubbed clean with the cuff of her sweater.

"I want to buy a house with a yard where I can plant all kinds of tomatoes. But every time I go to an open house, there are too many people lined up to buy it. They make offers over the asking price, put down thirty percent or more, all cash. How can I compete with that?"

She grabbed a plastic spray bottle from a shelf and began spritzing the plants.

"There was one house that I loved. I worried so much about getting that house, I couldn't sleep. I lost seven pounds. I went to church and prayed. I even went to the psychic because I wanted to win that house so bad. It was at the edge of the city, but still in the city limit. A big pink house with a real backyard, three bedrooms plus a sunroom, wide streets, quiet, no traffic. Like you're not even in the city. People were lined up for that house! Even way out there!"

My mom threw up her arms, causing water from the spray bottle to sprinkle across the room onto my face.

"Maybe if I had your dad's half and if I was young, like you, and had a good job," she said, sighing, "but I can't take his money and I'm old."

"The plants are nice," I said. "You did a good job in this room."

My mom beamed.

"Thank you, Jane," she said.

Even though our history suggested otherwise, sometimes it didn't take much to make my mom happy.

"I hope you don't decide to stay in New York," my mom said. "You're going to come back, right?"

"Of course I'll come back to visit," I said.

"But you're not going to stay there forever. You'll move back, right?" she said. "I can't travel on an airplane all the time. The flight is so long. I hate to fly. It's so hard now since the towers fell. What if you meet someone and decide to stay and have a baby? What will I do?"

"I don't know," I said.

"You won't want to travel with a baby," she said. "It's so cold over there in the winter. I can't live somewhere so cold. I'm getting old. Old people don't like to live in cold places."

"I'll visit you," I said.

"If I get a house that's big enough, I hope you'll stay with me."

"Okay."

"If I'm still here in this apartment, you can sleep in this room."

"With the plants?"

"Of course with the plants!" she exclaimed. "Don't you know, plants are good for your health? They clean the air and help you get more oxygen. They help you breathe. Do you ever feel like you can't get enough air, like everything is closing in on you?"

I stared at her. I was amazed at how the literal could turn so metaphorical.

"I think you should sleep in this room before you leave for New York," my mom said, gesturing across the room stuffed with overgrown plants and household supplies purchased in bulk. "You can stock up on air and prevent something bad from happening that would have happened."

"What would plenty of air now prevent later in New York?" I asked.

"Could be anything," she said. "You never know what's going to happen. It's best to be as prepared as possible. You want to be ready for anything."

"Okay," I said.

"I don't want you to suffocate there," she said. "I would never be able to sleep again."

KEVIN CAME TO haul away what I'd set aside for the Goodwill, which turned out to be almost everything. He'd brought his truck and bungees and a coil of rope to tie everything down. I hadn't seen him since our last family trip to Bodega Bay, almost a year earlier. There had been other gatherings since, but he hadn't shown up. I'd sent him occasional emails, but he'd responded so cursorily when he responded at all. I now realized that we hadn't even spoken since Bodega Bay. I wasn't sure how my mom had even gotten him to show up. My guess was that she'd guilted him into helping out and doing his duty.

I could hear Kevin removing his boots at the entryway, my mom murmuring softly. Kevin had always been light on his feet, his soles like silk rugs that muted his footsteps. It shouldn't have surprised me when he suddenly appeared at the doorway as I was sealing the last of the boxes, but like an idiot I was startled.

"Lotta stuff," Kevin said.

Kevin's persona was quiet and low-key; underneath, a slow burn that could explode unexpectedly. He had a youthful, unlined face, small and egg-shaped like a K-pop star, with large eyes and a delicate mouth, his hair thick and black, cut in a fade. He was strong and muscular, though his figure was lean. He was only thirty-one, but he somehow resembled an elderly man—his movements slow and deliberate, as if his body ached. A pair of wraparound sunglasses perched on the crown of his head like a headband, and he wore relaxed jeans with a plain black T-shirt that was neither tight nor loose. His face had a slight sheen.

"You don't want to look at any of it?" I asked.

Despite all the changes of the past year—our parents' separation, our mother's move to San Francisco, our father's new life as a truck driver, my upcoming move across the country, and the sale of the house where we'd all lived together as a family—we were both behaving as if it was no big thing.

"Nah," Kevin said. "I don't want to clutter up the garage." He wasn't much of a talker, but when he did speak, he spoke slowly and carefully, as if holding back the words he really wanted to say. As a child he'd been yelled at constantly, by everyone outside our family, for being rude. It wasn't that his thoughts had become nicer, it was just that he'd learned to keep them to himself.

"I can't really take anything," I said. "I'll be living in a studio in New York, and there's no storage."

Kevin nodded. We hadn't spoken about my impending move because we hadn't spoken to each other about anything of substance in years, though I knew that my parents kept Kevin updated on details about my life the same way they kept me updated on his.

We were interrupted by our mom beckoning us from the other room. We gathered to find a fresh pot of boricha, Korean melon and apples peeled and sliced into sleek white wedges, and an assortment of rice cake, all of which had been arranged on platters and set upon trivets in a neat row on the coffee table. My mom was sitting on a floor pillow, motioning with her hands, in the style of a game-show host, the signal for us to take seats. I sat in a side chair and my brother took the couch.

As soon as Kevin was seated, my mom jumped up to fix him a plate and pour a cup of tea. I helped myself to some cashews from a little bowl, waiting my turn to serve myself the same refreshments that my brother was about to enjoy.

To my mother's chagrin, I'd always refused to fill the role of caregiver when she was absent. She'd tried many times to teach me how to cook and clean, to serve my father and brother, but I could never make sense of the idea that one gender should serve the other—the roles seemed arbitrary and nobody could explain why they weren't assigned the other way around—and I couldn't accept the explanation that this was just the way things were. Had my dad stepped in and sided with my mom, I wouldn't have gotten away with abdicating the role that was expected of me, but he never did. He only held my mom, and any other Korean woman who was not me, to her fate. Maybe this is why I remained resistant to cooking and cleaning well into adulthood, making my life more chaotic and wasteful than it should have been.

While my dad didn't want me to belittle myself by serving men, while he expected me to be independent and have a lucrative career, he frequently told me that I needed to watch how I talked to men. If he knew that this undermined his desire for me to have the power and authority that men had, he never let on. Always, he'd caution me: You're going to get yourself in trouble if you don't watch how you talk to men.

I took a bite of apple, noticing that it was slippery and tasted of olive oil. I decided not to ask.

My brother didn't meet my eye. I watched his face darkening, and the more time passed, the more I felt something hard and cold inside me that I'd forgotten was there begin to expand like a balloon.

Kevin wasn't in the mood for talking. It could have been our mother's presence or that the time that had passed since our last encounter had caused the tension between us to fester, growing and becoming uglier. I watched him, making myself small and quiet. As I tried to remember what had gotten us to where we were, I felt myself shrinking into the person that I had thought I'd grown out of, leaning into that little ball I'd hidden inside myself.

"Is everything done? The boxes are packed?" my mom asked.

I nodded. We sipped tea.

"Kevin, didn't Minjoo give you something? For Jane? She said she sent something with you." My mom nudged a small shopping bag leaning against the coffee table. I didn't know who had put it there—my mom, or Kevin, perhaps shortly after he had arrived.

"Oh, yeah," Kevin said. "I almost forgot. That's from Minjoo. It's a going-away present."

My mom handed the bag to Kevin, who then passed it to me. Inside was a present wrapped in a colorful abstract print, tied with a dark velvet bow. I didn't want to open it in front of everyone; I'd have to pretend. Gifts from Minjoo always revolved around Odie, Kevin and Minjoo's Pointer-Border Collie. A calendar with Odie in twelve different poses and outfits. A mug with Odie on it. Tote bags, socks, stickers with Odie on them. Later, when I unwrapped the present at home, I was relieved—it was a handsome leather journal. *How thoughtful,* I thought. But then I opened it to a picture of Odie mounted to the inside cover. Odie as a puppy running, mid-yap, his soft black fur shiny and white-speckled. It's not that I didn't like Odie—he just wasn't mine and I didn't think about him when he wasn't there. I suppose that was the point. We all did baffling things to draw attention to what mattered to us, to be perceived the way we wanted to be perceived. Kevin did baffling things, too. It should have been obvious what was going on with him, but we were too wrapped up in our own lives.

I HELPED KEVIN load the boxes of discarded clothing, housewares, and knickknacks into the bed of his truck. We tied it all down with the bungees and ropes he'd brought with him.

If you'd dumped it all on the street, you could have traced our family history, lined up our belongings down the city blocks, like layers of sedimentary rock in a canyon: Kevin's blue baby blanket worn to shreds; the Peanuts figurines and Brooke Shields Barbie from a family friend, which I'd once cherished because our parents didn't believe in buying toys; our mom's suede roller skates with bright orange rubber wheels that she'd picked up for five dollars when the roller rink went out of business and in which she'd skated in circles all around the neighborhood, hair permed, blue eyeshadow and peach blush, the neighbors staring, until our dad intervened, reminding her that she was a grown woman; my children's violin, that I'd been informed had a fallen bridge when I attempted to sell it in college, and which I'd played until Kevin demanded that I quit (he wanted the violin, I could have the piano), a conflict that would repeat itself with tennis (he wanted tennis, I could have the piano) and that I'd become well-experienced in, the one-sided feud, the single-participant contest, following us into adult life, every choice I made paired with a reminder by a cousin or aunt that Kevin might get upset because I was doing something that he had wanted to do; stacks of outdated graphite tennis rackets with chips and scratches; worn-out tennis shoes, holes in the soles and the toes; our combined collection of tennis trophies, piano awards, and piano books that could have been lined up for blocks and blocks; our dad's stuff, old and dated and forgotten, leather golf gloves and V-neck golf sweaters, the country club's logo of grapes embroidered on the chest; sleeping bags and tents and cooking equipment for camping; big clunky flashlights and a Coleman lantern that we used to pack up in the car on road trips to national parks, our pop-up camping trailer hitched to the back, our dad glowing with pride as he'd fold the camper down into a rectangular box and, later at the campsite, expand it like an accordion into a miniature house, and which he'd eventually pass down to his brother with young children when our own family life had become too full with striving, the luxury of recreational time squeezed from our lives; our mother's massive collection of clothing accumulated since the sixties, long flowy skirts and dresses, full-length coats in acid-washed denim and camel hair and quilted silk, oversized turtleneck sweaters, legwarmers and slouchy leather boots, coordinating pastel tennis sets, swishy nylon warmup suits in iridescent peach, shell-white, and fluorescents; all our mother's crystal bowls and candleholders; snow globes from Vienna; wooden music boxes from Germany; pinecones and potpourri and jars full of marbles and baskets and wreaths; abalone and conch shells; wooden tennis rackets from the seventies; tarnished silver platters and Korean lacquer trays; glassware from Swensen's, including sundae bowls, banana split bowls, tall milkshake glasses, big glass mugs for root beer floats (but the ice cream scoopers my mom kept); a shoebox full of handwritten notes I'd exchanged with friends on loose-leaf binder paper, folded into squares and triangles with origami folds, decorated with hearts and lipstick kisses; high school yearbooks, leather-bound, gilt-edged, the glossy pages filled with loopy signatures and the signoffs of the decade (Stay Sweet, BFF, Friends 4EVA, KIT, LYLAS, TLA, 2 good 2 be 4gotten); clothing for teenaged girls and boys of a past era, now "vintage" fashion (oversized Esprit tote bags, Billabong T-shirts and tank tops, Gotcha pullovers, Pendleton flannel, Guess denim, tie-dyed T-shirts, babydoll dresses and long hippie skirts, scuffed-up

Doc Martens, Birkenstocks worn through to the cork, and many pieces of solid black clothing from when Kevin and I went through an all-black phase). All these things were artifacts now: used-up, space-encroaching, no longer relevant. I couldn't believe we were giving it all up. I felt terrible thinking of how much money we must have spent, only for everything to be boxed up and donated. I thought of the memories each item held, every separate object representing a specific time in our lives, all of it together symbolizing us—the Kims in Napa—and all that we strove to escape and become, spanning across continents and decades. How would we remember everything without all our stuff?

After the Goodwill, Kevin and I decided to stop for ice cream in Japantown before going our separate ways. We hadn't been there together since we were kids, when our parents would take us anytime we passed through the city. There was a little restaurant in the main square run by a Chinese family that reminded my parents of the Chinese district of Seoul. Not the food you'd find in the Chinatowns of American cities, but Korean-Chinese food that Korean mothers cooked at home, that school children might have as an after-school snack along with kimbap and ddeokbokki. Noodles in black bean sauce, noodles with seafood in spicy broth, kimchi pancakes, fried pork. There was no Koreatown in the Bay Area. That little Chinese place in Japantown was the closest our parents could get.

Kevin and I didn't care for Korean-Chinese food, our mom said, because we were born in America and hadn't grown up on it, the same way we hadn't grown up eating sweets made with red beans, like red bean pastries, red bean porridge, and red bean popsicles. I had never liked the taste or texture of sweetened red beans or the thick black bean sauce that drowned fat, slippery noodles. Both were deceptive in appearance, tricking my mind into connecting what I saw to what I knew: chocolate, which was familiar and delicious and American.

Every time I'd give the beans another try, take a hesitant bite to see if I'd finally acquired the elusive Korean taste, I was without fail unpleasantly surprised by the mismatch between what I saw and what I tasted.

Kevin and I did love, unreservedly, the green tea ice cream in Japantown. It was perfection: subtly sweet, with just the right amount of matcha, and it was green. Our Swensen's diner/ice cream shop had served over thirty flavors of ice cream, but none of them were as interesting or unusual as green tea. It made us daydream about one day living in Japantown, something we would never actually do.

We took our little cups of oversized double scoops outside into the crisp, cool air. It wasn't dark yet, but the streetlights were already on, casting an eerie glow. The big square was empty but for a few families with children, city guides and foldout maps in hand. The big wooden tower with its old arched roof looked over all of Japantown, standing sentinel, having seen everything we hadn't seen and archived in memory, in the knots of the wood grain and the hinges of its very structure, all that we'd forgotten or ignored.

We moved over to the terrace that looked out onto the plaza below, where children skipped, ran, hopped, twirled. Beneath was the underground mall that spanned the entire block. A young couple stood beside us, speaking Korean and sharing purple yam ice cream out of a waffle cone shaped like a fish. Kevin and I watched the kids as they jumped in uncoordinated movements, arms gesturing wildly, mouths open with laughter and absurd pronouncements.

"I'm going to hammer your teeth!" a girl shouted in Korean at her brother. She clutched a plastic toy hammer as she flipped into a no-handed cartwheel, the crown of her head hovering mere inches above the ground. The children's voices sounded in high registers, shouting unselfconsciously, tiny people without vanity or loss. Their Korean was peppered with exclamations in English.

Another family walked across the square. A little girl wearing a red cape over a romper leaped into the air, foot kicked out, landing with a dramatic karate chop.

"*Hiiiiiiya!*" she shouted.

Her brother held a poster tube in both hands like a sword, taking the stance of a warrior. I couldn't tell if he was defending himself or about to attack.

"That's an aikido move," Kevin said, nodding at the boy.

The child was half-squatting, feet planted wide. He looked like a human chair, his upper body stick-straight and pivoting toward his sister. He pointed the poster tube at her, as if casting a spell.

"Defense," I said.

"What?"

"A form of self-defense," I said. "You used to tell me all the time when you were taking aikido in high school. You said that they teach you to defend yourself while protecting your attacker from injury. Defensive holds, pressure points, throwing people."

"You remember that?" he asked.

"You used to show me the moves every day. How could I forget? You tried to practice on me!" I said, laughing. "You made me watch all those Steven Seagal movies with you. My friends used to make fun of me because I knew so much about Steven Seagal."

I wondered what Kevin thought of the Korean American kids playing happily in the plaza. I couldn't remember us ever being that carefree. He'd once come home from a pool party at the Koidas, a Japanese family in Santa Rosa that he knew from Justin-Siena, the private high school—I went to public school—and he'd told me, flabbergasted, that the twins Kyle and Keira ran around laughing, pushing each other in the pool, singing, blowing out candles and eating cake, opening presents, and their parents were also easygoing, friendly, and kind. "Why are they so happy?" he'd said, incredulously. I learned that the Koidas had been in the Bay Area for generations, before and after they'd lost their homes and businesses and been forced into a concentration camp in the desert and then had to rebuild their lives from scratch. It had taken them two more generations just to get back to where they'd been before, but they did it, and from there they built higher and bigger and better. Kyle and Keira's parents were both doctors and so were their grandfathers on both sides. Stability and money and fulfilling work that other people respect can make a happy family, enough room and time to enjoy things. Was it because the Koidas were Japanese? Was it something about being Korean? About being new immigrants? But watching the Korean kids playing in Japantown, twirling and laughing, I envied how cheerful and comfortable they looked in their skin.

As a teenager, Kevin had been obsessed with aikido. He'd take me to a New Age bookstore in town, where he'd spend his allowance on books on aikido and Zen Buddhism and spirituality and meditation. Countless times he'd read *The Way of the Peaceful Warrior*, a best-selling self-help book about a young gymnast who meets a gas station attendant named Socrates who becomes his mentor and teaches him how to pursue an enlightened life. Maybe it was a fad of the nineties, but it all seemed to feed into a hole in Kevin. While not Korean, the teachings were often based in East and South Asian philosophies and spirituality, the books sold alongside incense and yin-yang medicine balls. Kevin was seeking to calm the chaos in his mind, the spinning and whirling and pushing and pulling, the self-critical thoughts, the abuse from our parents, the insults from people in our town that he took as truth, the bewildering cacophony of voices talking at him from all sides. Follow the path of the peaceful warrior, be at peace, be a peacemaker, resolve conflict with grace and sensitivity and the quiet certainty that should the situation descend into violence, you will win. He'd even bought our mom books on freeing your mind of stress, which she never opened. He was trying to fix things, fix himself, in the only ways that he knew how. Steven Seagal movies were violent, but the man preached Asian philosophy about pacifism and compassion and enlightenment, citing aikido as a peaceful martial art designed to protect the aggressor. Steven Seagal claimed to be a grand master of aikido as well as a former green beret, among other things. He was proven to be a fraud.

"I don't do aikido anymore. I don't have time for stuff like that," Kevin said. "I have to work. I pick up overtime whenever I can. I have a house to take care of and a mortgage. Have to make sure my wife is happy. I want to retire early. That's for people who don't live in the real world."

Name any person who has done something unforgiveable and you can always trace it back to a time when they were powerless and the unforgiveable was done to them. There's a circle that keeps going and going. It doesn't end because we don't pay enough attention to where it begins.

Kevin was born in that circle. I saw him in there, growing, becoming. I thought I was just a witness, that I was outside, but I was in there with him. We all were.

We spend too much time thinking about our victimizers, who never think about us, and our pain begins to define us even when it no longer has anything to do with them. While our victimizers may forget, we remember and remember, as if we're only living to remember. That's how it becomes so easy to never notice when we become victimizers ourselves.

We finished our ice cream on the terrace and watched as families and companions passed through the courtyard below. The mood was lighter now that we were away from our mom. The strain between us that I'd felt earlier at our mom's place was still there, but it was now like a wound that had healed and scarred over. We stood together wordlessly, the silence both awkward and comforting, as people continued to come and go, until day became night. That was the last time I saw Kevin before I realized he wasn't okay, that things were out of our control. It's funny how life can change overnight, from fine to not fine, but I guess it's just appearances that change so suddenly. Underneath, change has been happening all along.

7

HIDING

May 2002

THAT SUMMER, WHEN I thought our lives couldn't get more complicated, Kevin surprised us—surprised everyone—by committing an act of violence so egregious, I couldn't accept that he'd done it, except that I had to: it was all over the evening news and they kept naming him, kept showing his picture on screen. So, I stayed in my room. Each night when Samir came home from his job in Redwood City, he knocked softly and asked if I wanted to talk. I always responded in the kind of upbeat tone people use when they're trying to hide something: "Thanks for asking! I'm great!"

I turned my phone to silent, never answered it, and ignored the voicemails. The calls all came from unknown numbers. I didn't get a single phone call from my extended family. They'd never call me, the insignificant daughter—not only was I a girl, but I was the youngest child in my immediate family and not the eldest daughter on either side of my extended family. Aunts and uncles got in touch with my parents when they needed to, but only when related by blood. Cousins were not allowed to contact each other without permission through the mothers first. I didn't know whether it was a Korean thing or a dysfunctional family thing, but it was law and unspoken. I had lost contact with friends from my hometown, having become more discerning about friendship in my twenties and, with the exception of Samir, my current friends wouldn't have remembered that I even had a brother. They certainly didn't know his name or profession.

I answered only when my mom called. She cried into the phone, slow, heaving sobs, so close I thought I could feel her breath.

"Why did this happen?" she said. "Why did he do it?"

"I don't know," I said.

"That's not Kevin. That's not what he's like," she said, sniffling. "Kevin is kind and gentle. *You're* the bad one," she said, her voice rising. "You've always been the bad one, not Kevin."

"Okay," I said.

"This is your dad's fault. My family warned me that Kevin would turn out like him."

My mother's pain leaked out like water from a sieve. I kept mine close—Kevin's horrid act, my mother's blame, and her tendency to transfer Kevin's faults onto me, her desire to switch our places. My mother's lack of boundaries required that I keep everything contained, walled up, sealed. I listened, but I didn't have answers, none that could be put into words, that could be explained in a way that she would understand.

She didn't want me to come over; she feared that somebody would see me. People were looking in her windows, she said, though I knew it couldn't be true since her apartment was on the third floor. I imagined her sitting on the couch, holding a napkin with both hands like she was strangling an animal.

According to the news, the defenseless man Kevin had beaten was in stable but critical condition. Naively, I clung to this fact—the man was alive, which meant that he could get better and maybe it would all go away. If he took a turn for the worse and died, nothing would be forgotten. I tried to reassure my mom with this reasoning, which helped feed my own delusions. Anything I said in a soothing tone seemed to calm her, but at times it was like she'd gotten a jolt, an electric shock.

"Everybody knows!" she whispered. "Why did he do it?"

"I don't know," I said.

"I can't sleep. I've lost seven pounds."

I stayed on the phone with her for what felt like hours. I took her with me to the kitchen as I made myself a snack, to the bathroom when I had to pee, to my bed where I listened to her under the covers. Other than the man in the hospital, I felt most sorry for my mom. I wondered how she'd manage after her son had brought her such shame. Kevin had always been the most important person in her life; he symbolized her own value in the world and her chance at future stability. I let my mother talk incessantly, with hardly a breath. She began telling me the story of Kevin's life as she knew it: the sweet child he had been, the sensitive boy, the quiet, softspoken young man, the obedient and generous son. I had no idea who she was talking about. Certainly not the Kevin I knew. The person she described was someone I'd only seen glimpses of when we were small. I remembered an unhappy child, eager to please, wishing to find his place in a world that had no place for him. That vulnerable boy had faded away, replaced with an angry young man who grew angrier over time. He had a veneer of careful politeness that stilted conversation, but I knew that the veneer hid a rage that was ready to erupt at any moment.

But I didn't say anything. I imagined my mom in her apartment. She'd have the white pillar candles lit and incense burning. I felt powerless. I was an ineffective daughter and sister. I could do nothing but listen. My mother's grief spilled out, a continuous stream of anxiety and regret. She started cycling, repeating everything she'd said all over again. It felt familiar. Her sorrow took me back to when I was eight, when she and Kevin had started having their first big arguments. Kevin was ten and his grades were slipping, he wasn't listening to her, wasn't agreeing to the obligations that she said would be his when he grew older. I'd reassured her that it would be okay, but I wasn't doing that now.

At times, my mom just cried into the phone, never saying a word. The sound was so close, it felt like she had planted herself inside of me and I'd have to carry her with me for the rest of my life. It was my duty as the unimportant daughter to sustain our mother, to bear our burdens. As long as I could remember, our lives had revolved around Kevin and his future. He'd carry on our name and history—all our potential lived in him. But he took it away in one moment, blew up the whole structure down to the very foundation, and everything we'd built made no sense anymore.

THE TRUCK DRIVER

8

THE TRUCK

November 2001

THE END OF my parents' marriage coincided with my father's change in careers. Forced to shutter his auto repair shop at age sixty when a lawsuit put him out of business, he'd been looking at a long retirement with not enough money and had seen his chance to pursue his lifelong dream of becoming a long-haul truck driver. A month before my mom came to visit me, announcing that she was house hunting, my dad had made a similarly unannounced visit, acting like nobody I knew. He was going to see his new truck and wanted to show it to me.

"Finally, I get to see America," he said.

My dad had a lot to say. He spoke more to me during the half-hour drive from my apartment to the company parking lot than he had in all the years I'd known him combined. He'd just returned from training in Louisville, Kentucky, a place he'd never been, and it was all fresh in his memory as he described the flight they'd booked for him, the people, the weather, the hotel he got to stay in for free, the complimentary meals. He rambled on about the hundred-year-old trucking company he was about to start driving for, the cross-country routes he hoped to be sent on, all the states he'd get to see for the first time. Then he started over and said it all again as if to prove it was all true.

It was dark. Not late, but it was winter and the sun had begun to set before dinner, making the days feel short. The truck had just arrived in South San Francisco and the district supervisor had told him that he could come after five, when his truck would be ready.

"He said feel free," my dad said, chirpily. "I already have the keys. Ha! I have a boss now! I'm on a company payroll!" His voice bounced, chanting rhythmically.

We got into his pickup and headed toward South San Francisco. The space between us felt like the moment before a present is unwrapped, when the secret is still a secret but is about to be revealed. I stared at my dad's face. It looked new, rare. The dad I'd grown up with had hardly been around, always at work. Even when home, it had been like he was missing, because it never seemed like he wanted to be there. He'd been quiet and moody, and I'd never known why. I'd always been told that he'd once been very handsome, but I'd only seen evidence of this in old photos. He'd been slim with a baby face marked with an intense, heavy brow and a dazzling smile, and he'd had a penchant for custom-made tailored clothing. His good looks had faded by the time I was born, his body soft, his face, which had once been delicate and fine-featured, soft, too. But something in his expression was making him look young again, all the excitement about his new job bringing back the spirit of his youth. In his profile I recognized the cheekbones my mother had told me about, like perfect apples, the delicate tip of his nose, the strong brow. His full head of gray-peppered hair somehow also looked different, shiny and buoyant. He watched the road, beaming, hands loose on the wheel. The wind blew in from the open window, lifting the hem of his polo shirt.

"Shona!" he said, wiggling in his seat. He stuck his arm out the window, laughing as big gusts of wind whooshed under his sleeve and puffed out his shirt, like he was an inflatable tube man outside a car dealership.

Headlights illuminated the highway and the squat shrubby trees lining the shoulder. The slant light flashed gold.

"My truck is *huge*, the biggest one there is," he said, "and the container on the trailer is refrigerated. I had no idea those things were giant refrigerators. So the food won't spoil! Did I tell you it's brand new? I'll be the very first driver. Inside, it's all modern, everything high tech and computerized like a spaceship. I think it must be worth half a million dollars, more than some people's houses!" His voice rose and fell as he embellished the vehicle I had yet to see.

I just sat there, mute, as if I'd been kidnapped.

My dad had a particular way of speaking, as did my mom, my brother, me, and most of the Korean people I'd ever met. More than anything, we were direct—we'd insult you to your face, not couch our insults in subterfuge as other people did—because the whole truth was the only way to be decent, to show that we see you, to allow you your dignity and to keep our own. We were repetitive, circular, took forever to get to the point, then hammered it in relentlessly. We reveled in sharing our miseries, at times moaning on like the needle got stuck. We exaggerated, poked fun, like jocular cousins, up and down octaves within the same sentence, bouncy and rhythmic, expressive. Though many considered us inscrutable, like Sanskrit inscribed in stone, we couldn't have been easier to understand. Somehow directness confused people.

"I haven't gotten my first assignment yet. I wonder where they'll send me," my dad said, gleeful. He went on about all the sights he wanted to see, the national parks he'd never visited, the states he'd never set foot in, though some of it he'd already mentioned before. Soon he was circling, repeating things he'd already said and the things he'd said earlier that he'd already repeated.

I gazed out the window. I thought I heard him say something about Philadelphia cheesesteak. I tried not to laugh.

"Vegetarian," he said, smirking, his voice low, as if my dietary preference was an inside joke. He rapped the side of my head lightly and dug his knuckles in.

"I even have a benefits package! Ha ha ha! I've got health insurance and dental," he said, tapping his front teeth with his finger. "There's a 401K. I've got days off, vacation days, sick days. Ha ha ha!"

He laughed the way you might if you'd won the lottery. I remembered when a young man had punched him in the face, knocking out his bottom front teeth, after my dad confronted him for breaking into the bill-to-coin changer. That was when he'd owned the carwash. "That's *my* change machine," my dad said, recounting the story when he got home. His face looked like it had been dragged on asphalt. "Then he hit me, so I fought back!" he exclaimed, mouth open wide, and my mom noticed the missing teeth. She had a lot of things to say, about his teeth and the cost to fix them, the state of his face, whether the police would come knocking on our door and take my dad away, and who would provide for us then. I caught fragments from my dad, his remarks all bewilderment. "Looked like he was twenty," he said. "Kept calling me names," he said. "*Americans*," he said, mouth curled. When Koreans of my parents' generation said "American," they meant white. Didn't matter how many times I corrected them. Instead of replacing the missing teeth with dental implants, he got a retainer-like mouthpiece that held two fake teeth in place. When he removed it to show me, I flinched at the holes in his mouth.

"How's school?" my dad asked.

"Fine," I said.

"You're going to be a lawyer! Ha ha ha! You did the best of all the women in our family."

My dad rattled off summaries of my female cousins and aunts who'd chased men with the most money and status and the highest paying jobs. I'd heard it all before.

"You make your own money," he said, softly. "Will it be hard to get a job?" he asked. "What about the internship you did last summer? Will they hire you? You need money for the bar exam?"

"I know what I'm doing," I said.

Like my mom, my dad had no idea that I was struggling to attend classes. Graduation was only a semester away. I'd tell him my whole plan about moving soon, once he'd spent some time on the road and settled into his new job.

He continued asking about my future, my prospects, how soon a comfortable life would be mine.

"What about a boyfriend? Don't you want a family? What about that engineer? He has a good job. Doesn't he work for Google? At least he's Chinese," my dad said. "Better than nothing."

I gave him the side-eye, but he didn't notice or didn't care.

"We can set you up with someone. I heard there are Korean dating websites. Gomo says everybody dates online now," he said.

When I didn't respond, he kept chattering away.

"You're a very difficult person and you always have to have your way. You should marry someone a little bit stupid. Then you'll always get what you want."

I didn't know what made me more uncomfortable, the topic itself or my dad's nosiness and insults, even if his intentions were supposedly kind. I did know that what made me most uncomfortable was the one-sided conversation from earlier—the bragging about his truck, his pride about the benefits package. I was baffled. What was he doing starting a new career, as a truck driver of all things? Why was he taking me to some warehouse to look at a semitrailer truck? I was annoyed, embarrassed.

My dad had never asked questions, never wondered about my life. Everything before had been so different. I wanted to ask why he was talking to me now, telling me about his life, but in my head the query sounded like a challenge, which meant that I'd never say the words out loud, at least not directly.

At the company lot, he leaped out of the driver's seat and jogged toward the semitrucks parked neatly in a row alongside an old one-story office building that seemed to be closed for the day. Inside, most of the lights were off. My dad was standing in front of the line of trucks, a dull, yellowish light shining down on him, his face expectant and solemn.

"Mine is the black one," he said.

Up close, a semi is even more intimidating than when one barrels past you on the road. The eighteen wheels each come up to an average man's torso. Lined up next to each other, the trucks made a wall of metal as tall as a house and as wide as a city block, their menacing Darth Vader grilles staring down at me. I half expected them to transform into robots.

My dad grabbed a handrail near the driver's-side door, hoisted himself up, and stood on a metal perch. It looked like he was hovering in midair. He pointed at the cab behind the front seats and told me that's where he'd nap between truck stops.

"Like camping!" he said.

His excitement felt so big, I imagined it was his proudest day, bigger even than when he'd bought his first house. This was what he'd always wanted, while a house was what he'd been told he had to have. He'd brought it up only a couple of times when I was a teenager, so long ago that I'd forgotten about it. I was surprised he hadn't forgotten about it too. It had been less than a year since he'd retired.

My dad walked around the truck, his steps light, bouncy, looking like someone else entirely. He pulled himself up onto the little perch again and stood there for a minute, beaming. He disappeared inside. I waited, wondering whether he expected me to follow. His head popped out.

"Jane, come in! Look! You never sat in a car this high up. You can see the tops of all the cars. You can see over everything."

Who was this person? He was nothing like the dad I knew, the one who'd made us so fearful in our own house, who wouldn't let me or my mother make our own decisions, who told Kevin that he was weak, coddled, no better than a girl, who put down every choice Kevin ever made, whose memory was like a squid, reaching from the deep into the present, making us all stuck. The dad I remembered was replaced with a cheerful man who only looked forward. I couldn't bring the two versions of my father together. The difference was too stark.

I didn't want to go inside. I wanted to remain where I was, where at least life made sense and things were recognizable. I didn't want things to change now. I wanted them to have been different from the beginning. I wanted what I'd always wanted: to start over, for my life to be mine, to feel that I was beholden to no one. I was beginning to see that in my family the wanting of things that seemed impossible, that no one would let us have, was our one true bond.

My dad disappeared into the truck again. I could hear him whooping as he opened and closed compartments. The sound of his laughter ringing in the cool still night could have belonged to anyone else, not my dad.

"Look at that!" he shouted from inside.

It hadn't taken much to get him here. How easy it could have been, I thought, to have gotten what he wanted thirty years ago instead of buckling down with the businesses, making himself miserable and taking it out on us. I could still hear him exclaiming with wonder. The truck looked less menacing now with my dad sounding so jolly inside. In the moonlight, it lost its color. The glossy black big rig shone with a goldish hue, like a holy object blessed by a priest. I stepped toward the doorway as if I was approaching an altar.

9

MARRY THE LION TAMER

Summer 1985

WHEN KEVIN AND I were kids, our parents often took us camping. My dad had invested in a camper that folded into a compact rectangular box but could expand, accordionlike, into a little house with a queen-size bed on one end, a double on the other, and in between a tiny kitchen with a little sink, a mini fridge, cabinets, and a two-burner range next to a table for four and brown plaid upholstered seating. The camper was a new high-end model that my dad had picked out on a special trip to a trade show. He'd placed an order right there in the big coliseum packed with campers and motorhomes and salespeople passing out pamphlets and performing demonstrations. We had to wait a year for the manufacturer to produce the first batch. When my dad brought home the camper and set it up in our driveway, it reminded me of a boat, unmoored and stranded on land. The only time I'd seen him happier was years earlier, when he drove up in his brand-new BMW.

When our parents felt adventurous, we'd pack the camper and drive to Glacier National Park, Zion, Yellowstone, the Grand Canyon. Once we even made it to Niagara Falls. More often, we'd drive to Tahoe, just under three hours from Napa.

The last time we went camping together was our last trip to Tahoe, the last time we crossed the state line into Nevada, the last time we went to the circus. When summer was over I'd begin high school, when little things seemed like a big deal and big things got ignored.

On our way to Tahoe, we'd always stop in Reno for two nights. Kevin and I had begun griping about it.

"Why can't we just stay home?" I moaned. "How am I supposed to talk to my friends?"

"I hate Reno," Kevin said. "There's nothing to do but go to buffets. The food's not even good."

"Nobody I know goes to Reno. They just go to Tahoe and come home," I said.

We'd outgrown Reno even though we'd yet to grow into the age that one would have to be to really enjoy it.

This might have been when my dad realized that he was going to lose us, though he was the one pushing us to be lost, that we were forging ahead into a world that would accept us, but that he could not access. As we moved farther away from him and closer to American belonging, there must have been a quarrel within himself—let us go, take us back—that he would have to accept but would never resolve.

We crossed the border one last time to Reno and checked into Harrah's, made our way through the smoke and the gold-rimmed mirrored casino to the hotel's all-you-can-eat buffet and ate far beyond the point when our stomachs began to ache. The next night, we walked under the lights past the water show set to "The Ride of the Valkyries," me skipping ahead in rhythm with the music, Kevin at the water's edge, his face dark, then light, flashing with the shadows cast by the waterworks, while our parents chatted behind us, their tones low, syllables long and bouncy, the conversations tinged with secrecy, though only because my brother and I had forgotten nearly all our Korean. Soon, we arrived at the coliseum, where the circus was performing. My dad never failed to pay in cash, and the change at the ticket booth was always returned in two-dollar bills, which Kevin and I held up to the light, turning them over carefully in our hands, exclaiming that the bills looked unreal, too crisp, like Monopoly money. We settled in with hot dogs and popcorn, and we watched with attention as the curtain opened to the first act: the lion show.

This occasion was memorable for its finality and for the following bizarre suggestion from my dad: "When you get older, maybe *you* can join the circus."

Kevin, my mom, and I all looked at him. He was looking at me.

He continued. It would mean that I'd never have to settle down, no job or house or place to keep me, he explained, I'd get to spend my days performing and doing acrobatics, and, best of all, I could travel and see the world.

"You could marry the lion tamer," he said, pointing at the lion tamer's assistant.

Her mouth was red as a jewel, skin bare and marble-white, and she wore a gold sequin bikini that winked under the bright lights, paired with a headdress studded with gems.

"You could be her! Doesn't that look fun?" my dad said, pointing, still.

The lion tamer had wild eyes and no shirt, his tan chest waxed and oiled like that of a bodybuilder. He slid his head in and out of the lion's wide open mouth, smiling, flashing incredibly white teeth. With a flourish, he picked up a set of knives from a table and threw them in quick succession at his assistant in the sequin bikini who stood stock-still against a wooden plank. She smiled, never even flinched, as if posing for a photograph, but I could feel her terror, the way I thought I could feel the psychic pain of mannequins at the mall when I looked at them long enough.

"Don't you think the lion tamer is handsome?" he said.

"No," I said, incredulous.

"Are you crazy?" my mom shouted. "Jane isn't joining a circus! How would we explain it to everyone?"

The four of us were sitting in a row, Kevin and I in the middle, our parents on the outside, sandwiching us. My mom leaned in, speaking to my dad across the tops of our heads. Her voice was low, hushed, as if the suggestion was even an option.

"How would Jane have children? Would they be in the circus too, traveling from one city to the next?"

"Why not?" he said. "Why couldn't they grow up in the circus? Maybe it would be fun."

"How would they go to school?"

"Jane could homeschool them."

"It's not happening!" my mom exclaimed. "Jane has to go to college and get a good job and marry a man with a good job. Then they can raise children in a nice house in a nice neighborhood in a nice town. The circus is not a good life."

I couldn't believe this was even being talked about seriously, as if in a few years I'd be flying the trapeze or tightrope walking, getting knives thrown at me by some wild-eyed spray-tanned man I'd just married. I did not want to join a circus, nor did I want to be a mother and a wife in a nice house in a nice town—I'd yet to meet one who was happy. But it didn't matter what I wanted and didn't want.

I could see the allure for my dad. A traveling circus meant that your home and your family and people traveled with you, no mortgage, no bills, no tedious job the sole purpose of which was to pay the mortgage and bills. All his life he'd been tied down by businesses that he was responsible for. It was grueling work to run a diner or convenience store—long shifts that could run all day and night, always on your feet, interacting with customers, managing shipments and employees, stocking shelves, keeping the books, making sure everything was up to code, all with hardly a day off. It was uninspiring. How wonderful it sounded: a nomadic life, off the grid, no reporting everything you do and own to the government. Before anyone even knew where you were, the vans and campers and buses were packed up, and you were off to the next city.

No wonder my dad loved camping. No wonder my dad wanted to be a truck driver. Every day, he could wake up in a new place. He could drive around a mountain, right at the edge of a cliff, or watch the sun set over the ocean, or chase tumbleweeds through the plains, or pass through fields of windmills, or find himself in a world of big red rocks.

That's the thing about being unhappy. You think the answer lies in something else you know nothing about. So you go to that something else and are surprised to find unhappy people there, too.

THE FOLLOWING MORNING, we packed into the car, feeling bloated from overeating at the casino buffets, tired just thinking about the next few days of camping and hiking we'd planned for Tahoe. We drove down the dark multilevel parking lot, winding in tight circles with our camper. It took our eyes several seconds to adjust when we emerged into the light.

My dad had once worked for Shell Oil as a full-service station attendant—one of his first jobs in America—and he hadn't liked the job, but had retained a deranged loyalty to the company. He would only buy gas from Shell, would allow my mom to fill up only at Shell, and when Kevin and I got our driver's licenses, we were told that we should only patronize Shell. Once, we'd driven to Los Angeles with the tank on empty for miles, my mom panicking about how we weren't going to make it as we passed Chevron and Arco and Mobil, while Kevin and I scanned the signs on the long stretch of the 5 searching for the big yellow shell outlined in red—our beacon off the highway. My mom always paid with her gold Shell credit card.

This time, we didn't find a Shell station until we got to South Lake Tahoe. By then we were all a little tense, having kept our eyes peeled for so long. It was Kevin who saw it first: "There!" he shouted, his finger tapping the window as he pointed at the yellow sign in the distance. My dad took the exit and pulled into the station, which was packed full. With the camper, we were stuck waiting in the one line that gave us enough room to straighten out.

As my dad filled up the gas tank, an average looking white man with a puggish face pulled his pickup truck into the spot directly in front of us so that our cars faced each other. The man got out and began to fill his tank and his eyes settled on our car, a shiny coral BMW sedan, and then the camper.

The man turned to my dad. "Can I ask you where you got that camper? How big is it? Does your whole family fit? How much does something like that cost?"

My dad glowed. Then he laughed.

"It cost a lot. Too much for you. You can't afford it." He smirked and chortled simultaneously.

I watched the man's face turn from friendly to confused to contemptuous. We were all watching—my mom, me, and my brother—all except for my dad, who was so busy feeling his feelings that he wasn't seeing anything.

"Okay," the man said, nearly smiling again. "Sure, no problem," he added, as if he'd just called his bank and had been asked to wait on hold.

They turned away from each other, proceeding as if nothing had just happened. My dad ignored the man and the man ignored my dad while their gas tanks continued to fill and the space between them expanded with unspoken insult. The little screen at the pumping station ticked away the gallons and the corresponding price. The whole thing took a miserably long time.

My dad was the first to disappear into the mini mart to settle the bill. A few minutes later, the man followed. There was no way to know what their interaction was like inside, whether they interacted at all. There was a glare on the shop windows that made everyone inside appear ghostly. When my dad returned, he got comfortable in the driver's seat, beaming, looking as if he'd won a court case in which someone had unjustly accused him of a violent crime. He didn't stay smug for long. After turning on the engine and attempting to maneuver the car out of the spot, he discovered that we were very much trapped in place.

"Aiiieeesh," my dad muttered. He stuck his head out the window, craning his neck. He was measuring the space around us, of which there was very little, between our car and the pillar behind us, the row of cars lined up to the left, and the man's car in front.

"Why did he leave his truck here?" my dad said, indignant.

Both my dad and the man had pulled their cars very far forward, meeting in the middle of the lane, so that they could access their tanks with the corresponding gas pumps. A few more inches and the noses of our cars would have touched.

My dad didn't hesitate. He rolled down all the windows with the press of a button, adjusted the side and rearview mirrors, and proceeded to attempt to force his way out in the narrow space between the gas lanes. The people around us who noticed what was happening stared, mouths open.

The car crept along millimeter by millimeter. The amount of space between us, the man's truck in front, and the cars to the left was no more than an inch, not to mention the camper that my dad would have to somehow straighten out to follow the same unforgiving path. He kept trying to back up at an angle to allow more room in front where we were coming out at another angle, but there was a big cement pillar right behind the camper that my dad tapped lightly every time he moved in reverse. My mom was freaking out.

"Are you crazy?" she shouted. "Why don't you just wait?"

Ten minutes later, my dad had gotten the car about a quarter of the way out of the tight space, but the camper still had the whole way to go. He pulled in the side mirrors, got my mom involved on the passenger side, so that the mirrors wouldn't ding the cars that he was trying to slide past.

The man was back, holding a soda and a plastic bag.

"What the hell? What are you doing? You're gonna hit my car!" he said.

"I got it!" my dad snapped.

"Why didn't you just wait?" the man said. He came up close to the driver's side window.

"You can't just leave your car here while you go inside!" my dad shouted, although he had done the exact same thing. "How am I supposed to get out?"

"By waiting!" the man replied.

It was true. He could have just waited the ten minutes it took for this man that he didn't like to warm up a frozen burrito or whatever it was he was doing in the store. And now, the way that our car was angled had caused the traffic to stall and cars had pulled up behind the truck so that the man couldn't get out either.

The man took a step back, seemed to be meditating with his eyes open. He took a sip from the plastic straw of his oversized soda cup.

"Look, if you want to keep trying to squeeze your way out, be my guest. But if you put a dent on my car, even a scratch, you're paying for the damage. You can obviously afford it. I'm standing right here, man. All these people are watching. They're all witnesses."

"I know what I'm doing!" my dad shouted. "I got it!"

My mom was yelling at my dad to stop, exclaiming that he was crazy, while the rest of us, including the man, held our breath as my dad tried to swing the car and the camper around and through in such a way that everything attached to us would only touch air.

"I don't know why you want to do this in front of your kids," the man said.

He was still standing very close. The ice swished and clinked inside his cup. I could have reached out and tickled him through the open window.

"You have your family with you. They don't look happy," he said, nodding at me and Kevin.

I was sure the man was right. I was sweating. I felt nervous and fearful, and I wanted to be anywhere else. But while I was trying to make myself small, Kevin leaned forward and watched our father with reverence, transfixed. Later I'd blame myself for never having noticed what Kevin was like back then—what he looked up to, what he wished he had.

The slowness of our progress was agonizing. Several more minutes passed, though it felt like an eternity. The cars on either side of us hadn't moved since my dad had started trying to squeeze his way out, and the traffic had stalled in the lines behind and in front of us such that people close enough to the exits were backing up and leaving. Somehow, our little family had made time stop at the South Lake Tahoe Shell station. I slouched down as far as I could, trying to make myself invisible.

The man stood by. My dad scowled. All that time standing around in the lot with nowhere to go, watching my dad inch forward and backward, forward and backward, had given the man some time to consider their earlier exchange.

"How do you know what I can afford?" he said. "Whatever, man. I was just admiring your camper. Just trying to chat and pass the time while we filled up our tanks. You don't have to be a dick."

My dad ignored him. It was very quiet. Just the sound of the car starting and stopping. I was so far down in my seat that I couldn't know how close we were to getting out, whether we'd made any progress at all. Just when I thought it would never end, that someone would call the police to direct the traffic from the outside in, that we'd all get arrested or our car impounded at the very least—we finally escaped.

"See! I told you!" my dad shouted. I popped my head up and noticed that we were rolling along quickly, gaining momentum at last. My dad pumped his fist in the air, hooting, looking ahead triumphantly.

Kevin watched the cars beginning to move behind us.

"I can't believe Dad got out without scratching a single thing," Kevin said, his voice low. He looked bewildered, as if he'd just watched our dad walk on water.

I looked back and saw the disgruntled man still standing there, frowning as the cars snaked around him. He took a sip of his soda as he watched us leave.

"Yeah, you're the man!" the man said, not quite shouting, though loud enough for us to hear as we drove away. He was right where we'd left him, with his drink and plastic bag, in the same spot that my dad had felt was a trap that he couldn't wait for someone else to release him from.

"You're the man," he repeated.

WE HADN'T BEEN back a week when Sawyer Rhodes's mother knocked on our door to tell us that our sheepdog Scout was dead, that she'd witnessed the accident on her morning walk. She wept on our doorstep, dabbing her eyes with a handkerchief.

"They're waiting for you," she said. "They want to apologize."

My dad and I drove to the scene of the accident, where we saw the big rig parked on the shoulder of the thoroughfare that connected our neighborhood to town, the glossy red tractor in front, the silver semitrailer attached to it. My dad inhaled sharply and got out of the car, walking tentatively at first, then quickening his pace as he neared the two white men in jeans and flannel shirts standing over my dead dog, his fluffy white fur ruffling in the wind. The two men looked at us, solemnly, heads bowed.

"Hi!" my dad said, smiling. "Are you truck drivers?"

He shuffled into the bike lane to get a better look at the semitruck, craning his neck for a full view. A car horn blared as his foot teetered into the road. The older man stepped forward, right hand extended.

"I'm so sorry, sir. We didn't see the dog. We were driving under the speed limit, but it's fifty-five here, and at that speed there's no way to stop. The dog just shot into the road out of nowhere. I'm very sorry."

The man had white hair and a matching white mustache. He looked like a lot of the dads in my neighborhood who'd come home from their law offices and listen to the Grateful Dead and Simon & Garfunkel on the record player after dinner, but his excessive politeness and the deferential way he spoke to my dad made him different.

I reached them just as he finished talking. I'd been walking very slowly. My dog was lying on his side right next to the two men, not of his own accord, obviously, since he was dead. I surmised that he'd been placed there by either one or both of the men. I wanted to be polite and join my dad and the two truck drivers, but being near meant that I'd be closer to my dog, who was dead, and I hadn't yet seen anyone that I cared about dead before, only wild animals, like squirrels and rabbits, and birds and frogs, which I always steered clear of, afraid of being too close to death, as if a dead thing was sacred, divine, and I didn't know how to honor it.

The second man, who was young, swore under his breath when he noticed me. His body straightened as if attached to a spring. His face contorted into anger.

"You brought your kid?" he said to my dad. "Why would you do that?"

To my surprise, his voice was breaking. The older man held up his hand to his driving partner and continued speaking to my dad.

"The speed limit on this road is too high, in my opinion," he continued, "with these nice neighborhoods nearby. These are good people, fine families with children and pets. I've heard of that country club up the road," he said, pointing toward the entrance of Silverado. "I've seen the tournament on TV. Your neighbor, the doctor's wife, she said the same thing, said that your neighborhood council is trying to get the speed limit changed."

"How long have you been truck driving?" my dad asked. "How much do you make? What is it like? I always wanted to be a truck driver, but my wife and my family wouldn't let me."

I don't remember what the man said. I had a habit back then of blocking out conversations happening around me, even when spoken directly to me. Instead, I listened to the tone and the rhythm, which told me a lot, sometimes more than the actual words.

The man talked at length, his voice slow and measured, respectful. His language had the sound and cadence of someone speaking with great restraint: the tones of indirect, unspecific, and uncontentious chitchat, the real message hidden beneath layers of nuance, the kind that would take me another decade to decode and that would elude my father forever.

My dad listened attentively while the truck driver spoke. The younger man paced back and forth, head down, distress radiating. He was very tall, taller than the old man, who was taller than my dad. He glanced at me periodically. Suddenly, he stopped and pointed at my dad. My mom always told me that I should never point at another person, so I had a feeling that what came next might be unseemly.

"How can you be so insensitive?" he shouted. "People tell me that *I'm* insensitive," he said, laughing in a mocking tone. "Your daughter's standing there crying about her dead dog. Why'd you let her see that?"

he exclaimed, pointing, again, first at me, then at my dead dog. If my mom had been there to see all that pointing, she'd have whispered to me that the man had been raised by trolls under a bridge.

"How can you ask us about truck driving?" he continued.

By this point, I'd stolen several glances at my dog and had pieced together that there were no visible wounds nor any blood on or around him, which was beginning to make me suspicious about whether he really was dead. If I patted his head, would his eyes open? If I rubbed his tummy, would he stand up? Everyone else seemed overly confident that my dog was dead, and here was this young man shouting that my dog was dead, that in fact he had killed my dog, accidentally, and it appeared that the guilt of this accidental killing was making him crazy, turning him into a person who couldn't stop pacing and shouting and pointing.

The man walked back and forth in long, loping strides. Nobody spoke, not even when he paused. At times he stopped, planting his feet firmly, set far apart. He'd take a deep breath and glance our way, looking as if he was about to let loose another diatribe, but he'd begin pacing again, stewing. The whole time, the old man motioned to him, seeming to believe that he could control reality with his hands and eyes, like a magician, trying but failing to calm his partner down. But now the old man gave up on trying to ease the situation. The young man would not be repressed.

"I have a daughter too," he said. "A baby. She was born a month ago. She's at home with my wife. God help me, when she grows up, that I do right by her, that I protect her from something like this."

The man's voice quavered. I thought he might cry.

"I wish I could be home helping my wife with the baby," he said. "A job like this, you're always on the road, you're away from your family. Nobody *wants* to be a truck driver. It's just a job you do because you have to. If I could do it all over, I'd do everything different so I could have more choices. I don't *like* this job," he said, scoffing.

The man swept his arm in a semicircle before himself, gesturing at the landscape around us. His palm passed over the grand country houses joining the vineyards and the rolling hills, over the sun setting beyond the mountains and casting an orange glow on our skin like magic. He looked like a figure in a Renaissance painting explaining how everything got there.

"If you can afford to live *here*," he said, "why would you want to drive a truck for a living? Why would you want to leave *this*? What about being with your family?"

He looked at my dad like he'd just stripped naked right there in front of us. The old man put his hand on the young man's shoulder.

"Chip, it's enough," he said. "This isn't right. Mr. Kim is from a different culture. We don't know anything about their culture."

He turned to my dad.

"I'm sorry, Mr. Kim. Chip is still in training. That's why we're driving together. We don't mean to disrespect you."

The young man butted in again. His face could not have been more red.

"I don't care if he's from a different culture," he said. "Basic respect is basic respect. It doesn't matter what culture someone is. He's being so insensitive. Pay attention to your daughter, man! Look at her!"

My dad turned to look at me, and when he did, I saw that they were *all* looking at me, all at once. The angry and sensitive young man, already full of regret and pain about the cards he'd been dealt, burning with resentment and a sense of injustice about how much more other people had, unable to see his own power, power that was his at the expense of others, that belonged to him not by having earned it but simply by being born. The older man who had spent a lifetime driving a truck for a living, knowing what people thought of that and, by consequence, of him, which was perhaps why he was so careful not to judge a man of another race. And my dad, who had been called a Chink by his neighbor so many times that we'd finally moved; who had been held up at gunpoint three times at the convenience store he owned and manned alone for years before he finally hired an employee to work nights so he could sleep; who had defected from North to South Korea as a toddler, his infant brother drugged so that his family could escape quietly on their third and final attempt, led by a guard to whom they had paid the last of their money; who learned decades later, after immigrating to America and giving birth to a new generation, raising them the American Way, and sending them off to college, that the remainder of the family left behind in the North had been murdered, every one of them, that they'd been killed after the escape that changed his life and the lives of his future children, dead all those years, and no one had even mourned them. How could I expect him to notice me? What pain did I have that wasn't inconsequential?

I knew how I looked, a child standing over her dead dog. I didn't want them to see me. I turned around and walked back to the car. My dad picked up the corpse and carried it to our car and put it in the trunk. We drove home in silence.

MY DAD TOOK the body to an animal shelter since he was unsure what to do with it. Before he left, he hovered in the doorway of my bedroom, never looking me in the eye, shifting nervously, and asked if I wanted another dog, to which I replied no. My mom and Kevin had decided that Scout's death was my fault. They didn't give a reason; they just said that he was my dog and my responsibility.

My dad didn't say anything to me about my dog. It was like Scout never existed, even though he'd lived with us for years.

That night at dinner, my dad told my mom about the truck drivers he'd met, his voice shimmering. Why couldn't *he* do that? The men he met were paid well, had good benefits, had retirement plans. He wanted to see America. He liked driving. He could listen to music all day, drive, study maps of America, drive, sleep at truck stops, drive. He would have fun while making money. He listed all the reasons why truck driving was an admirable career and why he would enjoy it. But my mom wouldn't have it. She was shouting, all panic, in the particular tone that meant he'd never win—she was the queen at never backing down when she sounded like that, she had the stamina to outlive any opposition, and we all knew it. It wasn't enough money, she said. He'd be gone too much. Most important, how could she tell her family and friends what her husband was doing for a living? She'd be seen as an embarrassment, a failure.

For some reason, my dad turned to me.

"What do you think, Jane? Do you think I should do it? Do you think there's anything wrong with being a truck driver?"

My dad looked at me expectantly. My mom looked at me with disbelief. I was only thirteen. Why would a grown man ask a thirteen-year-old what he should do with his life? My brother, if he was even there, probably wondered, as I did, why our dad couldn't choose his own career.

I wish he'd never asked me. I don't remember what I said, but he wouldn't become a truck driver for another seventeen years. If we'd given him permission back then, maybe he would have given us permission—my mom, Kevin, and me—to choose the lives we imagined for ourselves, or to imagine at all. Maybe things would have turned out different.

10

AMERICAN SPIRIT

January 2002

A COUPLE MONTHS after my dad took me to South San Francisco to show me his semitruck, his boss sent him on his first job, a two-week cross-country route to the East Coast and back. Every other day my dad called from the road. Utah, Wyoming, Iowa, Ohio, New Jersey, upstate New York. I almost always answered when he called, though with my mom I answered approximately half of the time. A kind of self-protection: my father never wanted anything from me, while my mother's needs were all-consuming.

Every time we talked, first thing, he told me the state he was currently driving through, the distance in relation to where he'd been the previous day, and his exact location on the *Rand McNally Road Atlas* of North America, which was always at his side on the passenger seat. I worried about driving conditions that he wasn't accustomed to, especially in the winter, having lived in California for most of his life. In the spring there was rain and hail, in the summer scorching heat waves, in the fall there were winds, hurricanes, brushfires, and in the winter, sleet and snow and black ice. I wondered about the mountains, whether his truck swept along the edges of cliffs that dropped down to the ocean or the unforgiving earth.

"I'm in the Hudson Valley, delivering pineapples. My truck is refrigerated!" he exclaimed, as if he hadn't told me five times already. His voice sounded hoarse. Free of my mother's watchful eye, he was probably chain-smoking unfiltered American Spirits, eating junk food, and not sleeping enough.

"Are you okay? Do you have enough money?" he asked. I could hear the wind as he drove, pinging against the microphone of his headset, like paper crumpling.

My dad never failed to ask about my finances, an aftereffect of having become a refugee in the midst of war and having emigrated again in the aftermath. A hallmark of his personality was to worry, incessantly, about running out of money. When he asked if I needed help, my answer was always no, even when I was broke, choosing to skip meals rather than accept his money. My immigrant parents had taught me not to expect financial support from them. I'd always understood that I could only accept money if I was in a coma. If anything, I should be supporting *them*, should have been already for years, even if there was no need, and even if I'd been told that I'd inherit nothing of monetary value because I was a girl. Lavish presents with high-end labels that signified status—this is what a good daughter provided. In the new Asian America, they taught me, I was supposed to be a moneymaking machine. Failing that, I should marry a man who was a moneymaking machine and then I should be a baby-making machine.

"I'm fine," I said.

"I hit a deer today."

"With your truck?"

"I was on the highway and couldn't slow down. Too much black ice. I had no choice. I had to."

I was neither a moneymaking machine nor had I married one. My dad had steered me into a lucrative career through sheer determination. He'd always had more at stake in my life than I ever did, always focused on the long game. Not having a career was never offered as an option, even if I did marry.

"Don't ever expect a man to take care of you," he'd said. "If you don't earn your own money, you'll be trapped if your husband turns out to be bad. You have to be able to support yourself."

Now, during his phone calls from the road, he began to change his tune. "Don't you want to get married and have your own family?" he asked, his voice tight as a filled balloon.

I think now that he was overwhelmed by the array of choices before me. Everything seemed too momentous. If I could name one memory to represent my father's soul, it would be him saying, "I never had any choices," which I heard more times than I could count and as far back as I could remember, all the way up to the day he told me he had signed on as a truck driver: at last, he was doing something he wanted. It was also true that none of us had ever felt like we had choices, even if our lives were freer than his.

"Have you ever been to a truck stop?" he asked.

"I don't think so," I said. "I've never really noticed them."

"That's where I shower," he said. "They're pretty nice! It costs around ten dollars to use them, but it's free for us because we have rewards cards for buying fuel."

He chattered on, his voice booming about his new job and new life, still shiny with novelty. He described the private bathrooms and showers, how they were surprisingly clean, and how the really nice ones came with a soaking tub. He circled back, repeating some of the same details he'd already mentioned. This is how I knew which aspects of being a truck driver most impressed him.

"I like those little hotel soaps you gave me and the mini shampoo bottles. I'm using them all the time. I carry them in that shaving bag you got for me. If you have more of the little soaps and shampoos, I can use them."

"Okay," I said.

"I sleep at the truck stops too, when I can, but if there's no stop, I have to find a safe place on the side of the road, near other truck drivers. Have you ever noticed that trucks are usually not alone when they're pulled over at night?"

My dad spoke at length, sharing gruesome stories of drivers murdered in their sleep.

"It's best to be where there are people around if you're sleeping in the truck alone. That's why truck stops are more safe."

"Is it comfortable?"

"Remember I showed you the cab behind the front seat? I got *a lot* of space back here. There's plenty of room. It's like camping!" he exclaimed, repeating the same thing he'd said the day he'd taken me to see the truck in person. My dad's exuberance was just as difficult to reconcile as before. I couldn't bring the old dad together with this new one who only seemed to be living in the moment.

The semitruck was black and glassy, like a lacquered box—*brand new*, my dad had pointed out repeatedly the day he showed it to me in the company lot. I'd hesitated at first, watching him pop in and out from a distance. Eventually, I'd climbed in to check out the sleeper cab, which my dad wouldn't stop talking about.

"Come in!" he'd said. "Look!"

Stepping inside was like one of those dreams where you find in your own little house a secret door to an elaborate mansion. The cab behind the driver's seat was the size of a small jail cell with a ceiling high enough for a tall person to stand beneath. There was a full-length bed, a little square window above it, and an overhead storage bin like in an airplane, a mini fridge, a microwave, a fold-down table, recessed lighting and outlets for charging electronics, even a small flat-screen television. I've never flown first class, but while being shoved to the back of the plane I've caught glimpses of those high-end sleeping cabins reserved for very important and very rich people, and they looked a lot like the cab of my dad's semitruck.

When my dad first started calling from the road, we avoided talking about my mom. The house was on the market and they were unofficially separated. With my dad on the road and my mom spending so much time in the city, they were barely living together, though the finances were still in my mom's control, and there were no legal proceedings.

My mom's place was a far, far cry from my own place South of Market, with its basement full of rotting trash that no one ever brought up to the curb, the lack of laundry facilities, and the noise—street traffic, arguments, occasional shrieks from someone out of their mind, including my downstairs neighbor who talked to herself day and night in multiple voices, garage bands with their shouty, fuzzy music, the laughter and vomiting of people stumbling home from the bars after hours, the occasional Scotsman singing folk songs in a mournful baritone ringing through the night. Nevertheless, even my situation was better than what my dad had gotten, which was another job when he was supposed to be retired and no place to call home except his semitruck, even if he had been dreaming about it his entire American life.

"My pee is black."

"What?"

"It started a few days ago. My pee turned black. I didn't say anything to you last time we talked because I didn't want you to worry. I told your mom. She said to go to the hospital. So I'm here."

"*Why is it black*?"

"I don't know. I'm at the hospital. They're doing some tests and I'm going to find out."

I did a Google search as we spoke: *What causes black urine?* I clicked on a link that took me to a site that listed nondangerous, possibly dangerous, and very dangerous causes.

"Did I tell you I have good insurance? I'm on the company health plan!" my dad exclaimed. He laughed proudly. It seemed obscene under the circumstances.

"When will they know?" I asked.

"Soon," he said.

"Are you coming home?" I asked.

"Nah," he said. "It's just tests."

He coughed several times. Or sneezed. I couldn't tell the difference. Through the phone, the sound was tinny and harsh.

I had the feeling that I should be more concerned about my dad's health, but another feeling was telling me that he didn't deserve it. It was this, the pulling of opposites, that kept me in the middle, nowhere, not knowing which feeling to commit to, who to be, how to live. It's hard to let go of someone who was once so tyrannical but who will be loyal until their last breath. How do you separate out what harms you without losing the love and the good intentions?

As with every conversation with my parents, it always ended up with Kevin.

"I called Kevin," he said. "I tried twice this week and he didn't answer. I called Minjoo, too."

"What did she say?"

"She said he's been busy working nights and working overtime. I guess he's sleeping during the day."

"That makes sense," I said.

"Have you talked to him?" my dad asked.

"No. Not in a long time," I said.

"I haven't heard from him either," he said. "I guess he's busy with work."

"Probably," I said.

"Have you called him?"

"Just when he didn't show up at Gomo's house for the barbeque. He didn't answer, so I messaged him. He said he forgot."

"Make sure he knows about your graduation. He has to be there for that."

"Okay," I said, though I was hoping he'd forget and I had no intention of reminding him.

11

SWENSEN'S

The Eighties

MY DAD FELL in love with diners before he came to America and before he ever set foot in one, the way looking at pictures of the Grand Canyon before seeing it in person can warp the senses, never allowing you to see it for what it is. He was drawn to the classic diner, the kind you see in American movies set in the fifties with jukeboxes and milkshakes, men with greased hair, ponytailed women in poodle skirts and bobby socks. A diner made him think of American youth, American music, American culture. When he worked his way up to owning a diner, I could feel that we'd reached a new level. Things were changing; we would change.

The first diner my dad owned was in Sacramento, after he'd sold his carwash and 7-Eleven store. This was twenty years before he gave up small-business ownership and became a truck driver. He commuted daily from Napa, over two hours each way. The place was straight out of Archie Comics with black-and-white checkered floors, red vinyl counter stools that whirled around, and mini jukeboxes at every booth playing the classics of the fifties and sixties. We moved across town to a fancier neighborhood where my parents said our lives were about to get better. Our previous neighbors had been young families with hardworking fathers like mine—a fireman, a shoe salesman, a prison guard. Our new neighbors were also young families, again with fathers that were hardly ever home—mostly doctors, lawyers, and business executives.

Our neighbors often assumed, bitterly, that my parents had received help from their parents, that surely money had been passed down, for my dad to afford such suburban splendor, in our particular neighborhood and in our particular coastal town, when what he did for a living was own and manage a string of small businesses. How could someone who ran a cheap, greasy diner have a house in the same neighborhood as the town's reputable doctors and lawyers? Afford to pay for all those tennis and piano lessons? My dad hadn't even finished college and he was an immigrant (weren't they poor?), while the other fathers had graduate and advanced professional degrees from elite American institutions and had achieved a level of pedigree that had taken at least four sweaty-browed generations in America to reach. Turns out you can make just as much money as your average mediocre small-town doctor or lawyer running a convenience store or diner or carwash or auto shop. It's that nobody wants to do it. You have to work from morning until night, no weekends and no days off, no vacation or sick days—tedious, exhausting work. And no respect. A diner like my dad's serves nonorganic hormone-packed greasy burgers and fries—animals served here are not grass-fed or free-range anything—with standard machine-churned, unnaturally-sweetened and colored, chemical- and additive-loaded ice cream sundaes. This is not slow food. This is not farm-to-table. This is factory, to airplane, to truck, to freezer, to freezer, to table. There's none of the glamour or aspiration of the high-end hyperlocal artisanal culinary academy fine dining you can find on the 29 from Napa to Yountville and St. Helena alongside family estate wineries and rustic farmhouses that provide tours of cellars and caves full of barrels where you can sip from oversized wine glasses in the crisp, cool dark, swish and spit into a bucket. My parents had no savings, no retirement plan, no health and dental package, no college fund. At home, frugality was the rule, as if we were living in the Great Depression: paper towels and napkins and sponges purchased in bulk and cut in half, the fridge and pantry nearly bare, no gifts, no celebrations. Lessons and tutors and SAT prep, no matter what the cost, but no toys or going to the movies or clothing not on sale—nothing extra that didn't support our economic and social mobility.

One of my favorite movies of the eighties was *Coming to America* with Eddie Murphy, who plays a rich African prince looking for love in Queens, New York, where he falls for Lisa McDowell, an upper-middle-class girl next door, played by Shari Headley. I saw us in the McDowells, a Black family that owned a local fast food restaurant called McDowell's, a successful McDonald's knockoff, complete with double golden arches emblazoned above the entrance. The McDowells took nothing for granted. Everything depended on hard work and discipline—running the business, school, social and family relationships. They had a comfortable life and ambition for more: strivers, like us.

After a few years, no longer able to stand the long commute and the long working hours, my dad sold the diner in Sacramento, and though he would soon need another business, there was a brief reprieve. He started playing golf again, which he loved for the wide open spaces, lush lawns, and male fraternizing, particularly when he could get together with longtime Korean friends, the lot of them free of their wives, chain-smoking in polo shirts so bright you could spot them a mile away. Normally, he had no time for the game, even though our country club's main attractions were tennis, golf, and swim, with a full-service clubhouse, all of which he paid for so the rest of us could enjoy them, if that's the right word, though he never got to enjoy them himself.

My dad spent much of his newfound free time reading. He stuck to mass-market paperbacks—one, sometimes even two a day—the kinds of books that you never see on a college reading list. Stephen King, Michael Crichton, John Grisham, Nicholas Sparks. My dad wasn't educated, at least he'd never be considered so in the US: he'd been forced to drop out of Yonsei University when he was twenty-one for mandatory military service, then immigrated to America, and never returned to finish school. Even though Yonsei is arguably the most prestigious school in South Korea, requiring the top scores on entrance exams, in America this doesn't mean anything, and as an immigrant in America without money or connections or fluency in the codes and subtleties that we only notice when someone doesn't have them, it wouldn't have made a difference for my dad whether he graduated or not. Whenever I move to a new city and visit my local convenience store or greengrocer, if it's owned and managed by a Korean man, I always wonder what he left behind in Korea, if he regrets coming to America, if he has a graduate degree from a university in Seoul where he gained expertise in an area of specialty that remains unacknowledged in our American systems, and I wonder what it's like to stand behind the counter selling candy, cigarettes, fruit, condiments, beer, and lottery tickets all day, every day, the days turning into months and years that fall on you, slowly and all at once.

I knew that my dad felt bad that he didn't have a college degree. It was one of his many sources of shame, intensified by a society that confirmed that a college degree was the bare minimum for entrance to the middle class. Before I knew of these kinds of rules, I didn't see why it mattered whether or not he'd finished college, and I still don't, in theory, except I now understand why it does matter, in the game of life and survival, especially for people like us. Because not having a degree made him insecure, I tried to convince him to go back to school, but he said that it was too late for him because he was old, that he'd missed his chance, and something like that didn't matter for someone like him anymore. Whenever he wasn't working or playing golf or meticulously hand-washing his cars, his nose was in a book, eyeglasses removed, the pages held inches from his face—English language only, and only the kinds of books that most people I knew scoffed at. I was pretty sure he didn't know what people thought of his reading material, but I knew that if he did know, he wouldn't care. While it made him feel bad that he hadn't finished college, he looked down on people with pretensions, who were class striving and status seeking, even though class and status were what he thought he didn't have and were the source of his pain and self-consciousness, which is exactly why he despised them.

Eventually, this idyll of leisure had to end. He bought our little town's diner, a family-friendly burger joint that served malted milkshakes and classic sundaes, ice cream pies, chocolate-dipped frozen bananas, and ice cream cookie clowns dressed with gumballs, whipped cream, and sugar cone hats. It was also a walk-in ice cream shop with over thirty flavors to choose from. The diner/ice cream shop was called Swensen's—a Swedish name, which none of us ever thought about until my cousin Saehee's Swedish husband pointed it out, smirking, as if the fact that we didn't know the name's origin meant that we knew nothing. At the entrance, there was a framed poster with an old-timey vintage vibe, in shades of antique brown and eggshell white, featuring Mr. Swensen with his white hair and old man silver frame eyeglasses—same as my dad wore—in a brown striped apron holding a hot fudge sundae. Like the Garofalos who owned the flower shop, we were the Kims who owned Swensen's.

The new diner took over our lives—my dad working daily from morning until night and my mom on weekdays, while Kevin and I took turns over the weekends depending on which one of us had to travel for a tennis tournament or piano competition. There were weekends when Kevin and I both worked. We'd both clock in, put on the brown striped aprons, a little notebook in the front pocket to take down orders, and we'd scoop ice cream at counter service, whip up milkshakes in the blender, seat patrons, wait tables and bus tables, wash dishes, ring up the checks, work the registers. When we were all there, the Kims were the face of the restaurant. You couldn't walk in without seeing one of us. Kevin and I were like a doubles team, calling out shots and directives—which tables we were covering, who was still waiting for their food or the check, which booths needed to be cleared. When we passed each other, there was always a nod or a communication, the only time in our lives when we really worked as a team, trying to get through the day and the night without catastrophe. Once when it got busy, Kevin and I switched to Korean, talking for no more than a minute about a mix-up with somebody's sundae and how to fix it. It was a mistake. Yes, the sundae, but more importantly that we were speaking in Korean. Our dad rushed over. I don't know how he got to us so fast; there was a counter and a low swinging door between us. He leaned in, eyes shifting from me to Kevin, and spoke in a low voice that trembled, barely controlled: "English. No Korean," he said. "*English.*"

When we were younger, Kevin and I had only spoken Korean to each other. It was our secret language because none of the other kids could understand us. English was public, imperative for the social world, the language we spoke to communicate with outsiders, to be heard and understood. Korean was private, intimate, bonding us by blood and by birth, the language we slipped into when we wanted our world to include only the two of us. But by the time we were done with elementary school, our dad had forbidden us to speak Korean anywhere. He feared that if we grew up speaking Korean, even alongside English, we'd be confused, have accents, that we'd never be accepted as American. Little did he know that no matter how perfect our English, how lyrical our prose, how American we seemed, no matter how loud and clear we spoke, even with the right tone, inflection, the right views and perspectives, the right amount of confidence, the right sense of humor, there was nothing we could do to keep from being seen as perpetual outsiders. No language or amount of money or social status would make us less foreign.

Our parents spoke only in Korean to each other. To us, they spoke a mixture, but we were to respond only in English and to speak to each other only in English. When we forgot, our dad yelled at us. Sometimes he'd come out of nowhere, as if he was spying on us. We tended to forget when emotions were high—if we were fighting, or if we felt sad or excited about something. The older we became, the less often we forgot, until we stopped forgetting because we'd completely forgotten the language. That time at Swensen's was the last time Korean inexplicably came back to us. We were teenagers and barely talking to each other, but there we were, sharing a rare moment of connection, and even though we hadn't spoken Korean in years, we fell back into our old way of communicating—an instinct, like blind fish in a cave. Sometimes I think that if we'd held on to our language, we would have known each other better. We would have known our parents better. But then we wouldn't be us anymore. We'd be some other family, some other Kims.

12

STRAWBERRY SHORTCAKE

April 2002

MY DAD HAD been on the road for almost a month and had just returned from the Midwest to my aunt's house in Palo Alto when he finally had a week off. He was staying with my aunt because he had nowhere else to live, having sold the house and separated from my mom. He happily ran errands for his sister and made repairs around the house. When I went over to see him, he was in the driveway washing his car with his shirt off, shoulders glowing pink from the sun.

He looked tired and had a phlegmy cough, but he was still riding high on his new life. He recounted his adventures on the road. None of it sounded at all exciting to me, but I pretended to listen as he described his truck and the truck stops for the tenth time, listing all the new cities he'd visited and reporting the changing and inclement weather.

My dad had asked me to bring my camera and take some pictures of his pickup truck, which he wanted to sell. There was nowhere for him to keep it now that the house was sold, and my aunt didn't want it in her driveway.

"I have to get a small car. I can borrow Gomo's in the meantime."

I snapped a few photos with my Canon ELPH. My dad marveled at it, turning the little silver rectangle over in his hand.

"Amazing!" he said, pressing the button on and off, watching the lens pop out and disappear again.

He opened the hood of his truck so I could get some photos of the engine.

"Are you all ready?" he asked.

"For what?"

"Your move," he said.

"Oh. Yeah," I said, though I wasn't ready. I still hadn't set anything up.

"Your mom is worried."

"I know," I said.

I told him about the grieving party she'd thrown for me and the séance she'd held in my room with the Korean aunties. My dad laughed.

"Have you seen Kevin? You should see him before you go."

"I saw him at Mom's. He helped get rid of our stuff. Didn't Mom tell you?"

My dad busied himself wiping down the windows of his truck.

"Something seems off," I said. "He's hardly responded to any of us and then Mom finally got him to show up, but he acted like nothing was wrong."

"Kevin's always been like that."

"No, he hasn't."

"There's nothing wrong with him."

"That's not what I said."

I couldn't shake the feeling that something wasn't right, but I couldn't put my finger on it, couldn't say what it was exactly that we should do.

My dad wanted to test-drive the pickup, so we decided to go for a drive. He took the quiet backroads, cruising along parks and hiking trails as he talked about his life on the road. How happy he sounded describing all the new places he'd gotten to see, new experiences, new food. "I always wanted to!" he exclaimed, just as he had when he first told me about his new career. I was waiting for him to scold me and try to make me change my mind about moving to New York, but he didn't. He didn't even say anything about how irresponsible it was, both financially and because I'd be off on my own living very far away, shirking duties to my family.

He reminded me of a young dad I'd almost forgotten. It was easy to remember him as unhappy and trapped—the bad dad, the bad husband, the violence, the rage. But he'd also been the one who bathed me and Kevin gently in the kitchen sink, every night when he came home from work. He was the one who rocked us to sleep, cradling our warm bodies with hope and pride. I was a baby, so I don't remember the memory; I remember only my mom telling us the memory. But somehow, her memory has become my own.

Here's a memory I know is mine: I was four, and I asked for a Strawberry Shortcake doll. I begged for days, weeping—I wanted it so bad, I filled with sorrow knowing that I'd never get it because we weren't allowed toys. I kept begging until one day my dad came home from work, grinning as he plopped down an actual strawberry shortcake on the table.

"What's that?" I said.

"Strawberry shortcake! Like you wanted! I had to ask everyone where I could get it because I didn't know what it was."

"I said doll!" I shouted. "Doll, not cake!"

I cried inconsolably.

It was late, but the stores weren't closed yet. My dad drove to a neighboring town to find the doll at Toys "R" Us. When he came home and gave it to me, I played with the doll while he and my mom and my brother ate cake.

I wish I'd known my dad better. I wish I'd seen who he could have been if he hadn't been under so much pressure. If things had been easier, maybe I'd have more memories like this of my dad, good memories that come quickly, naturally. It shouldn't be so hard to remember love or to allow ourselves joy. I watched my dad smiling, happily chattering about his life as we drove around aimlessly. I wondered, what was it all for? All that hardness, everyone trying to win at everything all the time, cutting away every happy and fun thing until there's nothing left but the clean white bone of ambition.

THE ALL-AMERICAN BOY

13

CHUN'S BROTHER

KOREAN CHILDREN ARE told and retell stories about goblins, ghosts, magic, shape-shifters. The men and women in these stories represent *man* and *woman*, *good* and *bad* in the expected ways, on opposite poles with nothing between them: the virtuous young woman versus the selfish woman who never learns the value of sacrifice; the hardworking young man, devoted to his family, especially his parents, versus the lazy trickster. Folktales operate in stark contrasts: generous and selfish, hardworking and lazy, beautiful and ugly, rich and poor, young and old, loyal and untrustworthy, good and evil.

Kevin and I loved the stories our mother told us about dokkaebi, grouchy goblins known for mischief. Impatient and ill-tempered, they thrive on schadenfreude. Lost shoe? Dokkaebi. Bone broth gone sour? Dokkaebi. The wind carried your laundry from the clothesline down into the stream, to be lost forever? Dokkaebi.

Dokkaebi are harmless, known mostly as a nuisance—they might not be remembered if not for their magical wooden clubs. Dokkaebi can grant any wish with the magic club, and any person who gains ownership has the power to grant wishes, for others and for oneself. In the stories, a character either finds a magic club, by chance, or is gifted a club by a lonely dokkaebi as a reward for friendship. A sinister character might steal a magic club from the dokkaebi or from a good citizen who was lucky enough to have gotten one by legitimate means. To make a wish, you pound the club on the ground three times and declare what you desire.

Our mom had told us a dokkaebi story about two brothers who were very different. Chun was diligent and selfless, Chun's brother was lazy and greedy. Every morning, Chun woke at dawn to cut and gather wood from the forest, which he then sold in the village, sharing his earnings with his parents, brother, and brother's wife. Despite his work and sacrifice, he never, ever complained.

At the end of one long day cutting wood and collecting acorns, Chun got lost in the dark and took shelter in an abandoned house, where he decided to spend the night. It wasn't long before a gang of dokkaebi, fired up from a good day of causing trouble and disorder, gathered into the house, settling in a circle.

Chun climbed into the rafters to hide as he watched the dokkaebi below having a grand time. *THUMP, THUMP, THUMP.* They pounded their clubs and chanted wishes, calling forth a variety of riches: piles of food and drink, mountains of gold, silver, and glittering gems. As Chun watched the dokkaebi feast, he became hungry. He'd worked all day and hadn't eaten a thing. He got out one of the acorns he'd collected for his family and put it in his mouth, but to his horror, the first bite made a terrible sound: *CRRAAAAAAAACK!* The noise was thunderous. Fortunately for Chun, the dokkaebi were convinced that the roof was caving in on them. They promptly fled the house, leaving behind the entire bounty, including the clubs.

Chun gathered as much of the feast and jewels as he could carry, intending to share his good fortune with his family. Chun was not only generous and loyal, he was smart and resourceful and only for the benefit of others: he remembered to take a magic club, which would allow him to provide for his parents for the rest of their lives. When he returned home, the village celebrated him for being a good son.

But Chun's brother, seething with jealousy, asked Chun how he acquired such wealth. Chun, too trusting to be suspicious of his brother, rattled off in tiny detail, from beginning to end, the story about the day in the forest that changed everything. Imagining his own future of boundless wealth, Chun's brother immediately set off for the forest. He filled his pockets with acorns, intending to eat them all himself. He found the house and hid in the rafters, where he waited for the dokkaebi to make their grand entrance. When they arrived, they sat down in a circle just as Chun had described. Chun's brother got right to it. He took a bite of an acorn: *CRRRAAAAAAAAACK!*

But the dokkaebi didn't run away. They peered up into the rafters, where they spied Chun's brother. They chased him down, convinced that he was the thief who had scared them away the last time. The dokkaebi kicked and beat Chun's brother with their clubs until he became flat, long, and skinny, stretched thin as a carpet.

Chun's brother staggered home empty-handed. When Chun saw his brother, he simply shook his head. The brother's face was wet with regretful tears. "I have learned my lesson," he said.

Kevin and I both identified with Chun, the virtuous sibling. Being Chun meant that the other person was Chun's brother, the spoiled sibling who wasn't even worth naming. I don't know why either of us thought we were Chun when our parents and all the adults in our family were always telling both of us that we were bad, lazy, and selfish, just like Chun's brother.

Every family has a Chun, and there can be more than one. But for every family of Chuns, there's always a Chun's brother. I wonder if we don't sometimes create Chun's brother out of fear that if we don't attach that name to someone else, it will attach to us. As hard as he tried to be Chun, over the years, Kevin became more and more Chun's brother in all our eyes, including my own. I let him fall into that role because I knew if it wasn't him, it would be me.

14

THE KARATE KID OF TENNIS

The Eighties and Nineties

KEVIN AND I wanted to like *Sixteen Candles*. But there was the problem with Long Duk Dong, the foreign exchange student from an unidentified Asian country whose every entrance is accompanied by the sound of a gong.

"Whass happenin', haaht stuff?" says the Donger.

"Oh, sexy girlfriend," he says to his American love interest, a white woman who towers over him in height, triples him in width.

"No more yanky my wanky. The Donger needs food."

Kevin became quiet whenever Long Duk Dong was on-screen. I could feel my face turn red.

"They only do that to Asian men," Kevin said. "You're lucky."

We didn't watch the movie again.

The Karate Kid was easier. Mr. Miyagi was a caricature of a wise old Asian man, but we liked him. His corny lines felt warm even though they were so stupid. You couldn't deny the truth underneath.

"Man who catch fly with chopstick, accomplish anything," said Mr. Miyagi.

"Walk on road, hmmm? Walk left side, safe. Walk right side, safe. Walk middle, sooner or later, get squish just like grape!"

"When you feel life out of focus, always return to basic of life."

Kevin and I were young, so maybe we just didn't see ourselves in Mr. Miyagi. He was the grandpa we wished we had. Our dad, on the other hand, loathed Miyagi and what he represented. "Americans," he sputtered under his breath.

The Vietnam War movies, American classics, came out in the seventies, continued in the eighties, and have trickled in ever since.

"Me love you long time. Me so horny," says actress Papillon Soo Soo playing a sex worker in Da Nang in *Full Metal Jacket*. No one had ever heard the phrase before the film was released in 1987. The same year, 2 Live Crew debuted *Me So Horny*. Papillon Soo Soo's sampled line provides the chorus, her voice sung along with and danced to, blasting on the radio and at nightclubs all over the world.

My college published a humor newspaper called *The Heuristic Squelch*. The cover of one issue in the nineties was a cartoon of young Asian women in cheerleader uniforms scrubbing fancy cars at a carwash fundraiser. The women were drawn with giant heads and tiny bodies, big hair and fat, pouty lips. Cartoon bubbles ballooned from their mouths: "Me so horny. Me love you long time." Even my Vietnamese boyfriend laughed hysterically when he saw it.

Slutty. That's me. I'm a ho. My vagina is sideways. I'm a geisha—quiet, demure, too afraid to speak, except to say, "me so horny." Look, there I am. I'm the epitome of femininity, both the quietly submissive kind and the loudly sexual kind. And I'm genderless, androgynous, flat-chested, basically a boy.

Kevin's a gangster, a martial arts expert, a plotting evil criminal mastermind. Emasculated exchange student. Small dick. Nonnative speaker dork. Magical Asian man.

Haha. We're so funny. Inscrutable, unrelatable, comically nonsensical. We're inhuman, unfeeling androids. Stoic, impassive, we betray no emotion. We don't even have to talk, that's how funny we are. Our presence is the joke.

I READ THAT Gedde Watanabe, the actor who played Long Duk Dong, based the *Sixteen Candles* character on a Korean friend. Watanabe's

Dong had a vaguely Korean-sounding accent, an imitation of his friend who was an immigrant from Seoul. Born in Ogden, Utah, Watanabe is a Japanese American who speaks fluent English in an American accent.

Kevin, an American boy born and raised in Napa, California, was nothing like the exchange student Long Duk Dong. Kevin didn't see himself in him, but he knew what Americans saw when they looked at him—*him* meaning Kevin and *what Americans saw* meaning Long Duk Dong. Kevin saw himself as Daniel LaRusso, the Ralph Macchio character from *The Karate Kid*, the small, scrappy Italian American Jersey boy transplanted to the San Fernando Valley with his widowed mother, who overcomes the odds by winning the All-Valley Karate Championship tournament where the competitors favored to win are a group of his bullies, members of the elite Cobra Kai dojo. Everybody knows what happens in the middle. A love interest, the bullies, the cruel dojo sensei, Mr. Miyagi, wax on wax off, catch a fly with chopsticks, practice the crane kick on a wood stump on the beach as the sun rises and as the sun sets, waves crashing and seagulls soaring.

What happens at the end in the final scene is something we can all see coming—you almost don't even have to watch it. But Kevin and I played the end a million times and never tired of it. Oh, how a part of me loved the heckling members of the Cobra Kai team. The unhinged, maniacal shouting, "Kill him!" and "Get him a body bag!" So awful in their lack of ethics, even they know it, the guilt flashing in their faces when the callous sensei orders one student to take Daniel "out of commission" with a disqualifying hit, and instructs another to perform illegal contact to Daniel's already injured knee. "No mercy," he says when they look at him with horror. "Finish him!" he bellows before the final point. The absolute depravity of the Cobra Kai dojo combined with some of the members' realization of this fact sets us up for what is the only right outcome. Daniel, knee impaired, takes the hallowed crane stance, balancing on one foot, his wounded leg bent in midair, both hands above his head, wrists pointed in little peaks, and launches into a flying jumping kick, earning him the final point that wins him the title. His opponent/nemesis presents the trophy to Daniel himself, and the crowd carries Daniel—the hero, the champion—lifting him above their heads, while Miyagi looks on with pride. Watching Daniel win over all that's stacked against him and get the trophy, the girl, the approval of his mentor, and even the respect of his enemies—it makes your heart soar.

Kevin never even took karate lessons, but in Daniel LaRusso, Kevin saw himself like the Karate Kid of tennis. The Tennis Kid. Above-average talent combined with sheer determination can get you pretty far. When you're the best around, even your bullies take notice. For people like us, sometimes it's why we get bullied in the first place. I suppose it would have been less expected if his chosen sport had been baseball or football or basketball, but Kevin loved tennis. He'd cut school just to get more hours in. While I was a power player, hitting the ball flat and hard, Kevin was about touch, perfecting his topspin and slice, admiring how the ball responded to his will in the most subtle and instantaneous ways. I can't remember us not playing tennis. I only remember when we stopped playing.

Our coaches always said that I was the one who could make it. But we all recognized that Kevin was the one who really wanted it. I didn't care so much whether I won or not, what number I was in the rankings. I'd often find myself, in the finals of an important tournament, wishing it was over so I could go home. For Kevin, winning was all he cared about. Turning pro, his only goal. He was never ranked as high as me in his own boys' age category, but this seemed to fuel him. He wanted it so bad, I didn't want to outshine him, and I was burned out anyway. I'd reached a point where I couldn't just enjoy the game anymore—it had become all about strategy and psyching out my opponent, finding their weaknesses and wearing them down, all while knowing my coach was watching every move, notating on a graph every point played, each winning shot and each unforced error, which he would review with me sternly after every match, even when I won. I despised all competitive aspects of tennis, which was ridiculous—it's a competitive sport. Kevin thrived on it. He'd do anything that would give him an advantage. He ate plain pasta before every match because Ivan Lendl did it. He took gymnastics to improve his balance. He was all in on studying himself, talking over every detail with our coach. Together, they tracked his performance after each match—how did he play when he was up versus down, serving versus returning, and how did it all compare against different playing styles. He replayed videos of himself hitting strokes to break down what he was doing wrong and what he was doing right. He took on extra training: running, lifting, balancing on a narrow wooden plank atop a rolling cement cylinder. Kevin did it all while I complained. Maybe that was why I found him enjoyable to watch. Watching meant that I wasn't playing. Instead, I was watching my brother, who wanted nothing more than to be on the court, winning.

I WAS DONE for the day. It was the summer before the start of high school, and I'd just won my semifinals match and advanced to the finals. I'd return to the tennis club in Palo Alto the following weekend. After I returned the balls and reported the scores at the check-in table, I found Kevin's court where he was playing the quarterfinals.

I'd asked my mom and our tennis coach, Don Dixon, to stay away from my court; I could always feel their anxiety radiating. Silence was worse than when they were vocal, groaning about my missed shot or double fault or yelling about my opponent's bad call. The quiet created anticipation that made me choke. So, I'd effectively sent my mom and

Don to Kevin's court. When I joined them, they were sitting hunched over on the long grassy steps for spectators.

Kevin had gone a third set and was up 4–2. My mom and Don were so engrossed, they didn't even notice when I plopped down my racket bag and sat next to them. My mom flinched every time Kevin made a shot, ran for a shot, returned a shot, missed a shot. Her body was perpetually jerking inward, like a toy being pulled by a string, while Don's motions were big exclamations, arms swept open, feet splayed, face pushing out.

An audience seemed to give Kevin more energy and deepen his focus. He had certain habits that he performed during matches that perhaps only I recognized. He'd told me about the little ceremonies he'd developed for good luck. He bounced the ball methodically before each serve. He'd lean forward at the center mark, body loose, racket in his right hand, and with his left, he'd bounce the ball in sets of six—one set of six bounces, second set of six bounces—and the number of sets could be any as long as it was an even number. While preparing to return a serve, he'd spin the racket in his hands. Spin, spin, spin. Spin, spin, spin. He bounced on the balls of his feet. As long as he caught the grip with the right side up, indicated by the markings on the neck of the racket, he was ready to go.

If only commitment and discipline translated to winning every time, the way it does in many other careers. Guts, drive, sacrifice. If you want to be a lawyer that bad, unless you had brain damage, you'd probably succeed. Not in sports. There would always be players better than you and there could only be one winner. Then there was the matter of staying on top. In this particular match, I knew that no matter how hard Kevin tried, winning was unlikely. His opponent was Paul De Luca from Chico, a top five player, who'd never lost to Kevin. De Luca's concentration might have wavered in the second set and part of the third, but it was obvious that he'd snapped out of whatever mental block he'd been stuck in. In less than ten minutes, he was already up 4–4, forty–love, and he had the serve.

Long and lanky and loose, De Luca's style was all Edberg, relaxed and elegant, a strategy that relied more on dominating at the net than on the power of his serve. Kevin was smaller than De Luca, but he was quicker on his feet, and as an all-court player, he was comfortable everywhere, dictating from the baseline but capable at the net, balancing attacking and defending. Yet De Luca, at seventeen, was a year older than Kevin, which mattered at that age. It meant that he had an extra year of everything—physical growth, training, qualifying tournaments, mental toughness.

Kevin, down 4–5, had the serve in the deciding game. At the center mark, he faced the net, right foot behind the left, toes pointed forward. He leaned in, hunched a bit, right hand holding the racket in a continental grip, the left bouncing the ball—one set of six, second set of six—his wrist floating up delicately between each set of bounces, as if testing the weight of the air. He shifted his body, placing his feet parallel to the baseline, and swept the racket down and back behind him while tossing the ball in a straight line above his head. Knees bent, symmetrical, back arched, right elbow cocked like a gun, face and hand pointed at the sky, there was that quiet moment that happens with each serve, the moment of waiting for the ball to fall to just the right height, then the body pivots, the core acting as a fulcrum. Kevin swung down, hitting the ball flat and with such force that the sound carried across the adjoining courts. It wasn't an ace, but the ball landed right in the outside corner of the deuce court, sending De Luca wide, reaching out past the alley and having to return when the ball had begun to fall. Fact: on most points, you want to hit the ball on the rise, play off its force and redirect it. But De Luca had to scoop to save it, pushing it up into an unintentional lob, which of course made it ineffective.

Kevin had advanced to the net, he was already there, waiting, and the lob wasn't high or deep enough to go over his reach, land at the baseline and spin up and back, a soft winner. Wasn't even high enough for Kevin to take the point with a satisfying overhead smash. The ball came up soft and floppy over the middle of the net, right at Kevin's eye level, to meet his Prince Graphite Original, a big *P* painted in black on the white racket strings—strung and spray-painted himself—the ball floating easy like it had been pitched by a machine set up for an eight-year-old, giving Kevin time to decide what he wanted to do with it.

It was delicious to watch Kevin beat De Luca with a serve and volley, De Luca's own game. I wish I could say that Kevin came back and won that set, won the match, but the next few points didn't go his way. He wouldn't return the following weekend to compete in the finals as I would, but he'd keep going for years when I'd quit, giving all he had every time, never doubting what he wanted.

IN *THE KARATE KID*, the theme song, "You're the Best," plays during the tournament montage. The song is awful. It's an eighties power ballad performed by Joe Esposito, and was turned down first by *Rocky III*, then *Flashdance*, before it was accepted for *The Karate Kid*. Though it's a bad song with bad lyrics, the chorus is catchy, and Kevin and I thought it was funny to sing: "You're the best around. Nothing's gonna ever keep you down." That line makes up the chorus, repeated over and over. The sentiment is conceited and self-absorbed, capturing the egomaniacal spirit of the underdog, perfect for people like us who felt superior and unjustly victimized. In the song's bridge, Esposito sings about never giving up until you win, while background voices shout in unison: *Fight!*

"Fight 'til you drop, never stop, can't give up 'til you reach the top," Esposito sings.

Fight!

Kevin and I loved that part. *FIGHT!* we hollered. In the same verse with the voices shouting *Fight!* there's one line that's never repeated—*A little bit of all you got*—but is noticeable in the way that it's drawn out, Esposito stressing each syllable as the phrase comes down, and then climbs right back up: *They'll never bring you down!*

I could hear it every time I watched Kevin play. Tennis was the lens through which he viewed his worth. It kept him on top, above all the voices trying to keep him down and tell him he was nobody. He just had to keep fighting, give a little bit more, even if that little bit was all he had, and he had to do it again and again, find more to give every time—each point, each game, set, match—even though he just gave all he had, even if he'd just given the very last bit of it. The world would go on saying he was Long Duk Dong, but he knew who he was. He was Kevin Kim, the tennis star, and he was certainly better than you—he'd put you through the wringer, double bagel you, make you regret your insults.

I'd watch Kevin and think: How many times could he give all he had? At a certain point, wouldn't he run out?

15

DARLENE

The Eighties

IT WAS INEVITABLE that Kevin and I would get to know Don better than most kids might know their tennis coach. For years, Don Dixon lived in the guest house in our backyard. He didn't pay rent. In exchange, we got tennis lessons on demand, while we saw our other coach, Sam Stefani, once a week on his private court. Sam was renowned for having coached the US Davis Cup team. He was retired but occasionally worked with young players who competed at a high level, with aspirations of turning pro or at least of playing for a Division I college team. Sam was clearly the more elite coach, but we were closer to Don. He was drawn to us, as if we were some kind of buffer between him and the world, and something about him was irresistible—his lack of boundaries might have been a red flag for others, but for us it felt familiar and made him charismatic. During those years that he lived with us and coached us, Kevin spent more time with him, but I learned things about him that I don't think Kevin ever knew. Once when we were alone, Don showed me a picture of himself from fifth grade.

"I would have had a crush on you," he said.

I peered at the wallet-sized photo, the kind kids trade with each other at school.

"Would you have liked me?" he asked.

The ten-year-old in the photo had the same brown curly hair, same dopey smile. The boy's delicate features would sharpen into the strong jaw and brow of thirty-five-year-old Don, same as I saw on the faces of men in mail-order catalogs. In the photo, the boy's face glowed, as if someone had turned a light on under his skin.

I was ten, the same age Don had been when the picture was taken. Old photos of grown-ups always felt like getting punched in the stomach. The difference between then and now seemed impossible, the beauty of youth too effortless to be true.

"That's me in South Carolina," Don said. "You wouldn't have liked me."

"Why?"

"Because I was Black."

Don's eyes shifted from me to the window that looked out on the backyard. I watched Don, who watched me watching him.

"You can't tell?" he asked.

He brought the picture close to his face, eyes narrowed. He looked like an old man reading fine print who'd found a very unfavorable clause. He scowled.

"I look like a Black boy," he said.

Don turned to me, examining me the way he'd examined himself. I wondered what I'd done wrong to make him think I cared.

"Listen," he said. "Nobody around here knows what I just told you. Just forget what I said."

Looking at the picture of himself as a boy, Don's face twisted into pure revulsion, like someone had thrown dog shit on his head. It was the same look of disgust I'd seen directed at my whole family all my life. I'll never forget that look. It was mostly white mothers and some white kids who looked at us like that, but there was also the occasional Asian or Latino or Black kid to mix it up—they were turning back on us the hate that had been directed at them. White men, most of the time, were too comfortable being on top to care much about us.

"Forget what I said. I'm not Black, okay? I get to choose. I'm white. Look at my hair," he said, pulling out a curl from the top of his head.

"There's blonde in it, see? Look at these curls—they're big and loose. People think I'm Jewish."

DON TOLD HIS secret to at least two other people in town. One was his best friend, Elliot Nakamura-Wong, who was a quarter Chinese, a quarter Japanese, and half white. The second person Don told was a woman he dated on and off for years, Darlene Mahelona, one of those beautiful people from Hawaii. She was tall with strong shoulders and muscular arms. She wore white eyelet dresses to show off her deep brown tan. She told me once all the different kinds of people mixed in her, but I could never remember past Chinese, Hawaiian, and Dutch.

Darlene was once a high school athlete, a track and basketball star, but a knee injury had kept her from attending college since she was no longer eligible for scholarships. For the previous ten years, she had been stuck in our small town working at Papa John's, living at her parents' house along with her younger sister, though she'd found her love of sport again in tennis, which is how she'd met Don and Elliot.

She came along on a road trip to a tournament in Fresno. While my mom and Don were signing me and Kevin in, collecting the freebies, checking out the brackets, bickering with the officials about how Kirsten Stoltz had been awarded the number one seed when it should have gone to me, and while Kevin stood aside scowling, Darlene pulled me aside.

"Don told me that you know," she said quietly. "I don't think Don needs to hide it, but it's really important to him."

Darlene's voice never rose. It stayed low, a sharp, urgent tone. She had the kind of open face that made you listen when it turned serious. She leaned forward, knees bent, face jutting out, as if she was returning a serve.

"I know you can keep a secret. You're not like other kids."

I didn't know why Don's secret was a secret, how he could even keep a secret like that. Kevin and I couldn't pretend to be white and get away with it, and neither could Darlene or Elliot. But I was beginning to notice how few Black people I saw in our town. It would be years before I realized how deliberately they'd been excluded by landlords who refused to rent to them, banks who refused to give them mortgages, country clubs who wouldn't admit them. Our Asianness made us invisible because it was so visible. People saw us and they saw Long Duk Dong, Mr. Miyagi, and Anna May Wong as the Mongol Slave in *The Thief of Bagdad*, or they tried not to see us at all. But the town did its best to render Blackness literally invisible through the actual absence of Black people, enforced by rules both written and unwritten. Black people were not acknowledged, except in indirect expressions of Blackness as a threat, as people to be feared. It felt like any injustice directed at them could just as easily be applied to us. I didn't know if my parents knew Don's secret. If they did, they chose not to mention it. Easier that way. I once witnessed my dad shower praise on a Black woman who worked at the DMV, who he said he'd first met in the seventies when he moved into town. He complimented her for her hard work and for supporting herself with a stable job, which might have been a microaggression or just paternal—it was the kind of sentiment he often expressed to me.

There wasn't a single Black kid at my school. There was another Korean girl, who'd been adopted by a white family. Her name was also Jane, and somehow the two of us Korean Janes knew instinctively to stay clear of each other. There was a Filipina, another adoptee, but her anxiety about who she thought she was versus what people saw and questions about my own authenticity had overwhelmed me to the point that I'd begun avoiding her. Then there was Orlando, my Mexican-Cuban first boyfriend in middle school. Later, after he went to Napa High, he'd had a new girlfriend, Esperanza, a beautiful, tiny thing who fawned over me when we met at a party, exclaiming how I looked like a porcelain doll, how lucky we both were to have fair skin. Napa High, home of the Napa Indians, had a Native American man for their mascot. The logo was an Indian head in profile donning a feathered headdress. The head, encircled in blue and gold, was emblazoned on the walls and above the entrance of the school building, painted on the floor, even, in the lobby of the district auditorium, to be trampled on by Napa residents attending the latest student production of *The King and I* or *Oklahoma!* At football games, the Napa High Indian danced across the field to the terrible, raucous music of the marching band, clad in faux leather and faux fur and a beaded headdress, feathers trailing down the Indian's back like the spine of a dragon, face painted, swinging a big fake tomahawk. They say that the name "Napa" comes from the Native Americans who lived there for centuries before many were killed by Spanish explorers in the 1820s, before war broke out in 1850 when a white man's death caused white settlers to hunt down and kill all the native people they could find. The first commercial winery was opened in 1859.

I'd gone to Vintage High, home of the Vintage Crushers. Our mascot was a winemaker. The Vintage logo, set in burgundy and gold, featured an old-timey picture of a man crushing grapes at a wooden barrel. At halftime, the winemaker danced incompetently, an oversized fake head teetering on top of his shoulders—angry-faced, bushy-eyed, butt-chinned, a burgundy headband tied across the forehead—inexplicably brandishing a trident. Each year, the two mascots—the Indian and the winemaker—faced off at midfield during the coin toss before the start of the Big Game.

I remembered Don's secret again when I met Jean-Robert, a Black man from Haiti who was hired to teach me driver's ed. We'd barely pulled away from the house on my first day of training when

Jean-Robert told me that when the other parents saw him walking up to the front door, they ran to their phones to call his office and demand that he be replaced with another teacher.

"Look at me," he said, pointing to the dark skin of his exposed forearm.

The day we practiced two- and three-point turns, he was still talking about it, as if something cold had invaded his mind and froze there, locked in.

"They wouldn't even answer the door. That's how much they don't want a Black man teaching their kids. You and your friend Anaïs are the only ones who've stuck with me," he said.

When I'd first met him, Jean-Robert had been overly cheerful in a way that reminded me of a version of myself that appeared when I felt the need to put others at ease. In the car, his façade fell away as he became comfortable with showing me his true self. He was a compact man with a booming voice, made sharp by his indignation. I felt envious of the effortless way he expressed his anger.

Jean-Robert was the first person to say out loud in my presence the word *racist* in reference to the way he was treated, who asked me if I felt it, the cold wind that he felt from people in that town. Nobody had ever asked me that before, and the possibility of it—what it meant about me, my family, the world—was terrifying. Talking to Jean-Robert, I understood that Don must have felt that same cold wind all his life, but unlike Jean-Robert, Don seemed to hate himself and therefore, anyone who liked him.

I REMEMBER A particular day, soon after finishing driver's ed with Jean-Robert, when I heard my mom and Kevin arguing, as they often did when my dad was at work. I could hear the noise through my closed door, my mom leaving and returning to Kevin's room, shrieking like a broken toy, about his grades and money and how he needed to figure out how to make some so he could take care of her.

This time Kevin fought back more than usual, which only agitated our mom more, causing her to return in shorter intervals, her voice high and squishy. When things had escalated to a point where it seemed like it couldn't get any worse, I heard Kevin shout in rage—no words, just a roaring bellow—followed by a yelp from our mom and a loud thunk, like a heavy object had fallen to the ground.

I hurried to Kevin's room and found my mom standing at the door, holding the side of her face, looking bewildered. When she pulled her hand away, I saw that the skin on her cheekbone was pink and blossoming. There was no blood, but she had an angry mark that was beginning to pus, right on her face.

"Kevin is just like his dad," she said, eyes vacant, still stunned.

A gold tennis trophy lay on the ground at the foot of Kevin's bed. I imagined the corner of the wooden base hitting my mom on the cheek. She disappeared into her own room and turned on the TV to drown out her feelings. Kevin got up and walked out. I followed him across our back lawn to the guest house. Don let us in, studying our solemn faces.

"I kept telling her to stop, but she wouldn't leave me alone," Kevin said, "so I picked something up and threw it."

"What did you throw? Did you throw it *at* her?" Don said.

"I don't remember. I think it hit her in the face," said Kevin. His cheeks were flushed and he was looking at the ground, as if he'd been caught stealing. "It's not my fault," he said. "Why did she move? She's so stupid, she must have stepped right into it."

"Your mother is crazy," Don said.

Kevin looked up and locked eyes with Don.

"That's what my dad says," said Kevin.

I was standing right there in the room with Don and Kevin, but in the course of the conversation, they seemed to have forgotten all about me.

Don lowered himself into a wooden chair. He held Kevin's attention with his understanding, his acknowledgment of the bad hand my brother had been dealt.

"You got stuck with a terrible mom. We don't get to choose our parents, but listen, you have your dad. You're lucky you have your dad. I wish I had a dad like that."

Don leaned forward, hands on top of his knees. The hem of his shorts shifted, revealing white skin in stark contrast to his dark brown tan, as if someone had drawn a line on a piece of paper and colored in one side. Even though I had the same tan lines, as did Kevin and most tennis players, I felt that I'd seen something obscene, illicit.

"Everything your dad does is for you and your sister. He's one of those dads—I see a lot of them around here—who just work all day to provide for their families." Don began to laugh, as if he'd just remembered a good joke. "They're whipped! They do whatever their wives say," he said, still laughing.

Kevin laughed awkwardly.

"Listen, you can't depend on your mom. She's a narcissist. She's not the kind of mom you can go to when you need help," Don said, leaning closer. "But you have your dad. He'll always be there for you. He'll be there until he's *dead*," Don exclaimed, emphasis on the word dead, which only made me think about my dad being dead. I didn't know what Kevin was thinking, but he was rapt with attention.

Don opened the drawer of his desk and took out a pocket-size recorder with a miniature tape deck. He set it on top of the table.

"Maybe this will cheer you up," Don said. "I haven't played this for anyone. Oh my god, it's fucking hilarious," he said, squeaking as he tried to stifle his laughter.

When he pressed play, the room filled with Darlene's voice, but she was nearly unrecognizable. I'd never heard her shouting before, never heard her sound so out of control, never heard her sobbing. I could barely decipher what she said, but I caught pieces—anguished, animal-like—about not feeling loved. Like all big arguments, there was a peak, where the thing that you're trying not to say erupts into the open: *You never touch me anymore,* she began. *You don't even kiss me,* she said, voice rising. *Don't you want to be close to me? How do you think it makes me feel?* Darlene paused long enough to squelch a cry, to take a haggard breath. *We haven't had sex in four months!*

Don was barely on the tape. Anything he said was being recorded just like Darlene—he wouldn't want to put himself in a bad light. When he responded at all, his voice was unfeeling, monotone, like he'd been plugged into a wall. His longest sentence: *Calm down.*

I felt both like a spy and like an animal in a cage. Darlene was in another cage, and I could hear her, but I couldn't set her free. I'd never heard anybody cry like that before except for my mother.

Don burst into laughter so uncontrollable he doubled over in pain. He stopped only long enough to pause the recording. Then he continued laughing, clutching his sides with both hands, head thrown back. Kevin joined in.

I imagine Kevin was just as confused as I was about what Darlene had said on the tape. I recognized something unspeakable about her confession of desire and Don's refusal to meet that desire, though what shocked me more was that he had recorded her private life without her knowledge, to play and replay after the fact and expose her secret self, her desire and feelings of rejection, the expression of all her pain, and share it with people who looked up to her, all with the intent to humiliate her. It was an unconscionable act of power and control.

"See," Don said, once he caught his breath. "Women are crazy. Listen to that," he said, pointing at the tape recorder, the proof. "Can you believe this shit?"

He rewound and played the tape again from the beginning. Don and Kevin huddled close, shaking with laughter. Don howled. They carried on for so long the room began to darken. Finally, Don turned off the tape player, but instead of putting it back in the drawer, he passed it to Kevin with the tape still in it.

"You can have it," he said. "It's a present."

When I followed Kevin back to the house I thought about Jean-Robert's anger. He was the first person I'd met who named the source of his anger and directed his anger at that source, the people in our town who treated him like a wild animal that had gotten loose. He called them crazy because he could see that they were crazy. He was angry at them, not at himself for being what they hated. Don's anger came from the same source, but he directed it at himself. He loved the power that white men wielded just for being white men, and he hated anything weak or vulnerable, including women who voiced their unmet desires.

LATER, AS I walked past Kevin's room, I heard the tape. The sound of Darlene's voice chilled me. I couldn't stand to listen to her cries ringing through the house.

I found Kevin sitting at his desk, hunched over the tape recorder, hypnotized.

"Will you stop listening to that?" I said, standing in Kevin's doorway. "Don shouldn't have given that to you. I can't believe he even made that tape in the first place. Can't you see he's crazy?" I said.

Kevin stared at me.

"He recorded Darlene in secret and then made fun of her behind her back and then he gave the tape to you. It's demented."

Kevin got up from his desk and walked toward me, calmly, wordlessly. His hands came up—light, gentle—and pressed down on my shoulders, pushing softly. It felt like courtesy. Push. Push. Push. Kevin guided me out the door, his expression tender almost, the way one looks when they have a suggestion. Push. Push. Push.

I found myself halfway across the living room.

Kevin turned around and walked back to his bedroom, where he replayed the tape again.

I can still feel it. The chivalry in Kevin that could twist into something else.

Push. Push. Push.

16

BLACK FLAG

The Eighties and Nineties

DON MOVED OUT after a fight with my mom. My mom was mortified to learn that Darlene—who was not married or even engaged to Don—would sometimes stay the night. Don accused my mom of jealousy, there was a lot of yelling, then Don made a comment about her sexual frustration and how he could help her with that. This did not sit well with my mother. She told my dad. My dad kicked Don out. For years afterward, he trash-talked us to everyone we knew, though when it was repeated to me, it was clear that it was his behavior that people were questioning. His reputation had been tarnished even though we'd said nothing. It was then that I recognized the power of silence, though I can see now that the structural powers in place put my family at an advantage.

Don moved into a loft in a warehouse downtown, but he and Kevin remained close. He had become a mentor and father figure to Kevin. I suppose it was nice for Don to have someone who looked up to him, but he probably also wanted people to see that not all the Kims had soured on him. If one of us still cared about him, he couldn't be the one who'd done wrong. When Kevin had problems at school or at home, he went to Don. Sometimes I'd run into Don in town, and he'd mention some way in which I'd undermined Kevin—once it was about how I'd purposely woken him from a nap, or how it was unfair that I had friends and he didn't, or how our parents treated us different because I was a girl, which was true, though obviously this didn't usually work in my favor. But I never said anything back. When someone speaks ill of you, silence gives you power, which Don and Kevin had yet to learn.

That year, Kevin's grades, which had always been average, declined to a new low. When his bad grades caused things to take a turn at our house, Don was the person Kevin confided in, and Don was the one who told a version of the story to people we knew and didn't know. I remember what happened so clearly. It was surprising but also not surprising.

WE STOOD AT a distance from each other, my mother, brother, and I on separate sides of the yard, while my dad squatted on the concrete under the basketball hoop. You could've drawn concentric circles around us like a solar system, the three of us orbiting my father, who stood at the center wielding an axe as he chopped up Kevin's tennis rackets, graphite shooting off sparks, gut strings curling into tendrils. The sparks felt like my father's rage transferred into physical form, his fury at my brother and his dreadful report card that had just arrived in the mail—two failing grades among a column of Cs—and everything else: me, my mother, the world. We all watched, entranced.

I was fifteen, Kevin seventeen. My parents were forty-five.

The chopping of the tennis rackets was not methodical. Rage is chaotic. My dad raised the axe high above his head and brought it down again and again. At times, he successfully cleaved into the pile, splitting through the rackets, though mostly the bit clanged onto the concrete. He even tried to chop up Kevin's racket stringer, squatted right over it as he swung the blade, but the thing didn't crack because it was made of solid steel. The effort left my dad breathless and red in the face, which only made him more angry. He had little experience with an axe and didn't have much use for one in the mild climate where we lived. In Napa, winter was mustard season, when the hills and vineyards and the floors of the valleys became carpeted with canary-colored mustard flowers that you could wade in knee deep, that blossomed in January and bloomed until March, when winemakers plowed them back into the soil.

My father must have felt a certain satisfaction and comfort in the release of rage. For the three of us watching, what we felt most was terror, an incoherent helplessness that bloomed within us, took root and lived there, following us everywhere, without our even knowing it.

Kevin stood near the guest house, watching. The cottage was empty, the floors and counters collecting layers of dust. No one had been inside since Don moved out. Kevin began to pace along the sliding glass doors, hands balled up like wads of paper. My mom was shrieking and crouch-walking toward my dad, whose work of chopping up Kevin's tennis rackets seemed to go on forever. She moved in, closer and closer, wanting to save Kevin's rackets, too expensive to replace—then she stopped, started and stopped again, at times retreating backward. I worried that our neighbors could hear us. I wished that my dad would do my rackets next.

Kevin walked toward me, arms pumping, his pace quickening as he approached. When he reached me, his hands came up, spread out flat, and pushed, palms socking into my shoulders. I was surprised how loud the sound was. I didn't fall over, but I took a few steps back to keep my balance. He never stopped, just continued storming into the house. I watched him through the glass as he walked to his bedroom, where he disappeared.

I followed Kevin inside. His room had one of those pocket doors that slides in and out of the wall. At least it used to, before Kevin broke it during an argument with our mom. Now the door remained permanently open. He had a habit of breaking doors. He'd even broken the door to my bedroom during an argument when I'd locked myself in my room; he'd bashed the door down with his shoulder and pushed me until I fell to the floor. "He's just like his dad," my mom had said, crying. "It must be your fault. You must have done something to make him mad."

I sat on the bed as he stuffed clothes into a duffle bag.

"What are you doing?" I asked.

"I'm running away," he said, head down. "I'm going to Don's."

He looked up, meeting my eyes. His face was small and heart-shaped, like our dad's, and he wore wire-rimmed glasses with thick lenses, had since grade school, one of those things, like being too thin or too fat, or too short or too tall, you never shake as a grownup, even when glasses become hip and you're no longer too anything. He was small and skinny and had a voice that broke, like a toy that needed new batteries. He'd gone through puberty, but seemed to be still adjusting to his new voice. He also had allergies and sensitive lungs—he'd had severe asthma as a child, had been rushed to the emergency room several times, once even by helicopter. I, on the other hand, had no ailments, had never required special medical attention, started walking at seven months, potty-trained at eighteen months and never wet the bed, learned how to read and play the piano at three years old, won my first piano competition and tennis tournament at eight, all of which our parents never failed to point out, how I learned everything faster and better than Kevin. At fifteen, my voice was lower than Kevin's, though he was two years older. People couldn't tell the difference between us when we answered the phone. Kevin had a classic bowl cut until Don gave him a flattop, tall and thick and even as a hedge, like the Fresh Prince of Bel-Air. "Parents Just Don't Understand" was Kevin's anthem.

"Don't tell mom and dad," he said.

I thought about how I was the one who'd be there when the shit went down, when our parents discovered that Kevin was gone. I had a sudden stomachache. Kevin continued packing.

"Why can't you just get better grades?" I said.

"I can't. I tried. I'm not like you," he said.

Kevin never cried, had learned not to, shamed by our dad. The last time I'd seen him cry, he was eight, running from our mom chasing him around the garage with a broomstick, yelling that she was going to kill him. When our mom would say in Korean, "Do you want to die?" I believed that death might follow. It wasn't until I was much older that I realized, while watching Korean dramas, that "Do you want to die?" doesn't literally mean that the following action might be murder, at least in most contexts. It was simply a Korean expression, like Americans saying, "I'm going to kill you." From the sound of Kevin shrieking, trapped in the garage with our mom chasing him, I could tell that he was just as fearful and gullible as I'd been. Our mom had always said that her role was to train us to submit to her authority, so that when she grew old, we'd know our place was to care for her. I remember him screaming, running in circles, "Umma, I love you!" The terror in his voice paralyzed me. "Why are you mad at me? You're scaring me! I'll do what you say!"

As Kevin finished packing, I was already regretting what I'd said about his grades and the way I'd blamed him, like everyone was always doing to me. Now it was too late—the moment was gone, too awkward to bring back up.

"I can't get better grades," Kevin said. "I tried. This is the best I can do. I can't do geometry and calculus. Why are people always saying that Asians are good at math?"

"I don't know," I said. "I'm not good at math either. They say that if you're good at music you're supposed to be good at math. It doesn't make any sense."

"But you still get *A*s," he said.

Kevin and I had math tutors, but there was only so much a tutor could do when a student had no interest in the subject. We'd both resorted to cheating, though I was better at it, or luckier. I sat next to a friend who was a math whiz and let me copy off her exams. It wasn't until years later that I realized the irony of an Asian kid cheating off a popular white girl in math class.

My eyes roamed around Kevin's room, resting on his prized possessions, from the jar of marbles on his desk to the bookshelves that contained a hardcover early edition box set of *Doctor Dolittle*, a gift from our English tutor before he moved away to find something more lucrative to do with his PhD.

"Don't touch my stuff," Kevin said, watching me. "If you touch anything, I'll know."

"I'm not going to," I said. But I was already planning it in my mind. After Kevin was gone, I'd look through his books and put them back exactly as I'd found them. In the past, I'd used a ruler to measure the distance between the spines and the edge of the shelf.

"You think everything is yours. Fucking greedy. That's what dad says—that women are greedy," he said. "Everybody gives you what you want because you're a girl. I wish I was a girl. You get what you want and you get to do what you want. Life is easy for girls."

I picked at Kevin's bedspread, which was black like the sheets. He was obsessed with black. Even his tennis clothes were black from head to toe except for splashes of neon yellow—socks, shoelaces, logo. The bright accents and the athletic style made him look more like Andre Agassi and less like a goth theater kid. He was often written up at Justin-Siena, the private school he attended, for deviating from the dress code. I went to Vintage High because our parents didn't think that they had to send me to private school. They could barely afford to send Kevin, so the justification was easy enough, though they soon learned that it would have been better to cite financial reasons rather than say "because Jane is a girl" when other parents asked. It just gave everyone another thing to fuel the gossip about the Kims.

Kevin's room was wallpapered in a mix-and-match blue-green color scheme that our mom had picked out years earlier. He'd asked for black paint, but she wouldn't even agree to white. That's when Kevin got the black flag from a man selling flags out of the back of a pickup truck. It was emblazoned with a skull and crossbones, a pirate hat on top and a red eye-patch over an eye socket. The pirate flag covered almost an entire wall. The rest of the room was plastered with Spiderman posters (Black Suit Spidey only) drawn by Stan Lee, who Kevin liked to imagine was Asian, like us. Maybe underneath that suit, even Spiderman was Asian.

"You don't have to go," I said. "Don't leave me alone with them."

Kevin looked up, eyes narrowed.

"Why does it matter?" he said. "They're nice to *you*."

"No, they're not," I said.

"I can't believe dad broke all my rackets. What am I supposed to do now?" he said, voice tight. "It's better to be a girl. Everything is easier. Mom and dad leave you alone."

"They don't," I said.

"They're not always yelling at you and telling you what to do. Dad didn't touch *your* rackets. How could he do that to me? He's fucking crazy!"

Kevin punched his fist into a pillow. His mouth became small and pointed.

"Dad thinks you're perfect. Is it because you get good grades? Because you're a girl? They leave you alone but they're always on my back, telling me I have to get a good job and make money," he said.

"But— " I said.

"I try to do what they say," Kevin continued, "but nothing I do is ever good enough and nothing is ever right. I say I want to be an engineer, and dad says, *That's what Asians do.* I say what about a doctor, and he says, *That's so Asian.* What can I do then? I want to be a tennis pro, but he says I can't because I won't make money."

"They do the same thing to me," I said.

"No they don't!" he shouted. "You get to do what you want because you're a girl. Whenever you ask for something, they give it to you. Sometimes you ask for things you don't even want—you only ask because I said *I* wanted it, but they won't let me have it, and then dad goes right out and buys it for you."

Kevin was right that I was given more stuff, but he was forgetting that he was set to inherit everything. He was wrong about everything else—nobody was getting what they wanted. But Kevin was so certain, so adept at making others believe in his victimhood and my role as victimizer, that sometimes even I believed him.

He swung the duffle bag over his shoulder and walked out the back door. I waited, listening, until I heard the sound of his car starting and driving away. Though our parents wouldn't buy him frivolous things, they bought him big-ticket items like private school tuition, an Apple computer, and a pickup truck because they believed a man needed a good education and a car.

The house became quiet, hollow. I didn't know if my parents had come inside, if they'd seen Kevin leave. If they knew that he'd gone, they'd assume that he was just letting off steam and, since he was a boy, they wouldn't question where he was going or expect him to ask for permission. There were certain choices that they never challenged, that were his birthright, while others were nonnegotiable. That was my impression. Kevin apparently felt differently.

I picked up the jar of marbles from Kevin's desk and let the weight sink into my hands. There were all different kinds inside, perfect little glass globes in a swirl of colors. I liked the ones that were transparent, that you could see through to the center, a whirl of blues and pinks curlicued like pigs' tails. I scooped up a handful and let them clink together, the clean sound of glass tapping glass. I put all but two back in the jar, holding one in each hand. I rolled them on my face, up and down the length of my cheeks. The marbles were cold and smooth, little orbs of energy that felt like static inside me, buzzing in my brain and my bones. I wanted to swallow them.

A WEEK OR two later, Kevin was back home. My mom bought him some retired demo rackets and convinced my dad to let him keep playing as long as he got his grades up, and, anyway, it was made clear by his high school counselor and our other coach that Kevin's best chance at getting into a decent college was earning a spot on the tennis team. So when, soon after, he was accepted to UC–Davis as a men's singles player, we were all happy and relieved, even though he wasn't offered a scholarship. He was lucky to get in, lucky to be accepted on the Division I team. He wouldn't have gotten in on his grades alone. Entering freshmen had a 4.0 average GPA.

Tennis got him into college, but not much farther. Not long after he started college, he reported that he wasn't happy because the coach had made him a redshirt, practicing with the team but not competing, because there were upperclassmen who were better than him. Eventually, he quit so he could try his hand at turning pro. Then in his sophomore year, he quit tennis for good.

After that, Kevin struggled to find purpose. He got a part-time job ticketing illegally parked cars for the campus police to earn money to take Minjoo out on dates. His peers heckled him for doing this work, but he admired the camaraderie among the uniformed men at the police station. On one of his visits home, Kevin told me, his voice shiny with appreciation, that they were nice to him and had encouraged him to join the force.

During this in-between time, after Kevin quit tennis, before he married Minjoo and enrolled in the police academy, the world was open. He should have been able to do anything. He would soon have a college degree from a good school, the promise of a big future ahead of him. Why couldn't he see it? Why couldn't we see what was happening to him and show him what he couldn't see?

Like most kids in college living away from home, Kevin moved often, apartments and roommates frequently shuffling. At one point, when he needed a new roommate quick, Minjoo lined up her friend Eugene from high school, another young Korean American man, to share the two-bedroom apartment that Kevin had found. Kevin and Eugene met when they signed the lease. It was a convenient arrangement, one that both no doubt believed would blossom into friendship.

Right from the beginning, they didn't get along.

I never knew what started it. Maybe it was competitive jealousy on the part of my brother because of Eugene's friendship with Minjoo. Minjoo had never dated Eugene, but she had a longer history with him than with Kevin. The few times I'd visited, Eugene had been friendly and kind. He was a social, easygoing guy, the opposite of my paranoid and intense and competitive brother. Kevin insulted Eugene behind his back and even to his face, calling him a girl and too soft, physically and emotionally, though to me he just looked like a handsome, well-adjusted college kid—polite and talkative, with floppy hair and a face like someone who'd say the right thing when you were down. Eugene recoiled in Kevin's presence, responding not at all to his slights. What they had in common was they were both self-conscious. The difference was Eugene turned it into kindness while my brother had become mean trying to hide it. The first time we met, Eugene remarked to Kevin, "I can't believe this is your sister! She's cute!" Kevin never liked when his male friends made comments like that. I never knew whether it was protectiveness or possessiveness. When Kevin would put me down in front of Eugene—I was spoiled, greedy, stupid, or simply, pronounced with disgust, a *woman*—Eugene was quick to defend me and call my brother a misogynist. I was still a teenager and I'd rarely heard the word used and, before that, never once to protect me.

AROUND THIS TIME, I learned that my dad had given Kevin a gun. He'd never given me a gun, because I was a girl. I wasn't even allowed to skip rocks or learn chess or tae kwon do. Kevin was proud of the gun, especially because it was a gift from our dad. They'd bonded over it while our dad taught him how to shoot and clean and care for it. At the apartment that Kevin shared with Eugene, Kevin would invite a friend over, and they'd hang out in the living room with their guns spread out on the coffee table. They'd sit there for hours—cleaning the guns, talking about the guns, comparing the guns—before placing them into a duffle bag and heading to the gun range.

I was there once, when the guns were out and Eugene came home. He flinched and kept his eyes lowered, mouth tight as he headed straight to his bedroom. I felt that I should apologize, but it was impossible with my brother in the room. What would I say anyway? Sorry about my crazy brother? He's had a rough time? I think he has PTSD, chronic pain, mental illness, unresolved anger stemming from injustices enacted against him, and other ailments that are not visible? If you feel unsafe, maybe you should find a new place to live? I couldn't say anything. It felt like someone had chopped off my legs and then told me to put my shoes on.

I wasn't there the day things really changed between Kevin and Eugene. Kevin told me the story later. He and his friend were hanging out in the living room with their guns again when Eugene came home and, for the first time, made the mistake of mocking them. He didn't know that you couldn't mock my brother. What happened was this: Kevin chased Eugene around the apartment with a loaded gun until he barricaded himself in his own bedroom. Eugene moved out that same week. He pleaded with Minjoo to break up with Kevin.

"I scared the shit out of him," Kevin said. "He's such a woman."

"Why did you do that?" I said.

"Eugene was making fun of me. He was like, *Yeah, you're so awesome*," Kevin said. "So I shouted, *What'd you say? What'd you say?* I put the cartridge in and pointed the gun at him and I chased him into his room."

Kevin's eyes grew wide and he squeezed his lips together, cheeks puffed out, as he tried to hold in his laughter. In that moment, I didn't recognize him—he looked like no one I knew.

"He ran like a girl! He couldn't even get the door closed. I had my shoulder wedged in and got my gun in there. I was pointing it and waving it in his room. You should have seen him, ducking all over the place, trying to close the door on me. He was on the floor. All of a sudden, he had nothing to say. He wasn't laughing anymore, just kept apologizing. He was actually screaming, begging me not to shoot him. I've never heard someone say they're sorry so many times. I've never seen someone so scared. I bet he shit his pants!"

Kevin laughed, his open mouth a little pink cave. He held his stomach with his hands, eyes squeezed shut, lines creasing his face. He was only twenty years old but he looked like an old man.

"What a fucking pussy. He's such a woman."

SEVEN YEARS LATER, Kevin finally got a full-time position at the police department. Proud of himself, he became very chatty. Whenever I'd see him, he'd keep talking about the police station, his squad car, his department-issued Beretta, his Kevlar vest, the arrests he'd made and how terrified the suspects had been—all kinds of things that I knew nothing about. What made me most uncomfortable was when Kevin talked about how he didn't know whether he could kill someone if it came down to it. This came up often.

"I don't know if I can pull the trigger," he said. "I don't think I can just kill someone, even if I have to, even though I know that if I don't, I'll be killed instead. If I hesitate, I'm dead. I have to shoot first, but I don't know if I can. I won't know if I have what it takes until it happens. Maybe I won't be able to do it and I'll be dead."

Despite teasing from his coworkers, Kevin began wearing a bulletproof vest anytime he was on duty. His vest was higher quality, thicker and heavier, than the department-issued vest—he'd paid extra for it. But it was worth it, he said, a matter of life and death, and he wore it whenever he clocked in, even though vests were recommended only in high-risk situations because they were heavy and hot and restrictive.

His first assignment included a patrol of the 101 near the peninsula, between Palo Alto and San Francisco, where the highway loops and curves in sharp angles alongside a mountain. Where the pavement ends, a cliff drops to the ocean. Above the road, up high on a peak, sits a little stone house, hutlike, with no edges, curved like a mushroom. It's straight out of a fairy tale with gnomes and forests and lost children and wolves and witches in gingerbread houses. But the little stone house isn't a fairy tale. The house lives in the real world, a world in which a house may be carved from a rock the color of a terracotta pot and a family may actually live inside—the chimney, the driveway, the little garden and mailbox are all proof. The stone house sits far above the highway at the cliff's edge, and the view from up there must be like loneliness, the earth going on forever, all ocean and sky and distant mountains.

When Kevin and I were kids, we visited our aunt in Palo Alto once a year. My dad's two brothers also lived in the South Bay, in San Jose. We always gathered at my aunt's, since she had a big house in a nice neighborhood with a pool and a deck to grill bulgogi and kalbi. Our parents often took the scenic route along the ocean, though the drive was longer. Kevin and I preferred the detour, partly because there was less traffic and thus minimal stress radiating from the front seat, and also because we loved catching sight of the stone house on the mountain. The anticipation set in as soon as we could see the ocean. We knew how close we were to the house by the place markers we'd committed to memory: the curves on the road, the stubby trees, and the big, jagged rock formations that flecked the landscape. Sometimes I even claimed to know exactly where we were by the particular shape of the mountain that passed alongside us, by the distance between us and the rising waves of the ocean. *See how that edge is all crusty and porous and resembles the top of a rose-cut diamond*, I would say, trying to sound like a geologist and a fine jeweler. Then I'd say something nonsensical about the ocean and the moon and tidal force that I'd once heard on a National Geographic special. I always managed to trick Kevin into thinking I was smarter, but I had no idea what I was talking about. *How do you know things like that*, he'd say before going quiet.

Right before the final curve below the stone house, I sometimes turned to look at Kevin, who was always looking up, lips parted.

"Who do you think lives there?" he said once. "Do you think it's a family? Or someone who lives alone?"

"I don't know," I said.

"I think it's an old person. A grandpa, all by himself."

KEVIN WAS PATROLLING the 101 alone at night when he got a call that a deer had been hit. He drove a short distance up the highway to the location. When he arrived, the driver was gone. The deer was lying by the side of the road, still alive. Kevin stood over the deer, its breath slow and heavy, uneven. Blood pooled around the torso, Kevin said, where its stomach had been torn open. He touched the deer with the toe of his boot, nudging it softly. The deer didn't respond. He knelt beside it, running his fingers along the length of its neck.

"Like how I pet Odie," he told me, referring to his dog, "when he's falling asleep."

The deer's eyes were open, wide-set and blinking slowly. Kevin got on the radio to ask what he should do. The responder told him that if the deer was dying, he should shoot it to end its suffering and animal control would come pick it up.

"I didn't want to shoot him," Kevin said, "but I had to. He was dying. They said it was better to put him out of his misery."

Kevin put his palm on the deer's chest, his hand rising and falling with its breath. He could feel the life drain from the animal's body, its heart beating slower with each moment. He stood up, aimed his handgun at the deer's head, and pulled the trigger. The body bounced and the shot reverberated, sounding across the open landscape like a bomb had gone off in the sky. Blood pooled around its head.

"I felt so bad," Kevin said. "He couldn't stop me. He couldn't do anything. He couldn't even defend himself."

AFTER HE'D BEEN with the police department for a year or so, Kevin asked me to join him on a ride-along. If you want a day pass at a gym, you're required to sign multiple forms and waivers with several pages of small print, but for some reason, at the police department, any civilian can request or be invited on a ride-along without signing a single thing.

Kevin was proud of his job and wanted to show me what his typical day was like. I never let on that I wasn't proud, that I'd learned never to mention to anyone what he did for a living, which after some time meant never mentioning him at all, because one thing Americans can always be counted on to ask about someone they know little about is their line of work. The overwhelming response before I learned this lesson was shock and disgust, like it was scripted into their DNA. My social world didn't include the type of people who had police officers in their families or social networks.

In his first years, Kevin worked the night shift. It was already dark when we arrived at the station in San Jose, but the building glowed, the fluorescent lights streaming yellow. We passed the boss on our way in, the captain of Kevin's division, a middle-aged Chinese American man who was exceedingly friendly and polite, just like all of his coworkers. Kevin introduced me to everyone in the office, all the uniformed men smiling and warm and respectful, ribbing each other and even me when I tried to make a joke. *You sound just like Kevin! So sarcastic! Jesus, you're like twins!* The station bustled with energy and good manners, everyone either heading in for a shift or heading out to join families waiting at home.

"This is my sister!" Kevin said to anyone we passed. "She just started law school!"

"Fancy!" they said.

I smiled, nodding.

"You won't arrest me, will you? If you pull me over and I'm hopped up on cocaine. What if I rob a bank? Remember my face!" I said, repeating some version of the bad joke as we continued down the hall.

In the patrol car, I sat in front in the passenger seat. The backseat—the cage—was empty and dark and gloomy, so exceptionally spare, I could hardly look, couldn't help thinking of the inhumanity and the shame stewing in there. As we left the parking lot, Kevin showed off his new driving skills, flooring the gas with his right foot and hitting the brake pedal with his left.

"It takes a lot of practice, but if you can master it, it's more efficient. You don't lose time moving your foot from the right to the left," Kevin said. "You might need that split second in an emergency. Could be life or death. But if you can't get used to it, it's just dangerous."

My head pressed back as we sped up dramatically, bounced forward when Kevin slammed on the brakes. It wasn't a relaxing way to drive, but nothing about my brother was relaxing.

We drove like that down every city block, Kevin flooring it all the way up to each stop sign where we came to an abrupt halt. I was thrown forward and back as Kevin kept talking, explaining his daily routine. He always arrived at work early so he'd have time to stop somewhere secluded to prep the equipment in his cruiser.

We pulled into the parking lot of an abandoned warehouse. He turned off the engine and flipped on the switch of the overhead light. Under the yellow glow, dust particles floated between us. He looked up and pointed at the ceiling where there was a shotgun attached, secured with a metal contraption that had been bolted in place. I didn't know how I hadn't noticed it before. He explained that the firearm was from his personal collection and hadn't been issued by the police department.

"Most cops don't carry shotguns," Kevin said. "People use them for hunting, but I like to have it for extra protection."

"What do you mean?" I said, shrinking, as I peered at the long barrel of the shotgun attached to the ceiling.

"You only get one shot, but if you want a man dead, if you shoot him with this, he's not coming back up. It's extra protection," Kevin repeated.

I thought of all the action movies we'd watched where Clint Eastwood or Steven Seagal singlehandedly shot and killed swarms of men with a shotgun.

"The cops at work think I'm crazy," he said. "They're like, What do you need a shotgun for? They think I'm paranoid, but I don't care. I'll be alive and I'll be the one laughing. Nobody can shoot me if I shoot with this first."

Kevin removed the gun from the ceiling where it was fixed in place, jerry-rigged with clamps and bolts. There was a moment where the barrel was pointed at me and I instinctively flinched, hands up to protect my face.

"Good," Kevin said, nodding his head. "Always make sure you're out of the line of fire."

I looked at him with disbelief. He was the one who'd put me in it.

He turned off the headlights and got out of the car. He leaned over, head cocked sideways, grinning through the driver's side window. He held the gun casually in both hands.

"I want to show you something," he said.

I got out and joined him, zipping up my sweatshirt. I was wearing one of those black hoodies that seemed to get Black kids killed, but were ubiquitous among privileged, mostly white kids in San Francisco at the time. Kevin took off his jacket and the top of his uniform. Underneath, he was wearing a black T-shirt and his bulletproof vest.

Kevin flipped a switch on the shotgun. A light came on, shining a bright, straight line from the top of the barrel. The gun glowed like a magic weapon sent from the future. In the dark, the light extended longer than a sword, and I remembered how when we were small, we'd pretended that our flashlights were light sabers that could touch the stars in the night sky.

"I had this light installed," he explained. "It's two thousand lumens. Wasn't cheap," he said, laughing. "But I need to see what I'm shooting at."

He walked into the center of the empty lot, nothing but pavement and gravel and the faded outlines of parking spots. Then he began. With swift, fluid movements, he pointed the shotgun into the dark recesses of the parking lot, pivoting with precision and intention, as if he'd performed the ritual a hundred times before. Each time he aimed the gun, Kevin nodded, confirming that the thing the light revealed was exactly what was meant to be: the rust-colored stain on the dumpster, the peeling paint on the sharp edge of a building, beyond the chain-link fence a field sprouting with dandelions. The white light shifted and shifted again, shining everywhere, glowing up every piece of garbage, every weed, every mound of dirt, like it was the star of a show. Kevin covered the whole damn parking lot, shining the light on each spot for exactly two beats and with an approving nod. He swept to the next—hands still, body in motion—gliding swanlike, in perfect rhythm, quick and controlled and purposeful. He hunched over, holding the gun close, swiveled around and around again, boots crunching into the gravel and kicking up little clouds of dirt.

I thought of when we used to train all day on the tennis courts, the sun beating down on us, browning and freckling our skin. I'd break for water and watch Kevin practice drill after drill, his focus equal in intensity from the beginning to the end of a session as he glided from side to side and up and down the court on the balls of his feet, his whole body moving in one fluid motion, beautiful and precise and graceful, like a dancer.

WITHIN A YEAR on the force, Kevin was full of confidence, all uncertainty behind him.

"I'm ready," he said, mouth tight. "I know I can do it. I'm ready to kill someone. Just put me there and I'll do it."

I could almost see him inflate, chest expanding, head rising, like a balloon.

I don't know how Kevin got there—from the fear of not knowing whether he could shoot someone, to the overwhelming need to shoot someone, as if anything short of that was a disappointment. I tried to tell myself that he just wanted to be rid of his fear, like we all do, though we all have different ways of coping. Some people work too much or exercise too much or use people to get a leg up. Some people give up. Kevin chose—what exactly? He wouldn't be a victim. He'd have the power. He'd make others fear him. He decided to stop being afraid as if you can just flip a switch, the same way I imagine young men summon courage when charging into battle—fearful, but willing oneself into fearlessness, a kind of heartbreaking bravado. I don't know if Kevin knew what he was fighting for exactly, but what I saw was someone fighting to be seen as a man.

17

PARADISE COVE

Summer 2001

THE SUMMER BEFORE, we all got together in Bodega Bay. It was the last time I saw Kevin before San Francisco, when we met at our mom's so he could haul our stuff to the Goodwill, and the last time we came together as a family before the very final time—the summer when everything changed.

The beach house in Bodega Bay was supposed to be our summer escape, but it was just another place for us to be uncomfortable together. My dad drove us in his coral BMW, so glossy it was almost invisible, a mirror reflecting the shapes and colors of the world as they passed over it. Every three months, my dad waxed the car with his shirt off, white stomach puffed out. He'd always start with the hood, hands moving in little circles, pressing down on the surface with soft round pads, cloudy swirls and spirals gradually covering the entire coral finish. In the twenty-odd years that my dad owned the car, it never once broke down, so attentive was he to the lifespan of parts, wires, and tubing. It was the first expensive car he'd ever owned or purchased, brand new from the dealer, unlike our hand-me-down Vanagon or the little brown Datsun hatchback he brought home after bartering with a stranger who'd posted a FOR SALE sign in the rear window. The car was one of those markers of success, and my dad's feeling of accomplishment extended to us all—my mom, Kevin, and me—a symbol of where we stood, our legitimacy.

The beach house was another achievement, acquired after two luxury cars and one regular one, a new house in the hills, and the country club. I was embarrassed about it and didn't mention it to people who didn't already know.

I LEARNED EARLY on that, though we owned the beach house, it wasn't ours to enjoy. It was a service for other people so long as they paid for it, much like the restaurant. The purpose was pure economics, to generate income as a rental and serve as my parents' retirement home—since it was both smaller and the location more remote than our house in Napa, its value was much lower—and, of course, my parents loved to brag about it. Depending on the context, the way in which they were winning had a different spin. Compared against Korean friends at Korean churches across America, they were on top—the top Koreans from Korea, the top family, the top parents with the top Korean American children—as if our superiority was in our blood. For my mom's two doctor brothers and Korean friends who were American doctors, the response was sputtering frustration—they'd worked tirelessly to get where they were and here was my dad taking a "shortcut" to get the same thing. Compared to them, my parents were equals, having shoved their way in. For Korean friends back home in Korea, some still living in banjihas, my parents were gods. For our white neighbors and all the families in our small town who looked down on us: my parents were giving them the double middle finger.

When Kevin and I still lived at home, where the space between the four of us bristled with stifling silence or noise and terror, we piled into the car with our overnight bags and a big red cooler packed with kimbap and kimchi, and we unknowingly crammed that prickly space in with us, trapping it against each other for hours all the way to Bodega Bay, where it settled into the dark corners of the house, simmered and smoked like lifting fog. I sometimes thought I could see it in the mornings on the beach, drifting between and above us, receding into the ocean only to arrive again, an endless loop.

My dad always drove. My mom sat in front, while Kevin and I piled in the back. We fought over the dividing line that separated his half of the back seat from mine. After we spent some time jabbing our elbows at each other, we propped up our travel set of Connect 4 on the center console and played for a while. Kevin couldn't stand to lose, and even when he won he was angry, calling me stupid. Our mom would tell us to quiet down. "Don't talk back to your brother," she said, pointing her finger at me.

The farther we got from Napa and the closer we got to Bodega Bay, the cooler and thicker and cleaner the air became. I could tell when we'd crossed the border from country land to beach land—the trees near the road turned to brush, the earth tumbled and flattened into dirt patched with white sand, and the air grew dense with moisture and salt. We could see the ocean from the car, the sun shimmering in rolls and bobs and long waves that folded within themselves, a mirror reflecting the world into light and unfurling like a scroll from the horizon to the water's edge, where foam melts into sand. Kevin and I asked for taffy when we passed the market, but our parents rarely bought it for us. When they did allow it, we were given one small bag to share between us, which of course we fought over, bickering about who got dibs on which flavors. I usually ended up with most of the cinnamon taffies even though they were Kevin's favorite too. He caved in like that, always giving up what he wanted, because our parents had taught us that men should give up things and women should be given things. I remembered that later, the unfairness to us both, how one of us was granted power and authority but forced to sacrifice personal desires, while the other was made powerless but granted the right to material things.

On our way through town, we'd drive past downtown, a one-way street with a little market, a post office, and an antique store with an old wagon wheel set on a lawn of woodchips. Our house was in a gated community on the beach. One side of the neighborhood abutted the water, and the other a rolling eighteen-hole golf course. Each visit, we had brunch at the clubhouse, as if it was a chore, sitting uncomfortably in the wood-paneled dining hall with exposed beams, barely looking at each other, maintaining the most stilted conversations as the other diners stared at us, the only people in the room who weren't white. I used to get upset about it and sit there holding my anger inside, though my face inevitably turned red, frustrated that our parents kept putting us in the same position, the Asian family getting stared down by a bunch of white people, and that we were supposed to pretend that everything was normal. My parents and brother, in their discomfort at trying to maintain the guise of fitting in, would shift their attention to me and tell me that I was acting spoiled.

One summer when I was sixteen, we stopped in for Sunday brunch. Our waitress was a woman in her twenties with frizzy red hair and cakey foundation. I thought to myself that she was a townie, though I myself was a townie in Napa, where we lived year-round. She was new or I'd never noticed her before. Her nametag said CELESTE.

"Can I take your order? Would you like to start with drinks or appetizers?"

Celeste's skin was nearly translucent and covered in ginger-colored freckles. It's probably why her foundation was the wrong shade and why she wore too much of it. She didn't smile at us, though she glanced around the dining hall repeatedly, and I noticed that she was smiling at everyone else. She nodded agreeably at a family sitting at an adjacent table and winked at a pigtailed girl. A pair of waitstaff passed by, prompting her to flash a perky, toothy grin. There was a small gap between her two front teeth. When she looked at me, or Kevin, or my parents, her face turned hard and she looked annoyed.

"Chink," I blurted.

Celeste stared at me. "What?" she said. There was a crease between her eyebrows.

"You heard me. I called you a Chink."

"*Jane*," my dad said, his voice low.

"Shut up," Kevin said as he glared at me.

"What happened?" my mom said, looking up from her menu, her eyes roving around the table. Since everyone else was looking at me, she settled on my face, which I imagine was radiating with smug indignation.

"What did you do?" she said, her eyes boring into mine, her tone sharp.

A white cloth napkin was set on the empty plate in front of me, folded into a floppy crown. I picked up the napkin and shook it, releasing the inscrutable folds with an elaborate gesture—a flick of the wrist, all flourish—and I laid it down in my lap, smoothing out the creases.

"Origami," I said.

I looked at Celeste, who was still staring at me. There was a little dot of spit right in the groove above her upper lip. Her mouth moved, forming words she didn't speak aloud.

"Um, okay," Celeste said, slowly. "I'll give you a few more minutes." She turned around and walked away. I could hear her starched white shirt brushing against her black waist apron.

I could tell when someone didn't like me because of my race, which might not seem that important, but it's everything, almost.

The difference between knowing and not knowing when something is unjust is almost everything.

BACK AT THE house, my dad would often sit on the deck in the backyard, smoking American Spirits and reading the latest best-selling thriller. My dad valued privacy more than most things. The backyard deck was his little oasis, a quiet place to be alone. When he retreated to the hammock, my mom walked my brother and me down to the beach. Kevin and I buried her in the sand, chased each other into the ice-cold water, and climbed onto giant porous rocks that jutted out of the ocean, where we ducked and shielded our faces when the waves came crashing down and splashed all over us. We waded back to the shore and lay down on the pebbly sand, sunbathed until we got headaches.

Once during this summer ritual, my mom told me that she wished that Kevin had gotten some of my luck. I asked her what she meant.

"It's okay that he's not handsome," she said. "He's not a girl, so it's okay. It's important for girls to be pretty. I just wish he was smart. One day he'll be a man—he should be the one who gets to be smart, not you. I wish he was talented. Everything is so easy for you, but he tries so hard and he's never the best."

I didn't think it was true. That one of us was better. I thought that we were the same, and being good at something was a matter of what you believed about yourself, and what people thought of you was a matter of what you could make them believe. In high school I learned that everything was about maintaining a façade. Faking confidence, making people think that you're special, making it look easy. Kevin couldn't do that. It was as if he had a disability, and his disability was not knowing how to lie. Back then, that was the only difference between us.

⁂

IN THE SUMMER of 2001, we all had the sense that this was our last time at the beach house. It was difficult for all of us to get there, and with each of us coming from different places, living our separate lives, aligning our schedules to get together even for a weekend wasn't easy. A rocky inlet of the Pacific on the coast of Northern California between Sonoma and Marin, Bodega Bay was far enough away to be inconvenient for all of us. My parents, in Napa, were closest, but they were sixty and got grumpy when they had to travel by car for more than an hour. They were thinking about selling the beach house. They'd been renting it out more frequently, favoring long-term renters, and for this one week the house was between leases. Before putting it up for rent, my mom had asked me to come up with headlines for the listing.

"The manager of the club wants me to give him three possible titles and they'll pick the one they like best," she said. "Can you do it for me? You were an English major."

After some thought, I wrote her a list.

Already Gone, the title of an Eagles song that Kevin liked. *Paradise Lost*, the first book assigned to me in college, which I managed to read about halfway through. *Paradise Cove*, because the first two choices were clearly too depressing, though they represented the spirit of our family, and *Paradise Lost* made me think of Paradise Cove, a beach in Malibu where Kevin and I had surfed for the first time while visiting cousins in Los Angeles. Afterward, we'd hung out on wooden lounge chairs underneath palm trees and thatched umbrellas. We'd sipped virgin drinks served in hollowed-out pineapples and whole coconuts, imagining that we were in Hawaii.

They went with *Paradise Cove*. No surprise. What choice did they have? Given multiple realities, we fall on delusion more often than not.

Minjoo had been joining us on our summer trips to Bodega Bay ever since she and Kevin began dating in college, but this was the first time she'd been here as his wife. I'd hoped that she would feel more secure of her place in his life and wouldn't feel the need to attack me as she usually did, but I was wrong. Through the course of a single dinner Minjoo asked if I'd gained weight, declared that I should stop running because my legs looked too muscular, and wondered aloud why my face and chest were so flat. When I felt defensive in those days, my snobbish instincts kicked in. I took a long look at her permed and orange-tinged hair, her theatrical makeup, and her too-tight clothes, and thought *this person is beneath me.* She was even more bewildered about the signifiers of American belonging than my family.

She caught me staring at the little white Louis Vuitton bag she had draped over the back of her chair. She had a collection of Louis Vuitton bags in different shapes and colors. I'd seen maybe a dozen over the years.

"Why don't *you* have one?" Minjoo asked. "Can't get someone to buy one for you?"

Kevin nudged Minjoo with his elbow. I wondered if this woman-on-woman bullying was about being Korean, or about being a woman, or both. Sometimes when I was talking, she'd whisper to Kevin, loud enough for me to hear: "Tell your sister to shut up."

I had learned, at times catastrophically, that of anyone in the room—with my family or in any other room in every other context I'd so far encountered—I was the person who wasn't allowed to speak. If I dared defend myself or anyone else, have any sort of opinion, I'd be stripped of not only the idea of agency that I made the mistake of thinking I had, but also the backhanded approval that I could have had, if only I'd known my place.

This is why I tended to keep quiet in situations with Kevin and Minjoo. All my thoughts were unkind. It was the same for them, only they said everything out loud. The same animal instinct that made Minjoo want to humiliate me is what made me describe her in my mind in ugly detail. Somehow my presence filled her with fear, which made me unforgiving.

I didn't share my dating life with either Kevin or Minjoo, or my parents, for that matter. Since no one knew if I was dating and whether I had prospects, there was no proof of my ability to attract a mate. Minjoo interpreted my silence on this subject as evidence of my failure as a woman, and she was fond of saying that I must not be able to find someone who would date me, that it was either because I wasn't pretty enough or because I was a high-maintenance pain in the ass. I've never met a Korean woman who wasn't accused of being both high-maintenance and submissive—polar opposites, yet attributed to the same woman, sometimes even in the same sentence.

Minjoo bragged about how her younger sister was marrying a doctor. "Why don't *you* get one?" she said. A doctor husband, she meant.

But Minjoo didn't marry a doctor. She'd thought that she was marrying a lawyer, but Kevin, who'd briefly considered law school, decided to join the police force instead.

You'd think that this would have been a deal-breaker, or when Kevin decided he didn't want children, but neither made her change her mind. Minjoo idolized him. Maybe that's why she was unkind to me—because she believed the things he said about me—and it wasn't just that I was his sister. Despite everything, it made me happy to see her doting on Kevin, to see him enjoy the attention, because those were the only moments that I saw him smile.

"My handsome husband," she announced. "My friends think I'm lucky that I got a good husband," she said. "They can't believe I get to live in a nice house and I don't even have to work. Everyone says it's because he's a good provider."

Minjoo had wanted to start a business in interior design, but Kevin thought it was too risky. He didn't want to invest the money in something she had no background in, without any guarantee that it would succeed.

"How do we even know if you're good at it?" he said. "Do you know what you're doing?" He pointed out that he couldn't recall anyone ever complimenting the way their house was decorated other than Minjoo's own mother. Then he nailed it in. "Whose houses would you make over? Koreans? I never met a Korean who hired an interior designer. You weren't born in America like I was, so Americans wouldn't hire you."

For Kevin, it wasn't an unusual or even very harsh thing to say. It was just Kevin being Kevin. We were all used to his tone, his way of controlling people. I didn't know anything about interior design, but he had a point: it seemed like if that was your thing, wouldn't there be a noticeable concept or style in the way your house was decorated? Their home looked like any other house belonging to a young couple starting out—a mix of old and new basic mismatched pieces, hand-me-downs blending with inconspicuous mall retailers and a bit of IKEA. I didn't exactly think that Minjoo was missing her calling, but I didn't like the way Kevin held her back.

Minjoo ran the household. She did all the shopping, cooked all the meals, washed and ironed Kevin's clothes, kept the house. Kevin was happy to be the recipient of Minjoo's care, the center of her life, the top boy, to hear the words "For the best husband!" as a big bowl of soondubu stew was plopped before him on the dinner table.

On this last trip to the beach house, my dad stayed inside and was more talkative than usual. He spent a lot of time lying down on the couch, resting, even in the morning. Earlier that summer, his younger brother, Jinu, had suffered a heart attack, the first of many before poor health would eventually kill him, but my dad was already acting like Jinu was dead. He stared at the ceiling, telling story after story—Jinu as a child in Seoul, taunted by other kids because his skin was so white and his hair was red.

"His hair turned dark when he got older, but he could never get along with anyone. He always thought people were making fun of him. The other kids thought he must be a war child, half-American, but he was one hundred percent Korean, like us!"

Kevin and Minjoo were sitting directly across from my dad, who kept craning his neck and propping himself up so he could see me. I was slightly out of view, sitting on a pillow on the floor.

"Jane, do you remember when Jinu tried to teach you how to ride a bike, he got on his bike and fell off? We couldn't stop laughing!"

My dad looked funny lying down on the couch, less like himself.

"Huh," he sighed. "Jinu always knew you were the smart one, Jane," he said, gazing at the ceiling. "He knew from the start. That's why he was nicer to Kevin."

I looked at Kevin. I hoped he hadn't heard that, but obviously he had. He stared deeply into his teacup. Minjoo set hers down on the table, too hard. My mom walked in carrying a tray with a fresh pot of boricha and placed it on the coffee table. We were all still processing what my dad had just said, dealing with it in different ways. Kevin closed his eyes and kept them shut. Minjoo picked up her cup, only to put it down again, three more times. I tried to gauge what might come next, unsure what move was best: disappear, make a joke, or change the subject.

My mom, who had missed it all, thought nothing of our silence. She made her way back to the kitchen, but stopped short just before reaching the door. She gasped, a sound so loud and abrupt that I thought she must have encountered an intruder, right there, in the hallway of our house. For a moment, I felt relief when I remembered that Kevin always carried a gun.

"OHMANA!" she screamed.

We jumped up, all at once, to see what the commotion was about. My mom was hunched over, inspecting the bottom corner of an antique mirror hanging near the entryway. Kevin and I rushed to her side to see what was wrong.

"There's a crack!" she said. "Oh no oh no oh no oh no! What do I do?"

Kevin took a step back. His hands were up as if he was about to catch something.

"Do you see this?" my mom said. "The mirror. It's cracked." She pointed at the corner of the mirror, where a series of lines of varying length bloomed from the original injury. I leaned in close, but my mom whipped around and pointed a finger at me.

"Did you do it?" she asked.

"Of course not," I said. "When would I have done that?"

She pointed at Kevin.

"Did you do it?" she asked.

Kevin shook his head. His eyebrows were raised, lips parted.

"It was probably the renters," I said. "Remember the stain on the carpet?" When we first arrived, we'd found a big ruby-colored stain on the living room carpet, the previous renter's fuck you gift. My mom had spent the first hour trying to scrub it out, spraying it with diluted white vinegar.

"We can't stay here!" my mom shouted. "How many times do I have to say it? Broken glass is bad luck, especially mirrors! We have to leave. We can never come back. What is wrong with these people?"

My mom turned around and gazed at the damaged mirror. The longer she looked at it, the more it seemed to offend her. In her wounded expression I could see the worry and sorrow that were imprinted in my memory from before I could remember—my mother's constant fear and resentment at having no control over her money, her health, or her future. Only people who feel powerless believe so firmly in the power of broken mirrors.

I returned to the living room and fell into a chair, feeling tired and numb. Kevin put his hand on our mom's back while he talked in a low, soft voice. I could make out only a few words, the sounds blending into a gentle rhythm. Our mom breathed deeply, consciously, except when a squelched sob escaped. I could smell her sweating.

"Maybe you should lie down," Kevin said. He led her to the master bedroom, hand in her elbow.

I worried that she'd get excited again. I remembered the night before when we discovered that all the mattresses now had deep indentations, sunken in like cake molds with the outlines of bodies larger and heavier than our own. All night we'd slept as if we were lying in hammocks. My mom had barely commented. "I thought you bought extra firm," she said to my dad.

MY DAD FELL asleep on the couch, though it wasn't even noon yet. Minjoo put a blanket over him. With his eyes closed and the blanket tucked snug under his armpits, he looked young, not old enough to be anyone's dad. Kevin went out to the back deck and I followed him there.

The sunlight filtered through the mist, thick with dew so fresh and clean it could've been bottled up and sold in a spritzing can. Kevin leaned on the railing and looked out past the yard toward the cool green hills of the golf course and the mountains beyond. He'd outgrown the younger skinny version of himself and no longer wore glasses, laser surgery having corrected his vision just in time for the police academy.

Not tall, though not short, he made up for what he lacked in height by bulking up. Police training workouts always involved weights: running laps in a weighted vest, obstacle courses with weights strapped on, weightlifting at the department gym. Kevin had told me about the game he and his coworkers played during their lunch breaks at Taco Bell, seasoning their chicken burritos with generous spritzes of department-issued pepper spray. I imagined the fleshy lot of them howling and sweaty and doubling over in laughter and pain. In training, they'd each gotten sprayed in the face so they'd know what it's like. *I thought I was dying*, Kevin had said. *You're blind, you can't breathe, and you're throwing up, all at the same time.*

Now he wore a blue baseball cap, an embroidered shield on the front panel above the bill: SAN JOSE POLICE DEPARTMENT. I could see the bulge under his denim jacket on his right hip, where a gun was secured in a holster. He was never without one. I wouldn't have been surprised if another gun was strapped at his ankle under his jeans, and a butterfly knife in his pocket. *Ready for anything*, he always said. *You have to be ready.*

His back was rounded, shoulders tense, and I saw the muscles in his neck twitch. I could tell he was angry. I wished that he didn't have to carry so much pain, that there was somewhere else he could put it. His pain was part of me. If I could take some away and hide it deep inside myself, we might both find relief. I wanted to be in it together so we could be on the same side, but he had never understood that what was happening to him was happening to me, too, and I didn't know how to tell him.

I cleared my throat. Kevin turned around. I took a step forward, wanting to touch him, but I knew that I couldn't. I was about to say something meaningless to kill the silence, but he was glaring at me, and I could tell that anything I said would be met unkindly. So I waited, watching my brother as his mouth shrank.

Moments like this were familiar. Kevin sulking, angrily; me not knowing what he was mad about. It could be something I did or said, or something he claimed I did or said, or it could be about something or someone completely unrelated to me that somehow he'd found a way to circle back—I was often to blame when something bad happened. I was always watching him to gauge how I should act to avoid setting him off.

I had no doubt that he'd added our dad's comment about Jinu to the pile of grievances against me—an accumulation of all I'd done wrong, everything I represented, all I'd taken from him.

Kevin made a sound that was a cross between scoffing and snorting. His eyes narrowed in on mine, holding me in place.

"You think you're so— " he began.

"No, I don't," I said, cutting him off.

He turned away, laughing scornfully. "You think you're better than everyone," he said. "You always have."

"What are you talking about? Where is this coming from?"

"You think everything is yours."

"I didn't do anything," I said.

"You don't have to. All you have to do is be you."

It was like we were reading a script written with no imagination. I could feel his anger rising with each exchange. There I was thinking it was all nonsensical, but Kevin was acting as if he knew the whole plot, hidden motivations included. His anger didn't surprise me, but the possibility of what it could turn into made me feel afraid.

"Bitch," he said.

He was looking at me with such intensity, I took a step back.

"You get everything you want," he said.

We stood there like statues. All was quiet except the sound of our voices, as if the universe had stopped and we had been sucked into a twilight zone where there was no time and nothing existed but the two of us having an argument that had no beginning and no end.

"You're just a stupid woman. You don't know anything," he said. "God, life must be so much easier when nobody expects anything from you."

"Yeah, life is easier for women," I said. I didn't even know if I was being sarcastic or agreeable.

"Why does dad care about *you*? Why are *you* the one?" Kevin said. "The thing that's fucked up is you don't even care about him. The only person you care about is yourself."

"It's not my fault," I said. "I don't want to be his favorite. He's crazy. You're mom's favorite and I don't care because she's crazy too."

Kevin wasn't listening. He was locked in, summoning Chun's brother from the dokkaebi in the forest, so certain he could prove that Chun's brother was me.

"I don't get why everybody thinks you're so great. *I'm* the one who's a nice person. Is the world really so stupid that nobody can tell? You just trick people into liking you because you act all fake and you know what to say. I never say the right thing and somehow that means that I'm the asshole while you're the one everybody loves, but nobody knows the truth!"

"Why do you say shit like that?" I shouted. "People are always telling me what you say about me—it's so embarrassing. All you're doing is making yourself look bad."

He came at me like a deranged animal. His face was blank as a napkin, holding in its empty space both illegibility and extreme clarity. What I saw was Kevin pretending to be Steven Seagal, whose movies he'd watched obsessively when we were young. I should have known what was coming. I shouldn't have been afraid, because my fear was what he wanted. He wanted me to believe that he was about to beat the shit out of me or at least give me one swift punch in the gut, and the second he sensed my fear, the moment I flinched or stepped back, he won.

I tried to dodge him, but I wasn't quick enough and there was nowhere to escape. Kevin pushed me hard, his hands flat, thwacking my shoulders. His blank face flashed with menace. He pushed me again, palms out, smacking my shoulders firmly, hard enough for me to lose my balance. I put my hands out behind me and grabbed the railing so that I wouldn't fall. I didn't say anything at first, afraid that he'd become more agitated, but somehow the situation had already escalated, and I didn't know how to stop it.

"What is wrong with you?" I said.

"I did everything they wanted. I tried as hard as I could. I can't be the best at everything all at the same time. How do you do it?" he said like an accusation, like I had somehow through treachery escaped the rules of reality that applied to everyone else. "Nothing I do is ever enough. But whatever you do everybody thinks is so perfect. How do you get them to think that?"

All that pressure and all his effort never got him what he wanted, never got him approval. They expected him to be a perfect American success story and a perfect Korean son at the same time. His frustration about this impossible, even incomprehensible, expectation turned into blame—I was always there, my presence mocking him.

"Somehow you always get it right. You're the perfect one," he said. "But you're a liar and nobody knows it. You trick everyone into thinking you're smart and you're a nice person, but *I* know who you are."

Part of me believed him. It's why I had to deny it was true.

"You're insane," I said. My voice was firm, but I could feel my legs tremble. "Listen to yourself. This isn't about me. It's about you. It's not my fault your life didn't work out. It's not my fault people don't like you. You're blaming me for what's happened to you, but I didn't do it to you. Why don't you look at yourself."

Kevin pushed me so hard, it was like an open-fisted double punch on each shoulder. I fell back, feet kicking up in front of me, and I landed on my butt and slid down the seven wooden steps leading from the deck to the backyard. Instinctively, I reached up and tried to grab the railing, a mistake because the wood splintered into my palms and fingers. Later that night, I'd sit in the bathroom for an hour trying unsuccessfully to tweeze out all the little wooden needles lodged beneath layers of skin. I tumbled onto the lawn, arms and legs splayed out. Other than my hands and a few nasty bruises on my rear end that bloomed the next day, visible to no one but me, I wasn't really hurt. I could have gotten up, but I chose to stay down. I looked at my hands, which were bleeding. My butt was numb.

"What the *fuck*," I said to myself. I looked up at Kevin, who was standing at the top of the stairs. He didn't look sorry. He peered down at me, squinting, as if I was at the bottom of a deep pit that I'd gotten myself stuck in by my own stupidity. He looked angry, still, and unsatisfied.

"What the fuck is wrong with you?" I shouted.

It was like he didn't even hear me. He was still in that twilight zone, while I had come back to the universe. His eyes glazed over. He began walking down the stairs, nodding his head while his boots dropped slower and heavier with each step, his eyes holding me in place. When he reached the bottom, his feet swished through the grass. He knelt over me, and he was so close I could see that the fabric of his jeans was wearing thin at the knee. I wondered if I should buy him a new pair.

"Remember when I asked dad for a sleeping bag and he said no, but then a week later he bought you a new sleeping bag?" he asked. His fingers swept the grass near my foot.

"Are you serious?" I said. I sat up, trying to seem unafraid. I held my shoulders open, but inside everything was gathered close together.

"Why did dad get it for you? You didn't even want it. I was the one who wanted it. Did you ask for it just because I did? Or did he get it for you for no reason?"

"I don't know," I said. "I don't remember."

It was true that I didn't remember, though I did remember that Kevin had already been given a sleeping bag—he just wanted a new one and I didn't have one before that. But I could tell that these were all details that he didn't remember or weren't relevant to the argument he had been having with me in his head all of this time.

Kevin's denim jacket was open, the hem pulled back and held in place with the inside of his wrist. I could see the gun holstered at his hip. It almost felt like he was showing it to me. He was still kneeling, his other hand dangling at his side, lazily, knuckles grazing blades of grass.

18

THE VIDEOTAPE

May 2002

IT WAS ALL over the news by the time we heard what had happened. It could have been worse. In another few years, he would have been the hot topic on the internet, a meme on Facebook and Twitter, and in a few more he'd have been recorded for all time via hi-res video making the rounds, shot from multiple angles by civilians with smartphones and posted to social media accounts, shared and reshared, tweeted and retweeted, ad infinitum.

You could say Kevin was lucky. The social media platforms didn't exist yet. But the man, Kevin's victim, definitely wasn't lucky, compounded with the fact that there were witnesses—Kevin's partner and an undergraduate journalism student with a shitty camcorder, though the college student is the person who changed everything for us, because without him life might have gone on as usual.

I was in my bedroom when Samir called to me from the living room. His tone was urgent. I figured it was something about the dishes or the trash, the usual things roommates bicker about, and I was busy sorting and planning, getting ready to leave California in a couple of weeks.

Samir pointed at the television, but all I could see was a blurry home video. A newscaster was speaking in the background, innocuous-seeming dialogue that I didn't pay attention to at first, but by the time the words sunk in and I had processed what was being said, it felt like I'd dropped down into a cave, dark and empty except the light of the television. I peered at the screen, trying to match the fuzzy scene before me with the information being reported. My stomach plunged as if the bottom had dropped from my cave and sent me tumbling down into another cave. I covered my mouth with both hands to keep everything in. I wouldn't throw up. I was on a seven-year no-vomit streak.

The video was on a loop, one minute of footage that kept ending and restarting at the same place. The image, shot from a distance, was blotchy, smudged like chalk. A few seconds in, the camera lens zoomed from a parking lot across the street to a grainy close-up of three figures. There was no way to identify the three people in the video. I couldn't even distinguish their gender. It looked like someone had taken an eraser to their faces. Two were standing and appeared to be dressed similarly in dark clothing. One stood aside, motionless, looking on as the other swung down a stick repeatedly on the third person who lay dormant on the ground, covering their head and face with their arms, knees pulled up to the chest. The news anchors narrated the scene, which is how I learned that the stick was in fact a baton and the two men standing were uniformed police officers.

The screen flashed. The image of the blurry figures was replaced with another that was so clear, so undeniable, I stopped breathing.

"A new video has just come in," a news anchor said.

The video confirmed everything. The facts that had been reported: it was all true. The baton, the police officers, and the fact that one of them—his identity indisputable—was whaling on the man curled into a fetal position on the ground. I didn't even have to see the assailant's face. All I needed was a clear shot of his build, his cocked elbows. One look at his stiff posture, the way he held his spine straight as a steel rod even as he brought the baton down on the man's body yet again, and I knew.

"Police officer Kevin Kim," the reporter was saying. She had said it before while narrating the blurry video, but by now reality had set in—the truth was right in front of me—and there was nowhere left for me to fall.

The first time Kevin hit the man, he pulled the baton back with his right hand, a big looping forehand groundstroke, the kind of flourish we'd been trained against on the court, and struck him across the side. Kevin swung again, lashing the man now with two-handed strokes, bringing down the baton from over his head and from both sides, onto the man's back and his ribs and his arms, which were covering his face. Then Kevin started kicking him in the stomach.

The camera zoomed in on the man on the ground. There was no telling his race—there was so much blood—but his exposed arms and hands were brown, sun- and weather-beaten, and his clothing was torn and ratty, feet bare. His hands fell away to clutch his stomach, and for a moment I saw his face. Instead of features and distinctions and identity, all I could see was blood and flesh like an animal torn open.

The beating and kicking continued. For no good reason. The man posed no threat. He had no weapon. He couldn't even speak. I couldn't imagine anything anyone could have done to deserve what was happening. *Just cuff him*, I thought. His lacerated hands were as swollen and raw as his face, all blood, all flesh, all red and pink oozing. When I thought it couldn't get any worse, a gun appeared in the frame, pointed at the man's head. At first, that's all I could see, the bloody man on the ground and the gun. I stared at the hand on the trigger, the barrel, the muzzle. I wondered which gun it was. I'd seen Kevin's entire collection, but never would have been able to tell one firearm from another even if you'd held one to my head. The camera zoomed out, framing all three men, though the lens centered on Kevin. When he came into focus, his image was incredibly clear. On TV, he looked like a celebrity.

Kevin held the gun with both hands now, arms rigid, neck taut. His face was so keen it hurt to look at it. In his features, I recognized everything. All that we had done wrong, avoided, ignored, and all the contradictory ideals he'd been told to embody. His face was empty, a blank sheet you could fill in with your own assumptions. There was no rage there, no pain or suffering. Complete calm. As I watched him, there was a moment when I saw a flicker—his mouth tightening, his brow shrinking. I thought I could see the boy he used to be, innocent and full of shame that swirled inside him, that grew from self-loathing into spite and disgust at the world that rejected and taunted him, that told him he was no man, no better than a woman.

Was the evening news really going to broadcast a video of a police officer—my brother—shooting an unarmed man in the head? Kevin stood as still as a statue of a police officer pointing a gun. He could have been a memorial in front of a federal building. For the next twenty seconds, we waited. The reporters had gone silent. The video appeared to be on pause except for the fact of Kevin's partner shifting his weight as he looked on. Kevin was stone and the dormant man just as quiet, frozen in time, either unconscious or trying to disappear. The nausea I'd felt earlier, from shock and disgust, was replaced with fear and terror.

So much of my life had been spent wishing that time would pass faster, that a future different from my present life would arrive and I could skip everything in between. Watching Kevin on the news, all I wanted was the future to never come, to go back, rewind as far as we needed, to a time when a different choice never would have brought us to this moment.

Kevin raised the gun high with both hands like he was chopping wood and swung straight down by the grip, the butt socking onto the crown of the man's head. The sound was soft and loud at once, like thwacking a sack of flour. I couldn't tell if the man even felt it.

SAMIR'S VOICE BROUGHT me back.

"Jane," he said. He repeated my name two more times. He turned off the television.

I stared at him.

"Oh my god," he said.

My mind was reeling. Was there someone I should call? My brother? My mom or dad? A lawyer? Should I continue packing or cancel the whole plan? How many people had seen the news? What would happen now?

"What are you going to do?" Samir said.

"I don't know," I said.

Samir looked at me with pity. Normally, I disliked when someone felt sorry for me, but what I'd just seen on the news was so unexpected, so violent, and so directly connected to me, I didn't care about being pitied. I felt implicated. I thought for a moment maybe it was all a terrible joke. But cameramen weren't jumping out of the shadows, and Samir wasn't shouting "You've been punk'd!" I felt a wave of sorrow and shame and guilt wash over me, and as soon as it hit me, so did the reality of what had happened and what was to come. I knew then that I'd never be rid of this new feeling.

AFTER THAT, KEVIN was on TV every day. He became a household figure for almost two weeks. The reporters spoke in even, deep tones, consonants sharp, as they described the incident that was the highlight of the evening news.

"San Jose police officer Kevin Kim," a newscaster said, "caught on film near upscale shopping district Santana Row, in San Jose, by a Santa Clara University undergraduate student who witnessed the brutal beating. The unarmed victim has been identified as Eddie Yeun, a thirty-two-year-old homeless man. His condition is unknown at this time."

Even when I changed the channel, all I got was another report on my brother and what he had done. Every station described Kevin's history with the police department, followed by a message from police chief Mike Martinez. The statement was often displayed in quotes while a reporter read aloud: "Officer Kevin Kim has been placed on administrative leave while we investigate the circumstances surrounding the event that took place last Wednesday in the Forest-Pruneridge district of San Jose. The department is looking out for the best interests of the city. Administrative leave doesn't indicate any wrongdoing by Officer Kim. Officer Kim has worked in law enforcement for the San Jose Police Department for four years. He has had no disciplinary actions or any recommendations for counseling on record in his years in public service. His attendance, performance, and conduct have been exemplary. Kim is a career street cop who has protected and served the community. He's a member of one of the best law enforcement agencies in California."

One station did a story on the victim, though they didn't have much to go on. For privacy reasons, his social worker wouldn't speak to the news, and the shelter that he frequented claimed to know nothing about his personal life.

"Eddie never caused any trouble," said a man in a black apron outside a café. "We all knew him by name. At first, we didn't even know he was homeless. We gave him free coffee whenever he stopped by, and at the end of the night we left out a bag of pastries and sandwiches. There's nothing that Eddie could have done to deserve getting beaten like that."

A reporter broadcast live at the intersection of Bascom and San Carlos, where Eddie Yeun had often been seen standing outside the Goodwill or the Dollar Store. A picture of Eddie retrieved from the shelter flashed on-screen beside Kevin's portrait from the police academy. They were the same age, in their early thirties, but they could have been mistaken as members of different generations. The photo of Eddie was a polaroid, but I could still tell that his weathered skin made him look older than he was. He wasn't even looking at the camera, and the flash made him appear washed-out and crazed, his eyes little globes of light. His greasy hair was parted in the middle and grazed the tops of his ears. In contrast, Kevin's photo was a professional yearbook-style portrait in which he looked his best. Kevin was shiny and promising in a dark pressed uniform, his hair buzzed close at the sides, short and combed on top. He looked handsome and proud.

Civil rights activists piped in, calling for police reform. Academics and professors of Law and American Studies held discussions on police brutality and excessive force. They were invited to debate on national television and radio, where opposing arguments brimmed with American fragility and righteousness. Ordinary Americans called in to rant about how the streets were overrun with illegal immigrants and criminals and America wasn't America anymore.

The academics lectured on racial profiling and systemic racism, Rodney King, Latasha Harlins, the destruction of Koreatown, anti-immigration laws, the model minority myth, Vincent Chin, Manzanar, the Chinatown Massacre.

The newscasters shook their heads in gentle disbelief. Why did some people always want to make everything about race? How could this have anything to do with racism when both men were not only the same race but the same nationality?

Kevin wasn't just my brother anymore. Now he belonged to everyone. They turned him into a symbol whose meaning they couldn't stop arguing about. Everyone seemed to have something at stake in Kevin. All that debate about what he did and what it all meant—they made my brother disappear. The person I'd known my whole life who was so many different things—he was gone.

19

SHAME

May 2002

KEVIN WASN'T ANSWERING his phone. My mom wouldn't leave her apartment and my dad was on the road, delivering perishables in his refrigerated Darth Vader truck. I hadn't heard from him since the news broke, but my mom had talked to him every day since the big event, so I knew that he knew everything.

When my dad finally called me, about a week later, he acted as if nothing was wrong. He chatted about his delivery of avocadoes in Maine, the heat, the truck stops. When I brought up Kevin, all I got was silence.

"Hello?" I said.

"We treated you the same," he said. "Why did he do that? It's his fault, not ours."

I drove to Kevin's house in San Jose with the windows down. I needed the noise. The sound of the traffic and wind at high speed somehow kept my mind distracted.

He and Minjoo lived across the street from a shady park in a neighborhood with a highly rated public school. The size and location of the house gave it a family vibe, though they had no plans for children—Kevin had decided after marrying Minjoo that he preferred a child-free life. Minjoo was always quiet on the subject and when prodded, Kevin would say: "I got Minjoo this house and the dog." There was a big deck and gazebo in the back where Minjoo could often be found painting.

A spare bedroom had become her crafting room. Another held small pets in cages—a bunny, a mouse, a guinea pig, a family of hamsters. The dog wasn't allowed in that room. At some point, between getting married and settling into a single-family house, Minjoo had become Dr. Dolittle, spending her days tending to the animals. When they got sick, she nursed them back to health, holding the smallest creatures with the utmost care in the palm of her hand while she fed them with an eye dropper. When they died, she cried inconsolably and buried them in shoeboxes in the backyard.

I knocked and then rang the doorbell. Nobody answered. I tried calling Kevin's home phone line, waited for the beep, and left a message on the answering machine, hoping that he'd hear my announcement that it was me at the front door. I wasn't about to go creeping around the house, spying into windows. One thing I'd learned from him was that you should never wander uninvited onto anyone's property, especially if the dwelling is occupied by a cop.

I rang and knocked, rang and knocked. Tried to be persistent, not annoying.

Kevin finally answered, opening the door in sweatpants and an old T-shirt. He looked exhausted. He turned and walked away, leaving me on the porch with the door wide open. I followed him to the living room, where it appeared he'd been sleeping. On the couch, there was a bed pillow and a balled-up quilt. The house, normally so tidy, looked like nobody had cleaned up for days. There were dishes piled up in the kitchen, the trash needed to be emptied, and there were takeout boxes on the counter.

"Where's Minjoo?" I asked.

"Gone," Kevin said. "She took the dog."

"What do you mean gone?" I said.

"She left."

Kevin sat down on the couch. He was totally calm. Minutes passed. I kept standing there. I shifted, blinked, looked around the room.

"Have you talked to Mom and Dad?" I asked. "I think they've been calling you."

"Mom called," he said, "but I haven't talked to her."

"What's gonna happen?" I blurted. "Are you getting fired? Are you going to court? Do you need a lawyer?"

"I don't know anything."

Kevin's passivity scared me. At least when he was angry I knew what to expect. Now I didn't know what would happen next.

There had been a time when things had been different, when we'd been on the same side and it was us against the world. It had been so long, I could barely remember the feeling. Now I realized that I'd never know that feeling again—a bond akin to looking in the mirror, our history and pain connected, shared with no one but each other. This was our tragedy: only we could understand each other's particular grief and sorrow, but we'd failed at keeping our bond.

I couldn't explain to Kevin how his pain grew from the same place mine did, couldn't even tell him that I suffered at all. The things that Kevin had done wrong were obvious. My failures had always been harder to detect, by others and especially by myself. As we'd gotten older and his pain deepened, became more complicated, I hadn't tried to help him feel less alone. I'd become cold, unwilling to connect. That coldness grew until it separated us.

"Why did you do that?" I asked Kevin. I tried not to sound accusatory, ridiculous considering the circumstances, but at the time it felt completely sane.

"I don't know," he said. "One minute I was trying to help Eddie, and the next I wasn't."

⁂

IT TURNED OUT that Kevin knew Eddie Yeun. Kevin had befriended the man and looked after him while patrolling the neighborhood.

"I tried to help him," he said. "I thought I could get him back on his feet."

Kevin began dropping off food to Eddie during his shifts. He'd order a burger and fries from a local diner and deliver it to him.

"There aren't a lot of homeless people around here, so he really stuck out. And he's Asian. How often do you see an Asian homeless man?" Kevin said. "He has an accent, but it's not that bad."

Kevin and Eddie were approximately the same size, just under five ten, which made it easy for Kevin to pass down his old clothes and shoes. Eddie had dropped out of San Jose State and his mom was in a mental health facility while his dad had moved back to Korea. An only child, with no relatives nearby.

"He's crazy, like his mom," Kevin said. "He's supposed to take medication, but he always forgets to have it filled."

Kevin would check Eddie into a shelter when it was very cold or raining or very hot, when Eddie seemed jumpy or was talking to invisible people. At the shelter, the staff would call his social worker and keep an eye on him until his medication got filled.

"I don't know what happened," Kevin repeated.

The rest of the story I had to imagine, based on what I'd seen in the videos and what I knew about my brother.

When Kevin got the call about a disturbance on Winchester, above the mall, Eddie must have been the last person he expected to find. Eddie usually stuck to San Carlos, never wandered past the Villas at Santana Row, where the shiny shoppers and luxury cars would have served as a kind of border that someone like Eddie wouldn't want to cross. Kevin would have been surprised to see Eddie behind the paint store, sunburned and barefoot, the soles of his feet black and blistered from walking the streets without shoes. *Where are his sneakers?* Kevin might have thought. *The ones I gave him?* If Eddie was off his meds, perhaps he was talking to someone who wasn't there, speaking in two different voices the way my downstairs neighbor did twice a day, at dawn and the middle of the night—one voice high and pleading, child-like, punctuated with wailing; the other low and stern, scolding.

I don't know what happened after Kevin got out of the patrol car and before the scene on the videotape. When had Kevin reached for the baton? Was there something that Eddie did or said that made Kevin snap?

I had seen the second video, the one that was crystal clear, that zoomed in on Eddie's swollen and bloody face, his raw, sunburned hands, then panned out, framing Kevin with the baton, his stance soldierlike. I don't know what was more painful to see—the man on the ground getting bloodier and more lifeless by the second or Kevin's calm, cool face, that left no room for doubt. I couldn't watch that video again. But the first video, the blurry one, I couldn't get out of my head.

"He was defenseless," I said.

"I know."

"How could you do that?"

He turned his head away and stared at the blank wall. I waited to see if he would say something, but I could tell the conversation was over.

I drove straight home and turned on the TV. Both videos were still all over the news. I recorded the blurry one on my VCR and watched it again and again, trying to make Kevin come into focus on the fuzzy screen, even though I already knew it was him.

I thought I could see the smirk on his face, thought I saw the way he strutted and puffed out his chest, though the recording was so grainy it would have been impossible to discern such detail. The scene was charged with violence heightened beyond reason, but everything was blurred as if someone had tried to erase the facts and identities and the event itself. The ghostly quality of the video, compounded by Kevin's actions—the repetitive hitting and kicking, the way his physical form had become so weaponized—produced an image that was hypnotizing, unreal. It was like a horror movie where the scariest moments arise when you can't see the actual threat, but you catch a glimpse of something monstrous—a shadow, a flash, a streak of smoke. What I saw on the video that had been recorded in San Jose was a faceless figure—a symbol, myth—that represented those inhuman, unforgivable cops that had beaten Rodney King, hammering him with their batons, using the same power strokes my brother had used, even after he was on the ground, as if letting him stand up was a weapon in itself, a bomb that would drop them dead right there. I had to keep reminding myself that the person on the screen holding the baton was not them, not a symbol, that the ghostly figure was my own brother.

I wondered what my dad saw when he watched the videos that kept playing on TV. Did he see a symbol, like I did? Did he see his own son? Did he see himself? Could he comprehend the rage and violence? Did he remember when he'd squatted over Kevin's tennis rackets with an axe and chopped into the pile with abandon? My father had been so full of unknowable rage that I could never comprehend and still can't, all these years later. Kevin grew into that rage, learned to inhabit the same space, and there was a part of me that envied them for what they knew and what they felt that I didn't, as if they were members of a secret club that I would never belong to. What was it like to act, to release all that anger? To open the lid after everything's been kept down for so long, teeming and growing and rising?

I could never reach the man who had cleaved into Kevin's pile of tennis rackets, or the man who had beaten an unarmed defenseless man to near death. There are many things I'll never understand, but I do know that my father must have been faced with an impossible task: how could he prepare us for a world that didn't accept him, that was encrypted with codes he couldn't translate, when his best hope was to push us toward the door that opened to the world he'd been waiting all his life to enter but never would, knowing that once we crossed the threshold to the other side we'd no longer belong to him?

Kevin never walked through that door. He had too many bad memories that he couldn't keep down and couldn't erase.

I'd always felt certain that I was different from my dad and my brother. But their rage was part of me. They'd fed it to me with every insult, every push, every time they hit my mother or me, every time they said that a woman is inferior by nature. They passed their rage on to me every time they were made to feel that they didn't qualify as men. Their rage combined with my own pain, so that I couldn't tell what was mine and what was theirs, because what was theirs was now mine. I'd swallowed it and swallowed it and I'd kept swallowing. It just stayed there, a little ball deep inside of me where all my anger had collected. I couldn't erase my bad memories either. I'd pushed them all down, kept them hidden, because I got in—into the world that we were all living so miserably to access. I'd felt myself disappearing and I'd come to understand that I had two choices. Either all the pain had to be kept a secret, or I could find the words and share it—to become a spectacle for some, but for you and me and anyone else who wants to be with us, a point of connection, an expansion of our selves, an opening of the world.

My brother couldn't keep his pain a secret, but neither could he find the words to express it, so he enacted it on the helpless body of another person, as if he too was helpless to stop himself. In the video, I couldn't make out his face, or any other detail that might have marked him as Kevin Kim, my brother. He looked like a ghost. It was as if the crappy camcorder had scrubbed away all the layers of politeness and silence that had formed his personality, leaving this wraith made of violence and shame, fragile, jagged, wielding the baton against a prone human figure that looked, in the grainy image on the screen, indistinguishable from himself.

20

GIJIBAE

June 2002

WE CAME TOGETHER one last time before my big move. By then, the media had moved on. First there was a Sri Lankan American attorney mistaken for an Arab man with a shoe bomb. Then there was another cop behaving badly on a college campus in Los Angeles—he shot a stream of pepper spray across a crowd of students sitting quietly in rows, peacefully protesting Bush's war on terror. "Before he sprayed us, he drank the coffee we offered him. He sat down and chatted with us," said a nineteen-year-old boy on the news, his face red and swollen.

Kevin was still on administrative leave. So far, no charges had been brought against him. Eddie's family had been informed, we were told, but they weren't getting involved. There could have been a number of reasons why, but if they were anything like my family, I imagine that they didn't want to call attention to how they had failed, the ways in which they were stained: Eddie's homelessness, his mother's institutionalization, his absent father, and the fact that no one had been looking after Eddie for so long. At the hospital, Eddie had come to, though he remembered nothing. There was talk about the ACLU stepping in, the DA pressing charges on Eddie's behalf, but the papers were never served. The unhoused population was not on the political agenda. If immigrants and their families had anything to express, it should only be gratitude. No one wanted to argue a hate crime committed by an Asian man on another Asian man. It appeared that in time the whole thing would blow over and Kevin would go back to work. But for us, it stayed fresh in our minds. Everyone in our extended family knew what had happened, the Korean community, our hometown—no one was going to forget. We were marked, all four of us.

When we gathered together, it was the last time we'd all be in the same place at the same time, though none of us could have known. We drove separately—my mom and me from our apartments in San Francisco, Kevin from his house in San Jose, and my dad from my aunt's house in Palo Alto. I wasn't sure who'd gotten through to Kevin and convinced him to meet for dinner. It wasn't me. He'd been ignoring our mother's phone calls, so I figured it was our dad, the only person Kevin wouldn't willfully disappoint.

We met at a Taiwanese restaurant, a dumpling place on Polk Street not too far from my mom's apartment. She wanted to keep clear of Chinatown and the sushi and Korean–Chinese places where we'd been before. My dad hated dumplings—Like eating nothing, he said, Where's the meat?—but my mom was insistent that we meet somewhere where we wouldn't be recognized. She didn't want to cook because her place was too small, she said, my apartment was a dump, Kevin's house was a mess without Minjoo around, and we couldn't go to my aunt's because she and my mom had been having the same argument since 1970. Despite everything, we would not fail to mark the event of my moving away.

At the restaurant, my mom ordered for the table. She'd heard of the place from a Taiwanese woman she'd befriended in one of the many classes she'd signed up for at SF State. She'd joined a women's rowing group for age sixty plus, and enrolled in classes on nutrition and farm-to-table cooking. Her biceps bulged from all the rowing in the early morning hours in the bay, and her newly muscled arms flexed unconsciously as she lectured me on the basic ingredients of California cuisine, rambling about the health benefits of extra-virgin olive oil and fresh tomatoes—old news for me, but new to her. My mom had learned about Taiwanese food from her young Taiwanese friend—younger than my mom, but older than me—and what really stuck in my mom's mind were the steamed dumplings, stir-fried mustard greens, and endless pots of tea.

"That's how she stays so skinny," my mom said after the waiter took our order. "She drinks so much tea. While eating and after the meal is over, pots and pots of tea."

None of us were in a good mood, but my dad in particular was noticeably grouchy. I was moving far away and I was too grown up for him to stop me, Kevin had publicly shamed himself and us on the news, not to mention almost killed another man, and my mom had just ordered food that he wasn't going to enjoy. My dad's mouth looked even smaller than usual. He kept making a sound that was a cross between a sigh and a growl, like a broken toy. I couldn't tell if he was trying to express a feeling or if he had a tickle in his throat.

My parents had yet to speak directly to Kevin about what he'd done. My mom had tried calling at first, but Kevin never answered, and she was too afraid to leave the house for fear of reporters waiting outside and the possibility of running into anyone who might recognize her as the mother of the bad Korean cop. As far as I knew, my dad hadn't even tried calling Kevin, except maybe to get him to meet us for dinner. I was the only one who'd talked to Kevin about what had happened, though I had the same questions I'd had before, compounded with more confusion after learning that he had been friends with the man he almost killed.

At the restaurant, we sat quietly, arms folded. Kevin's silence seemed to make the table between us expand like a balloon. We were all dealing with it by ignoring it, but the problem couldn't be swept under the rug like everything else. Even if my parents had managed to avoid facing Kevin, nobody else had let them forget—the phone calls from family and friends, the news and the radio, all reminders of how we had failed. We were marked for life.

As we waited for the food to arrive, I watched Kevin slowly move his eyes around the table as if he was taking a photo on panorama. When I met his eyes, he smirked.

At first, no one spoke. I didn't dare. I had no idea how to begin or what to even say. For some sick reason, I suddenly felt compelled to share my big news. It would have been a problem even under the best circumstances. The context was so inappropriate, it somehow felt like the perfect moment.

"I dropped out of law school," I said.

All eyes turned to me. The table was so quiet, I could hear a man nearby chewing. I explained how I hadn't finished my final semester of law school, and I was indeed moving to New York, but not to study for and take the New York bar exam and get a job. I'd been accepted to a fully funded PhD program in American Studies, where I would study Koreans in America, trying to understand what we inherit from generations of war and immigration. "The pressure to assimilate is toxic," I said. I kept going, trying to validate the scholarly research I was about to pursue, that they were hearing about for the first time. I expounded on the erasure of our histories, the denial of our experiences of discrimination, the way we'd been used as a tool to oppress other people of color. It was like a parody of a lecture. "Race is a social construct," I said. "But America is still the building." I pontificated about the patriarchy and misogyny and toxic masculinity and violence. One should always think of one's audience, but I was doing the opposite, completely stuck in my own head. I was about to embark on a new career, a new life, and I wanted it known that I was doing something meaningful.

My parents looked like they'd already convened because they were making the same face—surprised, mad, disappointed. I don't know how parents do it, get so many emotions in one look while matching each other simultaneously. I couldn't read my brother's expression. He looked pissed, but also like he was trying not to laugh. He must have been relieved that accusations about bad choices would now be leveled at me.

But something strange happened. The expressions on my parents' faces changed. I could feel it before I saw it, like the air had been sucked out of the room and then pushed back in. I don't know who started first, but for the next ten minutes my parents went on and on, heaping up not the scorn I'd expected, but praise. For taking charge of my life and doing things my way, for getting myself into a PhD program that I not only didn't have to pay for, but would pay me to attend. It was as if they were congratulating me for dropping out of law school.

Kevin and I stared. I don't think either of us could comprehend what was happening. We'd both been expecting a showdown, an attack on Kevin that would surely spiral out of control, a demand for answers and a parade of blame that might culminate in disownment. When I'd distracted everyone with my announcement, history showed that I'd be met with panic and denial and maniacal refusal to let me choose my course, a barrage of shouting until I'd agree to what they wanted, though they would claim later that nobody had forced me if I said I didn't like whatever it was I'd allowed myself to be pressured into. At the very least, someone would point out the obvious: grad school was for social misfits who couldn't cut it in the real world and in the end there would be no money, no job, just disappointment and struggle. Best case scenario: a job in a city not of your choosing. Instead, my parents showered me with approval. The sense of failure and embarrassment I'd expected about my quitting law school was replaced with hope and pride.

Kevin's face squinched with disgust. His mouth shrunk. His chin disappeared.

"Maybe you'll be a professor at Stanford!" my dad said, shouting. He must have liked the sound of it because he repeated himself two more times.

"When you buy a house, you can take the piano," my mom said, referring to our concert grand with ivory keys that was too big for anyone except the Changs, who lived in a gigantic old barn house full of foster children. The Changs were holding on to the piano for my parents, a fair exchange since their eldest daughter put it to use teaching piano for extra money while she finished a master's in ethnomusicology. "Just a master's, not a PhD," my mom pointed out.

Neither Kevin nor I spoke. We were still quiet when the food arrived, at which point my parents stopped talking. We ate quickly, in silence. Normally Kevin and I were very slow eaters, but my dad was right, dumplings don't take long. My parents resumed the praise.

"My dad was a professor in Korea," my mom said, "*and* a doctor. There's a statue of him on the campus of Seoul National University."

My mom had mentioned the statue before. I'd never questioned the veracity. I hadn't even remembered the statue until Minjoo returned from one of her trips back to Seoul and recounted how she'd visited the campus and looked everywhere for it, had asked campus officials where she could find it, only to be told that no such statue existed.

"Both of my brothers are doctors," my mom said. "But there's no woman who's a doctor in my family *or* your dad's."

"Your cousin Saehee wanted to get a PhD," my dad said. "Did you know that? She wanted to get a PhD, she wanted to go to law school. Now you're doing both. She didn't do anything because Gomo wanted her to marry that stockbroker. He's as old as I am. She just chased money because Gomo told her to," he said, snorting. "*Swedish*," he said under his breath.

I didn't even notice myself beginning to glow. The attention reminded me of childhood, when my athletic and musical abilities had silenced people. Having once been special for so long and then becoming nobody as a grown woman had both humbled me and made me needy. I felt myself easing into the spotlight. It felt right.

"Oh, come on," Kevin said. "A PhD isn't a real doctor."

My dad glared at Kevin.

"What have *you* ever done," my dad said. "How could you do that to us?" His face was tight. My mom began crying quietly.

"At least I know how to control my own wife," Kevin responded.

I'd never heard Kevin talk to our dad like that before. I thought he would get up and leave or return Kevin's challenge or maybe even break something right there in the restaurant, especially considering the ridiculousness of the statement. After all, Kevin's wife had left him, just as our mother had left our father. Kevin had denied himself the city life he'd wanted in order to satisfy his wife's desire for suburban comfort, just as our father had for so long denied himself freedom in order to maintain the level of respectability and income that our mother had expected.

My dad just sat there looking at his empty plate. He was different from how I remembered him. His body had become soft, his hair gray. My mom had tried to get him to dye it, but I'd told him that American men let their hair go gray, so my dad had refused, listing the names of powerful American men, all white, with gray hair as further evidence: Bill Clinton, Tom Brokaw, Walter Cronkite.

My dad closed his eyes. My mom continued crying quietly.

"Everything is so stupid," Kevin said. "What's the point?"

My dad opened his eyes and looked at Kevin with bewilderment.

"Everything I do is wrong anyway," Kevin said.

My dad closed his eyes again.

I should have followed suit, closed my eyes, shut it all out, but my judgment, which I had always thought was sound, at least compared to my parents and my brother, was clearly not, based on the decision I made right then to finally have my say.

"How can you be so crazy?" I said, too loud. "What is wròng with you people?"

My dad opened his eyes. My mom stopped crying. Kevin looked like he might punch me.

"I'm not afraid of you," I said to Kevin. "If you touch me in front of all these people you're going to prison. You think I care?"

They all stared. I actually thought I was keeping my voice down so as to not call attention, but in many ways I was just as delusional as everyone else at the table.

"How could you do that?" I said, shouting not just at Kevin, but my mom and dad. I blamed them for blaming, I said that their minds were irreparably warped, that they needed psychiatric help, and other things that I don't remember because what I said was too mean.

My mom had inexplicably taken off her watch and stuffed it in her purse. My dad squinted, as if he was looking at me through a spyglass.

"Kevin turned into *you*," I said, looking at my dad. "He's exactly like you."

My dad put his hands on his stomach and laughed sonorously. He turned away as if I'd just given him a big compliment.

I pointed, first at my mom and then at my dad, even though I'd been taught never to point at another person, particularly an elder, even more particularly in accusation, but there I was, my pointer finger hovering, stabbing back and forth between them.

"Why are you giving me approval now?" I said, jabbing my finger at the ceiling for emphasis. "Why are you proud of me? Why now? Where were you when I needed you?"

My mom had taken her sunglasses out and put them on top of her head. My dad looked longingly at the glass doors that led outside. I didn't look at Kevin. The little spark of bravery I'd felt earlier when I'd first confronted him was already half gone. I kept going, finger in the air, shifting between them like a little pistol. One thing about our family is once we start shouting, it's hard to get us to stop.

"You've never let me make choices about my own life. You think that no one should get what they want because somehow that makes a person spoiled. It's so stupid! We only get one life and we're all gonna die! What's the point of doing something you don't want to do?"

Like an idiot, I actually thought they'd answer my questions. I thought I was right, reasonable, that my arguments were sound. I was surprised when I didn't get the response I expected, though I still don't know exactly what it was I wanted from them.

They all began yelling at once. By that point, no one was sitting anymore. Of course, our presence in the restaurant was not under the radar. Everybody was staring.

The voices of my family blended into what felt like a strategic attack. I was selfish, they said, conceited, I'd always thought I was better than them even though we were the same. Then my mom said out loud the sentiment that they were all thinking.

"Gijibae," she said, almost a growl, her face hard and mean. It wasn't the way I was used to hearing the word, directed at little girls in a light, playful tone. I was a bitch, not a sly pretty fox.

"I'm not the same as you," I said.

The waitstaff and the manager arrived, forming a semicircle around us, a human screen to protect the other patrons from our unpredictable behavior. An older man in an apron sternly suggested that we resume our conversation outside. He didn't need to say it twice. We were already standing anyway. I was the first to leave. Didn't even bother to look back. It wasn't my responsibility to take care of the check. I was the daughter and the youngest.

SAYING OUT LOUD what I'd been thinking all along is how I saw how wrong I'd been. Keeping all those ugly thoughts to myself had made them feel so true, so justified. There had been no one to tell me I was wrong. Driving home, I felt disgusted with myself for having enjoyed the praise that my parents had lavished on me at the restaurant. My winning had always been dependent on Kevin losing. We couldn't both be on top. Only one of us could succeed, at the expense of the other. I'd been like a spy, moving back and forth across the border that separated my family from the world around us, changing who I was to get what I wanted.

Kevin now would always be the loser, and we had all played a part, especially me. I was a necessary element to Kevin's failure. I existed as his opposite, his mirror rival. I thought I was special, superior. I'd never even participated in the competition between us because I was never afraid that I wouldn't win. I thought I was the best. My ego was so big, the rivalry was one-sided. Excessive confidence undoubtedly helped get me on top, but it was Kevin's fear, the fact that he never believed in himself, that kept me there.

I had let myself become cold and spiteful. I was just as angry and could be just as cruel as they were, but my version of that cruelty emerged as a freezing out. Years of diminishment had kept me quiet, alone. I thought I could see things no one else could see. I'd made myself strong that way, through my willingness to expose other people's flaws, their selfish motivations, without holding back. But I'd become cold, proud, and unforgiving, and I never turned the lens on myself.

Being better than Kevin and everyone else felt like the natural order of the world, the universe confirming what was true. Winning was proof that I wasn't what they said I was, and winning means never losing the advantage, a never-ending task that keeps you from noticing what you've lost.

THE ESCAPE ARTIST

21

June 2002

SAMIR HELPED ME pack, partly to bond one last time before I moved away, but I also suspected that he was worried I wouldn't finish packing in time. While I was generally responsible and conscientious, Samir made me feel like I was always two steps behind. Sometimes in the middle of the night, I'd shuffle into the kitchen for a glass of water and find him up with worry and list-making.

We wrapped up my few dishes with paper and placed them carefully in a cardboard box. I filled up the empty space with pillows.

"How are things?" Samir asked.

"Good," I said.

"I mean with your brother."

"Nothing's happening to him."

I'd read in the *Chronicle* that Kevin's administrative leave was coming to an end. He was set to return to work in the fall. It was published on the back page along with other goings-on, in a little box with no caption. As I'd suspected, no charges were brought against him. Eddie was declared "indigent" and wasn't responsible for his medical bills. He had no desire to press charges against Kevin or the police department, nor did his family, or anyone on his behalf.

"Are you sure?" Samir asked.

"Yes," I said.

Samir taped the box shut, kneeling over it with a Sharpie.

"Are you glad?" he asked.

"No," I said. "I don't know. He deserves to go to prison, but I don't want to see him in prison."

What was worse, I wondered. Your brother a bad cop or your brother in prison?

"What do you think happens to cops in prison?" I said. "Nothing good."

I hadn't spoken to Kevin since that night in the restaurant. I couldn't bring myself to pick up the phone, and even if I had, I wasn't sure he would have answered. Whatever was wrong inside him, whatever had caused that outpouring of violence, the violence itself hadn't fixed it. I knew what he would do: get Minjoo back, stay married, keep going to work, keep sweeping the yard for trespassers every night with his gun drawn, keep withdrawing from us every so often. Maybe one day he'd disappear for a while and I'd find him hiding out in a cabin at the beach, firing bullets over the ocean. Sooner or later something even worse would happen, and when it did I would blame myself for not having known how to stop it.

Samir and I packed my stuff, taking breaks to brew coffee and snack. I didn't have a lot, but it took us three days because we were slow and inefficient about it. Each evening I treated him to dinner. It didn't cost me much since we ate, as we always had, at the kinds of places where you order through a window at the counter. The last night, we picked up burritos and sprawled out in the grass in Dolores Park.

"You can visit me," I said. "You could even move to New York, too. We could be roommates again."

"Why does everybody have a hard-on for New York?"

I shrugged.

"You're not coming back, are you?" Samir said.

We took the long way home, wandered through the Castro, rainbow flags flapping above us, walked up Haight along smoke shops and thrift stores and hair salons, and came back down Hayes past boutiques and cafes and gastropubs. I already missed Samir even though he was right next to me. It felt so final, like it was our last walk together. I had to remind myself that it wasn't the end, that our future held more good times, more memory-making, but I wondered when we'd be together again. The walk was unremarkable, one that Samir and I had often taken in the three years we'd lived together, but I craved familiarity—I wanted to see everything up close in all its ordinary detail, not a landscape view from up high, grand and unrelatable.

"Has anybody said anything to you about being Arab yet?" I asked.

"No," he said. "But I haven't tried to fly anywhere since 9/11. And I don't have a beard," he said, touching his smooth face.

I'd read the headlines about Muslims getting profiled at airports and on airplanes mid-flight, by both security and passengers, for looking suspicious, too Arab. I said a prayer for Samir, quietly in my head. No words, just a wish for the world to be good.

It was dark by the time we got home. I brushed my teeth while half asleep, the bristles wild and frayed from brushing too hard, a bad habit I could never kick.

MY DAD WAS supposed to arrive around noon the next day to help me carry my few belongings down the stairs and load them into the little trailer I'd rented. I didn't want his help. I was afraid he'd hurt himself and give me one more thing to feel guilty about, but he'd insisted. He'd helped me with every move up to that point in my life, and he wasn't about to miss the big one. It was all I could do to talk him out of driving across the country with me.

Early that morning, Samir went out to run some errands. I sat alone in his butterfly chair, leftover from college. The old box-style television with antennae on top also belonged to Samir. I hadn't turned it on since the days when the videos of Kevin were first looping on the news.

When Samir got back, he flopped down on the couch beside me and handed me a little paper bag.

"A going-away present," he said.

I opened it and took out a thick, floppy book. *Surviving the PhD FOR DUMMIES*. There was a cartoon picture of a man with googly eyes and an upside-down triangle face, pointer finger in the air. He was supposed to be a dummy.

"I love it!" I said, though I did not, at all. "I have a gift for you, too," I said.

I opened the drawer of the TV console. Inside I'd hidden an envelope that I'd planned on telling Samir about after I was gone, but the time seemed right. I handed it to him, and he opened it, shaking the contents into his lap.

"What?" he said, holding up a gift card.

"You can redeem it at a few different airlines," I said. "Now you *have* to visit me."

"Aren't you wiped out? With the move and everything?"

"I cashed out my credit card points. It didn't cost me anything," I said.

"That isn't my real present to you. It was a joke," Samir said. "You're good at lying," he said, laughing. "I couldn't even tell what you really thought about the dummy book."

"I love it," I insisted.

"No, you don't."

Samir took an envelope out of his jacket pocket and slid it across the coffee table.

"Here," he said. "Look inside."

I opened the envelope. Inside was the exact same gift card I'd given to him.

"Now you have to come back home," he said.

I started laughing first. Soon Samir joined in. I almost fell out of the butterfly chair, I was laughing so hard, doubled over with a cramp in my stomach. Samir was still on the couch, head thrown back and gasping for breath. I surprised myself when my own laughter turned to tears. At first I thought I was crying happy tears, until the crying felt beyond my control, a sadness that I couldn't describe, a longing for something that I couldn't even name.

At exactly noon I looked out the window and saw my dad walking toward the building, my mom beside him. It should have been strange to see them together again, but it wasn't strange. It felt right. From three floors up and a block away they looked like any happy couple, blessed to have grown old together. Whatever rift had grown between them, the disaster with my brother had healed it—maybe not forever, but for the moment completely. It made sense. It had always been disaster and struggle that bound them together. Lately their lives had gotten easier, and so they'd both looked up for the first time in decades and thought, "What else is out there for me?" But now things were bad again—maybe worse than ever—so here they were, practically arm in arm except that my mother's hands were each weighed down with plastic bags containing homemade food she'd brought, of course, to sustain me for the trip.

Feeling guilty, I ran down the three flights of stairs to meet them at the outer door.

"I didn't know you were coming, Mom," I said.

"Of course I am coming," she said. "I had to come. Don't you?"

Handing over the bags, she listed what was in them: "Kimbap and fried zucchini, your favorite. Don't leave it in the sun. And broccoli, and kkakdugi, and dubu . . ."

"Thanks," I said. I really was grateful. I hadn't packed any food for the trip.

"We'd better get started," my dad said.

"I'm sorry," Samir said sheepishly, "I wish I could stay, but . . ."

"You have work," I said. "Go."

I'd wanted to hire movers, but the emotional pain that would have inflicted on my dad would have been worse than any hernia, so there we were, me and him, hauling my mattress and everything I owned not only down three flights of stairs but up the block and around the corner to where I'd managed to park my car with the trailer attached, while my mom stayed behind to warm the food we'd eat when we were done.

It took us less than an hour, and all the time my dad kept talking, as if to show that he wasn't tired.

"You have to be careful," he said. "Don't drive late at night. If you get tired, stop and sleep, but don't sleep just anywhere. Find a good motel. And don't drive if it's raining hard. Pull off and wait for the rain to stop."

He went on like that, listing all the things I should do and not do to keep myself safe. It was the closest he was ever going to get to saying "I love you, I'll miss you," and I took it for what it was, knowing I was never going to say anything like that to him either.

After we finished, we sat at Samir's table and ate from Samir's plates. My mom had heated up the bulgogi, which I didn't eat, and rice and fried zucchini and the marinated broccoli she thought I loved though it was, as always, so undercooked it made my jaw hurt. We hardly spoke except to praise the food. There were four chairs at the table and only three of us, and I felt as if my brother was sitting in that empty chair, watching us. I'm sure my parents felt it too. I couldn't tell how old the ghost brother was. Sometimes he was his grown-up self, and sometimes he was a child looking up at us with wondering eyes, waiting for someone to fill him in on all the stuff he must have missed. I wanted to tell him to run. I wanted to tell him it's not too late, don't lose yourself, don't let them get you, but I didn't even know who

I meant by *them*—our parents, sure, Mom with her overwhelming tyrannical fear and Dad with his axe poised over the tennis rackets, but also America and Steven Seagal movies and Don Dixon mocking a woman for wanting him and all the people who'd told my brother in subtle and unsubtle ways all his life that he'd never be a man. I wanted to tell him to get away, but where could he have gone? And I couldn't tell him anything, because he wasn't even there, so I just sat there grinding the woody stems of the broccoli between my teeth and feeling guilty and sorry for him and for all of us.

We were trying to get free finally, me and my mom and my dad, each in our own way. Maybe it was late in the day for all of us, but it wasn't too late. Not even for them. My mom could buy her house on a hill or at least find an apartment to rent, and my dad could drive his big rig across the desert and over the mountains again and again for as long as he liked. Or maybe they would stay together after all, enough space in their lives now, finally, to see and hear each other for the first time in maybe decades, since before either of them had arrived in America, before my mom had run away with my dad and cried the whole way from LA to San Francisco because she'd disobeyed her family.

But for Kevin there was no escape. He'd beaten a helpless, innocent man to the verge of death and then gone back to his life as if nothing had happened. I'd wondered at first how he could have done that, but the answer was simple—he'd done it because he couldn't imagine anything different. It felt to me like he was already dead, like my mom and dad and I had survived some terrible disaster—our lives—but whatever pleasure we might take in having survived would always be tainted by the recognition that one of us hadn't made it.

"Shona!" my dad said, pushing back from the table.

I helped my mom clear the dishes, and she washed them while I gathered the last of my belongings into the backpack I would live out of for the next several days.

Outside it was cold enough to make me shiver, though two hours before I'd been sweating in short sleeves. A fragment of cloud had blown in from between the hills and swallowed us. I pulled my sweater tighter against my body.

"Where will you stop tonight?" my mom said.

"I don't know," I said. "Maybe Tucson."

"Call when you get there," she said. "Even if it's late. We'll be waiting."

I LIKE TO remember Kevin when he first moved out for college. When he left, he was thrilled and mostly relieved to finally be out of the house.

"Never again," he said, packing his bags, "will I ever live with them." He paused, his face brightening with realization. "Oh my god! I don't have to live with them ever again!"

Still, that first year, Kevin came back to visit once a month. These are the memories that I turn to when I need to remind myself of a better version of my brother. I knew he drove the two hours each way just to see me. For two days we'd go to the movies, out to eat, mountain biking. Occasionally, we'd play tennis, but only practice and drills, never a game, because Kevin feared that I'd win.

Not long after Kevin moved out, our mom became sick. When she returned from the doctor's office, she stayed in bed for months. An antique cowbell appeared on her bedside table. She clanged that bell with gusto when she wanted my attention. It was so old and rusted, it had a deep tone, almost like a gong. I hated that noise. It rang through the house, bouncing off the walls, like a ghost cow was following me, mooing about my mom's latest needs: a glass of water, a snack, an extra pillow and blanket, a better view of the TV, or just my presence to ease her loneliness.

Some days she'd tell me that she had a benign tumor in her stomach; on others she'd announce that she had cancer and that I'd given it to her by being a bad daughter. To this day, I still don't know what, if anything, had physically ailed her. I suppose I could ask her now, over thirty years later, but we're not the kind of family that addresses bad feelings from the past, no matter how far we've arrived from our history, no matter how much it has informed who we've become. A person can only live with so much guilt and regret about things that can't be changed. We don't meet problems at the root. We elide, we repress.

The fact that the stories were vastly different wasn't the issue. The first, perhaps closer to the truth; the second, I suspect, a way to assert power and control that she didn't have. The problem was that in my American mind, the daughter duties that she spoke of—cooking, cleaning, caregiving—were in fact mother duties, and I could confirm this as a firsthand witness of the American households in our small town, as well as a seasoned viewer of sitcoms and movies about American life that aired on our television daily. I didn't know if my mom's understanding of a mother's role was the Korean way or if Koreans in Korea would disagree with her. She thought that her duty to her daughter was to make sure that I knew my place, above all else, as last—the least important person in the room.

I called Kevin one night, when my frustration felt impossible to contain. On the phone, I didn't speak specifics. Who we are now begins with who we were then: people who didn't know how to talk about our problems except in vague, indirect ways.

"I'm thinking about taking the GED," I said. "I could move out a year early. Would it be hard to get into college with a GED? I could join a traveling circus. Or move to New York and be a stand-up comic. Do you think they could stop me? How much money would I need to get out of here?"

The following weekend Kevin came home to visit. I waited in the hall while he said hello to our mother, who was still in bed. Their voices were muffled, though I could hear hers increase in volume to the point where I understood that the tone was one of accusation.

Kevin met me in the hallway, his brow heavy, mouth tight. His eyes were glazed and out of focus and his steps were uncertain, as if he'd just returned from a trip at sea staring at the sun.

"Come on," he said, walking briskly.

I followed him outside. There was a Mustang convertible parked in the driveway. The color was a deep blue, almost navy, with a white top. The hood was incredibly long and the grille pointed forward, like a shark's nose.

"Where'd you get that?" I asked.

"My roommate let me borrow it. He owed me a favor. It's a sixty-four," he said. "Supposed to be a classic. His dad's some kind of car collector. I heard he has a five-car garage."

I peeked inside. The seats were upholstered in immaculate white leather.

"No headrests," I said.

"Yeah, wouldn't want to get in an accident in this car," Kevin said. "Not just because it's not mine."

"Talk about whiplash," I said, laughing.

We drove with the top down through the back-road vineyards, passing gangs of cyclists in indecently tight spandex on skinny bicycles, our hair dancing, ghostlike, the Mustang's engine humming so loud we had to shout into the space between us that seemed to reach forever, containing an endless sea of grievances. Our words got lost, carried away into the world outside of our world the moment they left our mouths, before we could hear each other or even ourselves.

I was fifteen years old with a learner's permit. Since I was just learning how to drive, I was not good at stick shift, and, of course, it was the only type of transmission that my dad would allow me to drive. Still, Kevin let me take over for a while, and for that stretch of time, as I peered over the steering wheel, hair whipping across my face, the afternoon sun reflecting off the hood, I had no memories—no past, no history, no identity—and all I thought about was the open road in front of us and how to stay on it without killing us or anyone else or the car.

We picked up deli sandwiches and apple cider at a farm in Sonoma, where a young bearded white man was selling "the best salsa on earth," homemade by his nana. There was a picture of his white grandma in glasses and a frilly collar right there on the jar. It didn't make sense to me, but I bought two jars anyway while Kevin wasn't looking and tucked them into his duffle bag before he headed back to his other life at college. Kevin took the wheel again and we passed cow pastures that never seemed to end, pinching our noses and holding our breath, cheeks puffed out, for what felt like miles. I waved my arms, red-faced, eyes bulging, and pointed at a farm of llamas. We looked at the llamas and then at each other, which for some reason made us burst into laughter, tears streaming down our faces. The thing is, we'd passed by that same band of llamas several times before, but every time, we'd laughed about it as if for the first time, just because we wanted to.

We drove to San Francisco and headed straight for North Beach, so we could drive up and down hills so steep that when we came to an intersection, we couldn't see the ground on the other side. Waiting our turn at a red light near the top of another vertiginous incline, I began to sweat, looking back nervously as Kevin pulled and released the emergency brake, one foot on the clutch, the other on the gas, to keep us from crashing backward into the cars behind us. Speeding down a hill, clear of traffic, I felt both afraid and free, as if we were being delivered from a wild and angry sea onto shore.

As we crossed the Golden Gate Bridge, the fog rolled over us, shrouding the rust-colored pillars that lengthened above us and fading into mist as we wound down the side of a mountain, the earth cut with rifts and valleys, dotted with orange poppies and peeling bark, the tree branches growing sideways, leaves flattening out like paper.

We ended up at the Pacific Coast, where the cliffs dropped to the ocean. We pulled over at Stinson Beach and ate our sandwiches on top of big rocks jutting out from the water. We stayed until the tide began to rise and the waves crashed too high, spraying our faces. We sprawled out in the sand and watched as the line of foamy water got closer to our feet and receded again and again.

Our favorite kind of sand was neither wet nor dry, or both wet and dry: the in-between sand, moist underneath with a hard layer on top that crackled like the magic shell of a dipped cone. Our heels and toes would break through the surface to the soft, cool underlayer. We rolled up our jeans, grains of smoky-brown sand between our toes.

We stayed until the sun went down, tried to guess the distance between us and the horizon, our salty hair turning crunchy as it dried. We shook the sand from our bodies before we got back in the car, brushing it off our legs and feet, hours away from feeling the sunburns on our skin. There was nowhere else to go but home, so we headed back the way we came. Kevin looked relaxed and content as he drove, a handsome and healthy young man with his whole future ahead of him. I watched as the ocean and cliffs and jagged mountain changed into pavement and open road and shopping plazas. I knew who Kevin was—he was my brother. He was taking care of me, and I was taking care of him.

ACKNOWLEDGMENTS

I STARTED WRITING this novel about ten years ago, shortly before my daughter Yuna arrived in the world and insisted that I spend large swaths of my days lying perfectly still on my back while she slept on top of me. I was a PhD student and had no childcare. Years began to blend. Before I knew it, she was a toddler, and she'd cry and pound on my bedroom door, which I locked when I was working. Her tiny hands reached through the gap under the door, squeaking on the hardwood floor as she slid them in and out. When she was a little older, she passed notes under the door. "I hope you're having a good time in there," she wrote, spelling awful, letters transposed and sometimes backward. "I miss you." And my favorite, to be read from bottom to top:

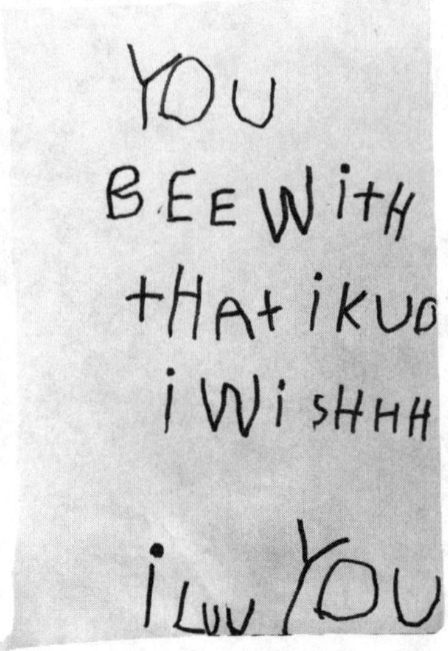

The first people I want to acknowledge are the parents out there who are trying to pursue a dream while raising children. I believe in you.

I wouldn't have been able to make this book without all the people who believed in me. I am deeply grateful to everyone who helped me get here.

Thank you to my agent, Kirby Kim, and my editor, Kathy Pories, for their dedication, talent, and extraordinary efforts in getting this book made.

To all the staff at Algonquin, Little, Brown, and Hachette, without whom this novel would not be the book that it is.

Much gratitude to *Ploughshares*, the Pushcart Prize series, *New World Writing*, and *North American Review* for publishing excerpts of this book in slightly different form.

To the University of Southern California, especially the PhD program in Creative Writing and Literature, and the MFA program in Creative Writing at the University of Houston for the grants and fellowships that facilitated my research and writing.

To Millay Arts, Tin House, Hedgebrook, the Jentel Artist Residency, and Debbie and Billy Gong for granting me time, space, and friendship. These residencies were so vital to completing my work.

To the Pushcart Prizes, the Center for Fiction, the Key West Literary Seminar, and the Rona Jaffe Foundation for fellowships and awards that granted me crucial support early in my career.

To the Inprint Foundation, Kundiman, the Korea Foundation, the Korean Studies Institute, and the East Asian Studies Center for awarding me fellowships and community.

To my mentors, Mat Johnson, John Weir, Dana Johnson, Aimee Bender, and Youngmin Choe, for their careful reading and generous feedback. To my undergraduate teachers at UC–Berkeley, especially Maxine Hong Kingston and Thomas Farber, for introducing me to the possibility of a life as a writer.

Enormous gratitude to Viet Thanh Nguyen for challenging me and always having my back, to Danzy Senna for humor and generosity, to

Percival Everett for friendship, inspiration, and honesty, to Banjo and Harry for listening.

To Barbara, Tod, and James Powers for welcoming me into their family.

To my parents, Hee Joo Lee and Kenneth Lee, for their sacrifices that made my life possible, and from whom I learned resourcefulness, hard work, and grit. To my brother, Gene Lee, and his partner, Hyun Chung Eom Lee, for always being there.

To Michael Powers for being the house chef, my most attentive reader and editor, my partner in life. And to Yuna, my proudest accomplishment—I love you all the way.

RAISING READERS

Books Build Bright Futures

Thank you for reading this book and for being a reader of books in general. We are so grateful to share being part of a community of readers with you, and we hope you will join us in passing our love of books on to the next generation of readers.

Did you know that reading for enjoyment is the single biggest predictor of a child's future happiness and success?

More than family circumstances, parents' educational background, or income, reading impacts a child's future academic performance, emotional well-being, communication skills, economic security, ambition, and happiness.

Studies show that kids reading for enjoyment in the US is in rapid decline:

- In 2012, 53% of 9-year-olds read almost every day. Just 10 years later, in 2022, the number had fallen to 39%.
- In 2012, 27% of 13-year-olds read for fun daily. By 2023, that number was just 14%.

Together, we can commit to **Raising Readers** and change this trend. How?

- Read to children in your life daily.
- Model reading as a fun activity.
- Reduce screen time.
- Start a family, school, or community book club.
- Visit bookstores and libraries regularly.
- Listen to audiobooks.
- Read the book before you see the movie.
- Encourage your child to read aloud to a pet or stuffed animal.
- Give books as gifts.
- Donate books to families and communities in need.

BOB1217

Books build bright futures, and **Raising Readers** is our shared responsibility.

For more information, visit **JoinRaisingReaders.com**

Sources: National Endowment for the Arts, National Assessment of Educational Progress, WorldBookDay.com, Nielsen BookData's 2023 "Understanding the Children's Book Consumer"